Out of the Blue

*Also by Sally Mandel
in Large Print:*

Portrait of a Married Woman

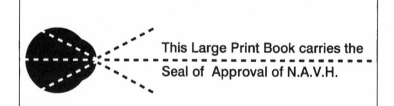

Out of the Blue

Sally Mandel

Thorndike Press • Thorndike, Maine

Published in 2000 by arrangement with The Ballantine
Publishing Group, a division of Random House, Inc.

Thorndike Press Large Print Americana Series.

The tree indicium is a trademark of Thorndike Press.

The text of this Large Print edition is unabridged.
Other aspects of the book may vary from the original edition.

Set in 16 pt. Plantin by Elena Picard.

Printed in the United States on permanent paper.

Library of Congress Cataloging-in-Publication Data

Mandel, Sally.
    Out of the blue / Sally Mandel.
      p. cm.
    ISBN 0-7862-2551-3 (lg. print : hc : alk. paper)
    1. Multiple sclerosis — Patients — Fiction.
  2. New York (N.Y.) — Fiction. 3. Large type books.
  I. Title.
  PS3563.A446 O9 2000
   813'.54—dc21
                                        00-027767

I could not have written this book without the valuable assistance of Sam Dworkis, Jen Carter, Terry Russo, Sam Barner, Steve Perlbinder, Hoot Sherman, and everyone at the Jane Rotrosen Agency, especially my rudder, Andrea Cirillo. And Jim Thomas, special thanks to you.

For Colette, and all the others

1

I pictured God feeling a little bored one morning and sifting through his files until he found my name. Oh yeah, that little jock, Annie Bolles. That flibbertigibbet who never sits still. Let's toss a thunderbolt her way and see how she handles it.

I knew there was something amiss when my legs disappeared. I was on my third lap around the Central Park Reservoir on one of those autumn mornings when the mist sighed from the surface and the gulls rose up through it like ghost birds. First, there was a tingling sensation in my toes, intensifying with each step until it felt as if my running shoes had been hot-wired. I tried to run it off, assuming it had to be some kind of weird cramp or shin splints. But within another quarter mile, the current had crept up to the knees, microwaving my muscles. And then my legs just pureed. I kind of collapsed against the chain-link fence until Armando, one of the regulars, came along and helped me hobble to Fifth Avenue and put me in a cab. It was my last great run.

MS — multiple sclerosis. For a while that was how I thought of myself. "Anna Marie Bolles, MS," as if it were some kind of advanced degree that followed my name everywhere. But as it turned out, getting MS was not the most significant event of my life.

That was five years ago, and I'd put in a lot of adjustment time before the Saturday afternoon I wheeled myself into the American Institute of Photography. During those periods when I was completely immobilized, I often surrounded myself with art books. Leafing through them gave me the pleasant illusion that I was strolling through a museum. Anyway, photos had always interested me. I can hear my mother snorting at that statement. What doesn't interest you, babe? Iguana shit? My mother has a mouth on her, but what's more irritating is that she tends to be right ninety percent of the time. So, more accurately, photography is one of many enthusiasms of mine.

This particular exhibit at the A.I.P. was called "Our Own Backyard," and it featured local amateurs. It was a summer afternoon, really steamy, and I hadn't done anything more than brush my hair back into a ponytail, a decision I lived to regret. The uptown bus wasn't air conditioned, but at least it had a functioning handicapped exit. As I wheeled across Ninety-fourth Street and glimpsed the runners loping around the reservoir, I had to admit to a twinge.

I saw him as soon as I got inside the gallery. Anybody would have noticed that striking face, but it was more than that. I found out later that he'd recently been on the cover of *Crain's* magazine, which is sold from wheelchair-eye-level at my neighborhood newsstand. But I wonder now if the jolt of recognition went a lot deeper. He was leaning oh-so-casually against the doorway, pretending to look at the photographs, but I knew he was faking. One of the advantages of this chair is that after people give me that first uneasy glance, I seem to become semi-invisible and I can stare at everybody to my heart's content. I figured he'd dropped by to check out the women. There was a stunning Italian specimen in a yellow sundress. In fact, most of the visitors appeared to be foreigners. Any New Yorker with sense and a subway token would have been at the beach on a day like this.

I started looking at the pictures, taking my time — also something I never used to have the patience for. Most of them were fairly clichéd. I, too, love that old lady in the park with pigeons perched on her head, but I think it may be time to give it a rest. I moved along, and then I stopped. I stared. I set my brake because I knew I wasn't going anywhere for a while. It was a bridge, but photographed from underneath so you could see the gridwork. It loomed upward in a pattern of delicate intricacy that contrasted starkly with the steel's violent power. The span thrust out over the river and then simply disappeared into a cloud bank. The image drew me totally inside the frame. I found myself shivering, imagining the cold breath of the fog, wondering if someone was cloaked there, readying himself for a final plunge over the edge. I don't even know how long I sat there gazing. But sometimes if I remain in the same position for too long, I begin to ache. Finally, I noticed that the backs of my legs had started to throb, and when I shifted in my chair, the man I'd seen when I first came in was standing beside me. God knows how long he'd been there.

"You seem interested in this photograph," he said.

"Very," I answered. I was rattled, disoriented, as if he'd shaken me awake from a disturbing dream.

"I wonder why." It wasn't a casual question — he *really* wanted to know. I took a closer look at him. He was about six feet tall, a little stooped and on the slim side, in a navy polo shirt and faded jeans. His hair was dark blond with sun streaks in it, and of the straight fine texture I always, after seeing too many Merchant-Ivory movies, think of as belonging to English aristocrats. He had blue eyes set deep into the bony planes of his face. He hadn't shaved.

I glanced at the picture again, pretending to consider it, but I was trying to make out the name on the placard: *Joseph D. Malone*.

"Well, Mr. Malone, I hope you've got a good shrink," I said.

His eyes opened a little wider, then he grinned. "That bad?"

"Or good."

"I've met you before, haven't I?" he asked.

"I don't think so." He had a look on his face that matched my own unnerving zap when I first saw him: *Where in the hell do I know her from?*

"I think it's brave of you to hang around while people look at your work," I went on.

"I've never had a photo exhibited so I was curious. But I'm not sure I'd do it again."

"Are all your pictures so tragic?"

"I didn't think this one was." He stared at it. "I wasn't in the best state of mind when I shot it, actually."

11

No kidding, I thought. "What about that one?" I pointed to the next photo by someone named Smith, a bicycle leaning against a bodega.

"You first," he said. I got the feeling he was testing me.

"It's an interesting idea, but not very well executed. It's too flat."

"I think we'd better get some coffee." Not waiting for a response, he took hold of my chair as if it were the most natural gesture and starting shoving me to the exit. Maybe he just figured since I was disabled, I wouldn't have anything pressing to do. I didn't know whether to be angry or embarrassed at my reaction, which was all too passive-female circa 1950. Not only that, I was revoltingly grateful that I'd pulled on my pale blue tank top because I knew it made my eyes seem almost navy. I looked up at Joseph Malone and got that compressed wheelchair view from below the chin. There was a little dent under the stubble. When I felt like reaching up and touching it, alarms went off in my head. Which I ignored.

"Who's got easy wheelchair access around here?" he asked when we hit the wall of heat outside.

"Jackson Hole's fine," I answered. I knew I could rely on the air conditioning there, and I was going to need it soon. I don't do so well when it gets over eighty degrees.

It's tough to have a conversation while you're under sail, so to speak, so I just sat there in silence wondering if maybe this guy had a kinky preference for the handicapped. I'd heard about such things on the MS website, but so far it had never happened to me. In the old days, men were always hitting on me, and to my surprise, I hadn't missed it at all, at least not up to now. There's a certain relief in not feeling like bait.

On the corner of Madison, a woman ran up in shorts and a bra and jogged in place, waiting with us for the traffic signal to change. "Hi, Joe," she said. Her eyes were far too full of him to take any notice of me. "Where were you last night? I thought you'd be at Michael's."

"Working late," Joe said as the light clicked to green. He didn't watch as she ran off toward the park, tossing her hair, but I did. She had great definition.

It took some maneuvering to get me through the narrow doorway into the restaurant. They seated us against the window where I wouldn't trip anybody up. Joe faced the interior of the room and I had a dazzling view of the street. Ordinarily I can't drag my attention away from the New York parade passing by outside, but now I had to force myself to keep from gawking at Joe Malone's face. Close up, his eyes held prisms of gold that lent them an unusual aqua tint. His eyebrows and lashes were dark, much darker than his hair. The effect served to further outline the extraordinary eyes. I felt like asking him about Michael's where he was supposed to be last night, but I kept silent while we ordered. He asked for one of those huge, politically incorrect burgers. I just wanted an iced tea. My stomach was doing flip-flops as it was.

Since I got sick, most people start out with, "Do you mind if I ask you a personal question?" It amazes me sometimes. Cab drivers, strangers on the street. One time a lady in the park sent her child over to do her dirty work. "What's wrong with you, lady? Did you have an accident or what?" So I was surprised when Joe said, "You're a perceptive critic. Are you a photographer?"

I laughed. "If you're partial to snapshots of people's feet with acres of lawn. I'm just an art junkie. Any kind of art."

"Maybe that's where we've seen one another, in a museum or a gallery."

An African-American woman passed by outside, swung around and tapped on the window beside Joe's head. He turned and gave her a wave. There was an elegance about the gesture. His profile revealed a bump about mid-nose. It wasn't one of those little porcine noses either, more like a real Roman schnozz. "You know a lot of women," I remarked.

"It's just New York," he said, as if that explained it. "You know, you really brought me up short. I always thought of that bridge shot as a comforting image."

"Well, it just shows what a good photographer you are. That the other feelings percolated up as well."

"Or what a sensitive eye you have," he said.

I was inordinately pleased, but I was dying to ask him about the unhappy time he'd referred to back in the gallery. Maybe he'd been breaking up with a girlfriend or getting a divorce. I looked at his finger. No ring. "So do you work in the art world?" I asked.

He shook his head and the eyes darkened a little. "My time's pretty much monopolized by a family business." Maybe he didn't want me to press, but I couldn't help it.

"Which is?"

"A small airline. I'm in charge of the New York office. What about you?" He sure hopped off that topic in a hurry.

"I teach English to high school kids."

"Don't talk to me about brave," he said. I put my brain into reverse and came up with the answer: my remark in the gallery. The man paid attention.

"Well, it's Cameron, the private school," I said, "so I don't have to worry quite so much about being gunned down. But I want to know more about your photographs." And about your family, and your childhood, where you went to college, your girlfriends (well, maybe not), your job that you don't like. Plus I'd just as soon take a close look at every square inch of your body. It had been a while since I'd allowed myself any of those fantasies. I could hear Ma buzzing in my ear: *Whoa, there, Annie, you're in deep doo-doo* — except she wouldn't have said doo-doo. I suppose it's my form of rebellion — I never use what I consider to be vulgar curse words, except to quote Ma.

"No, you first. I want to know every goddamn thing about you," he said, and our eyes snapped together with what seemed an audible click. I don't know who was more startled. "Jesus," he murmured.

But since I'd already jumped on the freight train, I decided to get it over with. "It's MS. Why I'm in the chair."

"How long have you had it?"

"Five years."

"Do you get remissions?"

"Mostly I do pretty well. I've only had to resort to this," I tapped my chair, "twice. I still work out at the gym when I can. I was something of an athlete in my day." All-state track, head of the Brighton University ski team, four years of dance, and on and on.

"Did something set you back?"

"I don't know, really. It just seems to happen periodically, and I'd picked up a cold." Actually, it was a urinary tract infection, but I was hardly going to tell him that.

I liked that he didn't get all maudlin about what a pity it was, wasted youth, etcetera, etcetera. He just nodded as if I was telling him how many siblings I had. "Usually, I prefer to weave a more imaginative tale," I admitted.

"Let's hear." His burger came, smothered in onions. He offered the first bite to me. It looked pretty appetizing so I took it. To be honest, what I really wanted was to share something with him.

"It depends on who's asking, the level of impertinence. Relative strangers get something like: it's Degenerative Antidisestablishmentarianism. It took me two weeks to learn that word when I was seven so I figure I might as well get some use out of it. For total strangers it's: I'm in disguise for undercover police work, or I only tipped a cab driver fifteen percent and he ran me over, or just that I prefer to sit." He started to say something and shook his head. "What?" I asked.

"I was wondering where I fit in. In the stranger department."

"Well. I don't know the answer to that." I reached for his plate and stabbed a french fry.

We spent an hour over lunch, during which Joe spoke easily and passionately about photography and reading, another of his avocations. He was reticent regarding his career, and it wasn't until we'd left the restaurant for the park that I got him to open up. I use the term advisedly since he imparted information in such a detached manner. But I did determine that he worked for a small charter enterprise started by his father, upstate near Utica. His dad was a pilot who had some kind of genius with airplane engines. His mother and older brother launched the business. Then when Joe got out of college, his marketing skills began to turn the enterprise into a multistate success story. Hence the article in *Crain's*, but I found out about that from another source. Joe never would have mentioned it.

As for me, I told him about my early years as a dilettante, how difficult it had always been for me to make choices when I wanted to do it all. I was crazy about music in high school. I resented having to settle on learning a particular instrument when what I really wanted was to become a one-woman band. Same thing with athletics. I aspired to the American Ballet Theatre and the Miami Dolphins with equal fervor. I confessed that I owed my career to my mother's bullying me into a teaching degree. Thankfully, as it turned out, since I'd had to give up my other gigs — tutoring tennis, teaching gymnastics on the West Side, coaching jazz dance. The Cameron School had been incredibly flexible, in part because I was an alumna but also, I suspect, because the headmaster thought it was instructive to have a disabled teacher on the staff.

Joe had pushed me down to the Great Lawn, where several ball games were going on. It took only minutes for the tops of my knees to turn pink in the broiling sun, but I wasn't about to complain. I knew the heat could make me sick, but I figured I was still semi-frozen from Jackson Hole and it might take me a while to defrost.

"You mentioned your mother," he said. I braked my chair beside an empty bench as he sat down and stretched out his legs. I noticed he was wearing battered Top-Siders with no socks. I could see the vein pulsing beside his ankle. "Is your father . . . ?"

"Left when I was six. He lives in L.A."

"Do you ever see him?"

I shook my head. "Not since before I was diagnosed. He's been married three times and there're a lot of kids. He's always sent money, but now Ma's got her bakery going in the neighborhood. We're all right."

"What about men?"

I gave him a stare.

"I told you I want to know everything," he said. When he smiled, lines crinkled beside his eyes and an indefinable sadness evaporated. I could see that his bottom teeth were a little crooked.

"Are you married?" He wasn't about to give up. "Do you have three children? A boyfriend? Come on."

I suddenly felt shy. Not just a little shy, but blushingly, stammeringly shy. "This time you. You go first."

"All right. I've dated a lot of women but there's only been one relationship that's lasted more than a few months. It hasn't been working out. I know what you're thinking. Can't commit."

"My record isn't that hot in the commitment department either. There was an off-and-on two-year thing, but it ended after I got sick."

Just then somebody hit a triple halfway to the West Side and a great roar went up. I watched a runner slide home and felt such a tug, a tearing sensation. It wasn't usually that bad, but I had to blink hard. I'd never minded getting dirty in a slide. Joe was studying me carefully, so I put a hand up to my eyes as if the glare bothered me. He took the other one and held it, palm up, staring into my future.

"So there's nobody now?" he asked. I shook my head, not trusting myself to speak through the lump.

"You know what, I think I'd better get going," I said, and withdrew my hand.

"Are you sure?"

I unlocked the chair and gave myself a push.

"I can put you in a cab," he offered. I liked that he didn't protest when he saw I was resolved.

"You can walk me out of the park, but I'm okay after that. It's good for me to flex my biceps." I did a body-builder's pose with my arms, showing off what definition I had.

As we wound down along beside the Metropolitan Museum, I was trying not to think, just to be. Live in the moment. It was hard when I'd spent so many years always looking ahead to the next challenge, the next choice. But it felt good to have a man's company, to remember what it was like to be touched, even if there was a sting to it. When we got to the street, he said, "Sure you'll be all right?"

"Oh, yeah."

"Anna, let me have your number."

"Oh, I don't think so. No offense. I'm just not . . . I don't think so."

"I don't even know where you live."

"I've got the light," I said, gave a mighty shove and sailed out across Eighty-fourth Street. "Keep taking those pictures!" I aimed a backward wave at him so I didn't have to see his face. I ought to carry air-sick bags for when I make remarks like that.

2

Instead of heading home, I found myself wheeling over to York Avenue. I stopped outside the bakery for a moment to see if there were any customers. Nobody. Ma was leaning on the counter over a magazine. *People*, probably. She was vocal about what a rag it was, but I happened to know she bought one every week and read it on the sly. I was grateful she wasn't busy. Ordinarily, she used free time to invent new recipes. She'd had some success with carrot-fig spice cookies, less with the latest effort to banish the tedium of chocolate chips, something called space-junkies. I haven't dared ask what's in them.

Norma's Crust had the widest smoothest wheelchair access in town. When the bell jangled, Ma looked up and quickly slipped the magazine under the counter. Her eyebrows drew together as soon as she got a good look at my face.

"What's the matter?" she asked me.

I opened my mouth to tell her "Nothing" and immediately burst into tears. I'm not much of a weeper, so Ma was out from behind that counter in half a second. I got the impression she vaulted over it, but of course that's ludicrous.

"What the fuck, Anna?" She had her arms around me while I just sobbed away, drowning her apron. I took a couple of great heaving breaths and started to laugh. What a spectacle. At this point, Ma straightened up and went for the scotch. She poured me a stiff splash in a measuring cup and watched while I downed it. Then she went over to the door, hung the "Closed" sign on it and pulled up a chair. My ponytail was somewhat the worse for wear. Ma reached out and tucked some stray tendrils behind my ears. "You ready to talk about it?" she asked.

"I think I must be cracking up," I said. "It's only that I met this guy at the A.I.P. and we had a nice afternoon in the park."

"Uh-huh," Ma said. She could speak volumes in two syllables.

"Well, that's it. You think I could have a tiny bit more?" I held out the measuring cup. She poured another half an inch, which I sipped at.

"Don't pull your deep-dive act on me now," Ma warned. "You know the deal."

When I'd been diagnosed, Ma made me promise to talk to her when I was low. Otherwise, she said, she'd kick my ass out. My father had not been one to share his feelings, and Ma said fifteen years of silent seething was enough. Still, there were certain things we'd never discussed.

"I haven't been with anybody. I mean men. Since."

"I figure you miss that," Ma said. "There were always a lot of guys around."

I nodded. "I guess I just never let myself think about it. Not after Bobby. That was such a mess." Bobby Zaklow had been my steady man for almost two years before that last great run at the reservoir. He stuck it out for another six months, but then he bailed. I couldn't blame him, and I didn't think I was in love anyway. I'd always thought that since I couldn't have Marlon Brando in *Streetcar*, I would never truly surrender myself to an all-consuming passion. Still, it didn't feel good when Bobby left, and I just shut myself off from men after that. I knew they'd all pull away from me once they found out what the future had in store.

"Tell me about this person," Ma said.

"His name is Joseph D. Malone. He had a really good photograph in the exhibit.

25

Maybe it was accidental. He's kind. He's troubled. He. He." I could feel the tears coming again. "He swept me off my feet, Ma," I wailed, "and I wasn't even *on* my feet."

"Oh, Jesus," Ma said, wiping my face. She let me cry for a while.

"Sorry," I gulped finally. I could see she was worried. It's not great for me to get agitated.

"So what're you going to do about it, babe?" Ma asked.

"Nothing." I looked at the desk in the corner where Ma did her accounts. There was a photo of me at college, accepting an award for the ski team. I was leaning on my poles, one hip cocked, one knee slightly bent. If I tried that now, I'd wind up on my rear end in a snowbank. God, I remember what it felt like flying downhill with the snow peppering my face. I still dream about it. "Nothing," I repeated. I made a goofy face at Ma. "You got a new cookie for me to try out? How about something with okra?"

It wasn't as easy as I thought, forgetting about Joe Malone. It was as if there were some cosmic conspiracy to throw him up to me at every possible juncture. First there was a copy of *Crain's* in the waiting room at my neurologist's. I always complained to Dr. Klewanis about the paucity of reading material there, assuming that he was trying to speed up the process of his patients' nerve-sheath damage by making us leaf through *Your Well Body* and *Scientific American*. But this time I snatched the business weekly up like it was a double issue of *Vogue*. Joe Malone's face was staring straight out at me with that plucked-chicken look of the recent haircut. In fact, he was one of half a dozen "new faces in the boardroom." There was a short paragraph on each executive. Joe's item said he divided his time between New York City and upstate near North Lockville, wherever that was, and that he'd persuaded his way into the offices of the CEOs of every major airline to pick their brains about co-operative air routes in the eastern U.S. Both Air East and Blue Skies Airways had been so impressed with him that they'd tried to snap Joe up and AirMalone along with him. I struggled with myself about whether to stuff the article in my bag. Then, after I'd left it behind, I stopped at all the news concessions on the way home until I found a leftover copy.

AirMalone chose that week to launch an advertising campaign that was broadcast daily on WNYC. I was listening to the radio and hauling my eight-pound weights around when suddenly there was this voice saying, *"AirMalone, the little airline with the big future."* Maybe it had been on before and I hadn't noticed.

Then the Sunday *Times* struck the final blow with an article in the Business section. I was soaking in the tub when Ma came in flapping the newspaper at me like a red cape at a bull.

"Isn't this your photographer?" She stuck the article in front of my nose, and there he was again, with longer hair this time. UP-STATE UPSTART FLIES HIGH. Either Air-Malone had hired a fantastic publicist or I was being pursued by some sadistic god of circumstance. Pretending casual interest, I grabbed the paper and got it soaking wet. I learned a few things about Joe Malone: (a) he was thirty-one years old; (b) he graduated at the top of his class from first Cornell, then the Harvard Business School; (c) his mother was described as "formidable"; and (d) he was "romantically linked" to someone called Lola Falcon. The name brought to mind a heroine worthy of Thomas Hardy, and what does "romantically linked" mean anyway? I think of a chain-link fence.

"There's no escaping the man," I muttered.

"What about this Lola broad?" Ma asked.

"He basically said he's a womanizer, so I wouldn't put too much stock in it."

"Oh, well, that's a relief," she said with one of her looks.

I gazed down at my legs floating like pale pink sausages on the bathwater. "He wasn't coming on to me, Ma. Believe me. I was in my chair, remember?"

"As if that gives you absolution." She took the soggy newspaper from me and pretended to wring it out like a dishrag. "I'd try the hair dryer. Just on the off chance you want to keep this."

By the time September rolled around, I was in remission. Thank God, because I always hated to start the academic year in my chair. I was one of those obnoxious faculty members who was unequivocably ecstatic to get back to work. First of all, it was a lot easier to forget my own complaints when surrounded by fidgeting, awkward, stressed-out, loopy, immensely touching and hormonally challenged teen-agers. I could never predict what was going to emerge from their mouths — observations ranging in intellectual acuity from Einstein to Daffy Duck. While almost continually unnerved, I was never bored. The third week of school, I took one of my classes on a field trip to the Pierpont Morgan Library to examine the illuminated manuscripts. We were crowded around some Blake when I looked up and saw Joe Malone's face glowing like a saint's, suspended over a display case on the other side of the dimly lit room. At that moment, he raised his eyes and spotted me. It was delicious to watch his face register the eloquent combination of confusion and shock. Last he knew, I had wheels instead of feet, and here I stood in all my five-foot-seven-inch glory. I could read his thoughts: *She been to Lourdes or what?*

I gave him a perky little wave. Michelle Cross, well turned out in Calvin Klein, sniffed drama in the air and peered at Joe as he crossed the room. He took both my hands and kissed me on the cheek.

"Anna," Joe said. The kids backed off as his gaze made the trip from my head to my toes. "What happened?"

"I'm better," I answered. I thought Michelle's Clinique-enhanced eyeballs were going to pop out of their sockets. "These are my students. We're getting illuminated."

Joe smiled at them. Michelle's best friend Sukey was mouth-breathing audibly. "I'm going to borrow your teacher for a minute," Joe announced. Of course, I had nothing to say about it.

I almost growled at Michelle. "Read the transliteration in this display. Take detailed notes because we're going to discuss it when we get back to school."

They made a big show of gathering around the case but they kept watching us. Except for good old oblivious Rudy Steinberger who was already scribbling in his notebook.

"Why didn't you call me back?"

"What?"

"I phoned the school a few times and left messages."

That reptile Chubb, I thought. Always grabbing for the departmental phone to see if he could get the edge on a colleague. Last semester he neglected to tell me the head-master had been trying to reach me for two days.

"But it's not that I'm really surprised to see you," Joe went on. He still had hold of my arm. "It's the lack of wheels."

"It just wasn't a great summer, that's all. When I met you, I mean. Not that it wasn't great to meet you." Oh, shit. Well, I do curse sometimes, but only when it really counts for something, and mostly in my head.

31

"I've been running into you all over the place," Joe said. I did like those smile crinkles, such gleeful punctuation.

"Where was that?"

"Well, let's see. I had a solicitation from the MS Society in the mail. I rented two videos that featured Cameron Diaz. Then I was trying to find my ski poles in the back of the closet and my brother's bowling ball rolled off the top shelf and almost gave me a concussion." He touched the spot. I had forgotten about his long expressive fingers.

"Oh. Bolles," I said. I wasn't about to mention the little shrine cached in my bureau drawer — the photos from *Crain's* and the *Times*. "Ski poles in October?"

"Next month there should be plenty of cross-country in the Adirondacks. I want you to come with me. Can you? I mean . . ." He gestured in the direction of my knees. I was annoyed I'd worn slacks. My legs are still good.

"I don't know." I didn't remember telling him about the ski team. Anyway, it wasn't the skiing that worried me. It was more the sensation that there was an earthquake underfoot, somewhere around 7.5 on the Richter scale. I glanced at my students, who were fooling around, whispering and shoving. "I've got to get back to them."

"Your home number's unlisted," he said. So he'd gotten that far. He had my arm and was clearly in no hurry to let go.

"I'll make sure you can get through at Cameron. Ask for the English department." I figured that if he did try to get in touch, I could dodge his calls more easily at work until I figured out what to do. He read the reluctance, or was it terror, on my face.

"Look, Anna, you don't have to commit to a weekend trip in the north country. We could have dinner."

"Great," I said. He let go and I backed off. "It was nice to run into you. I have to . . ." I made another feeble little wave in the general direction of the adolescents.

That was it. I picked up a paper airplane from the floor and rejoined the restive tribe, and none too soon. I didn't imagine that the ghost of Pierpont Morgan would have appreciated the decibel level. The next time I looked, Joe was gone.

"Is that your boyfriend, Miss Bolles?" Michelle asked. She'd applied fresh lipstick, the color of cappuccino.

"God, Michelle, you're so inappropriate!" Sukey piped up. The two had a difficult relationship, symbiotic and fraught with conflict.

"So is he?" This from Will Simmons who

33

was a knock-off of Johnny Depp. I would have done almost anything he asked of me except give him a passing grade which he truly did not deserve.

"No, he's not my boyfriend."

"Well, he wants to be," Will said.

"Oh, and you're such an expert!" Michelle was justifiably miffed that I'd chosen to answer Will.

Rudy Steinberger looked up from the display case. "Do you think they retouched these drawings? They look like somebody just did them this morning."

A-plus, Rudy, I thought.

There was a message on the English department voice-mail at the end of the day. I erased it without writing down his number. I figured I wouldn't have to mention it to Ma, but he'd phoned the bakery, too. I didn't remember telling him the name.

"No, I'm not going to see him," I told her over dinner. It was salad night at the Bolles household, and we were picking our way through a Brazilian rain forest assortment of leafy greens.

"Why not?" Just a trifle belligerent, I thought.

"Oh, do you have a point of view here?" I asked her.

"I liked his voice. As a matter of fact, we had a little chat."

It's an odd expression: *my heart sank.* But it felt that way, as if something inside my chest slid a couple of notches lower, into a dark place. "Didn't you swear you would never again interfere in my social life?"

"I was being polite."

"What did he say? Tell me exactly."

"That he wanted to see you and that he thought you were trying to blow him off."

I set down my fork. "He didn't."

"I swear."

"And you said?"

"That I'd encourage you to go out with him."

"Well, it didn't take you long to get cozy."

"I told you I liked his voice."

"He could be a serial killer for all you know."

"Well, then he's a very engaging serial killer with a nice voice." She tore off a hunk of parmesan baguette and scraped it around the inside of her salad bowl. She pretended it was a procedure equivalent to atheroscopic surgery so she wouldn't have to look at me.

"Kurt Finnegan," I said.

The scooping stopped briefly, then resumed. "I admit I overstepped in that case.

A tiny chat on the phone can't compare."

"Overstepped! You got the man fired from his job!"

She looked up at me now and her eyes were smoking. "He deserved worse. The guy was a shit."

"For two-timing your daughter."

"With the boss's wife."

I sighed. "Ma, I'm not starting up with Joe Malone. If he's on my case, that means he's got something wrong with him, and I'm not interested."

"So basically you're saying you've taken yourself off the market."

"Right."

"You do remember your reaction to spending the afternoon with him last summer? The tears, the *sturm und drang?*"

I got up and started clearing dishes. "I'm more vulnerable when I'm in my chair. He was symbolic of something, that's all."

"What a crapperful. You've decided you can't handle a relationship because you're sick. So, what, you're going to just cancel that part of you right out of the picture forever?"

I turned on her so fast that I lost my balance and had to grab the back of a chair. "Yes! That's *exactly* right. It's hard enough just dealing with myself. The last thing I need is some masochistic social-worker type breathing down my neck and congratulating himself for taking me on."

Ma's eyeballs drilled into me like mean little lasers. "I'm ashamed of you."

That's one thing Ma had never said to me in my life. I could feel my own eyes filling up as we stared at one another. Then a weariness passed over her face and she pushed her chair back and patted her lap. I sat down. It's pretty absurd, I suppose, but we've been doing this since I was a toddler and just never got out of the habit. We both took a little time out for some deep breaths.

"Anna, how do you see your life when you look into the future?" she asked after a while.

"I try not to," I said over her shoulder.

"Well, it's time you did."

"Does the future have to include a man?"

"It would be nice."

I sat back and looked at her. "You've done all right without one."

She smiled. " 'All right' is a fucking relative term, honeybun."

"Well, I don't need one. I'm a feminist."

That brought a laugh. "Look, I know how tough it was for an independent type like you to move back home with your mother. When I'm dead and gone I won't care if you live alone or with a pair of Rottweilers. That's not what this conversation is about." She plucked a thread off my sweater. "Is it?"

I shook my head, feeling about six years old. My nose was probably running.

"Joe Malone is not a symbol of anything," she went on. "He's a person you're drawn to, and you're scared. Be brave and admit it."

I took another breath. "Okay. I admit it."

"I'm not saying you should do anything about it. Just don't sling bullshit at me. I have no tolerance."

Ma always carried the warm scent of the bakery on her skin. Hugging her was like squeezing a giant loaf of bread. Then I climbed off and picked up her empty salad bowl.

"I'll figure it out," I said.

"Atta girl."

3

I listened to a lot of Mozart over the next week. I don't know what it is about Mozart, but he seems to cut to the core of things; there's no place to hide. It was in the depths of the final heart-rending movement of the *Requiem* that I got up and called the number I'd erased but not forgotten. I'd made this deal with Mozart that if I got Joe's machine, it wasn't meant that I should see him and I could just hang up.

"Joe here," his voice said. No hello.

"Well, Anna here," I answered. Wolfgang Amadeus could just wipe that smirk off his face.

There was a brief silence. Then, "Your mother's a piece of work."

"I'll say."

"The Met's open late tomorrow night. Want to meet me there to look around and then let me take you to dinner?"

"Okay."

"Six-thirty, so we'll have time with the pictures."

"Okay." Nothing if not pithy.

We hung up in a hurry, both of us grateful to get this part over with.

It was aggravating how happy I felt all day Tuesday. After spending one class cracking inappropriately jolly jokes about poor mad Mrs. Rochester locked away in the attic, Michelle Cross came up and asked me if I was using some new kind of moisturizer on my face.

He was waiting at the bottom of the steps. Nobody ever meets at the bottom of the steps, always in the grand foyer. I had to think it was because he was aware I might need help getting up that long marble sweep. I could feel a faint brush of stubble as he bent to kiss my cheek. Then he just grinned at me for a moment in a boyish kind of way. I confess a penchant for a well-delivered boyish grin. Joe took my arm to head up the steps. "I'm glad to see you. What shall we investigate?"

"Would you be depressed by the Dutch portraits?" I asked. "I've been thinking about them."

He laughed. "I don't know why I should be surprised. They're my favorites."

"How come?"

"Oh, all that drama, I guess," he said.

Everybody else was looking at the Impressionists, so we had the Old Dutch Masters almost to ourselves. He was very knowledgeable, talking about Vermeer's balanced composition and use of light.

"She looks like Mrs. Hendrix, my seventh grade teacher," Joe said, pointing out a particularly dour specimen in a gilt frame. "She carried a metal yardstick and whacked us with it if we didn't pay attention."

"Good God, where was this, the gulag?"

"Black River Falls, New York. She introduced me to the first book I actually enjoyed reading, so I have a warm spot for her."

"Let me guess. *Bleak House*."

"Nope. *Our Town*. Then she took us to Syracuse for an amateur production. I thought it was great even though Emily Webb was pushing fifty."

"I don't think of plays as books."

"That's what I read, almost exclusively. Sam Shepherd, Mamet, Ibsen. Shakespeare, to lighten things up."

"When I teach a play just from the text, I feel like I'm cheating the dramatist."

"There's a Tom Stoppard in previews. Will you come with me?"

"Maybe," I said. I was thinking we'd see how things went.

"Fair enough."

He chose a quiet neighborhood place that

served homemade pasta. Over linguini, he told me that he rarely stayed in the city if he could possibly get back up north. "It's ironic. My mother and my brother are much more urban, and they're stuck up there in the boondocks running the day-to-day. And here I am, Farmer Jones, wheeling and dealing in the big city."

"Oh, sure, Farmer Jones, I read about you in *Crain's*. That was a cute picture of you milking cows in your overalls."

"You read that?" He looked pleased.

"And the *Times*." What the hell. I'm too old to be coy.

"Then you're completely informed."

"Mm." Not quite. There was that little item about Lola Falcon.

"You said you'd tell me about the MS."

I obliged, describing the litany of early symptoms, the fruitless trips to specialists, the misdiagnoses of Lyme disease, hypochondria, Guillain-Barre, brain tumor. Ma didn't tell me about that one until later, and just lived through four days of hell all by herself. "It was actually a relief by the time I found a smart neurologist who figured it out."

"Are you on steroids or one of the ABC drugs?" He smiled at my look. "I've been putting in some time at the medical library. I

42

also have a physician friend upstate who won't take my calls anymore."

He was exaggerating, of course, but it was disarming just the same. "I'm on prednisone," I said. "One of these days I'll balloon up and they can use me in the Macy's Thanksgiving Day Parade."

"Well, it hasn't happened yet." He called the waiter. "The lady will have the Chocolate Sin for dessert."

"You're very bossy."

"It's how I got to be in *Crain's*."

"I see. Okay, Joe, I paid my dues. Now let's hear about the airplanes."

He pushed his chair back from the table just an inch or two. "I'm not very good at introspection. Sometimes when I think about where I've wound up, I feel as if it had more to do with everybody else than me."

"In what way?"

"Well, back in high school, for instance. I always got elected class president, but I never looked for it, never wanted to run. It just happened, year after year."

I laughed. "I was president, too, but I was always in there electioneering like a madwoman. Selling favors for votes, kissing babies . . . well, maybe not kissing babies. The thing is, you're obviously good at running things."

He nodded. "I know it."

It was hard not to smile. He acted as if leadership ability were some terrible character flaw. "Maybe you're just not interested in airplanes," I suggested.

"Actually, I like how they look. They're very pleasing. The shape. The grace. I'd rather fly in them or photograph them than sit in those endless board meetings with a bunch of people who think spread sheets carry the same moral weight as the Gettysburg Address." He actually ran out of breath. "Quite a speech. Sorry."

"I'm not so sure you're in the right line of work."

"Well, it's what I've spent a lifetime training for."

"Top of your class at the B-school."

"That's right. We've got a few hundred employees in an economically depressed county up there depending on us to keep things percolating. That's pretty gratifying."

"What about your father? Is he still . . . ?"

"Oh, he spends all his time puttering around with antique planes and talking to his cronies about the good old days. Your Chocolate Sin is melting."

I poked at it. I felt like poking at Joe some more, too, but he was looking so haunted that I took pity. And I suddenly had one of those waves of fatigue that feel like somebody dropped a heavy black drape over my head. He noticed.

"Are you all right, Anna?"

I tried to give him a reassuring smile, but my hand chose that moment to deck my water glass. If I could only predict when these things were going to happen I could just check into a padded cell until it passes and I'd do a lot less damage. The goblet went careening across the table, teetered at the edge and crashed to the floor. There was a fuss as the waiter mopped and swept. I wasn't so much mortified as very, very tired, so bone weary that it was an effort to open my mouth to speak.

"Do you want me to get the check?"

I nodded.

While we waited, he stared at me through the candlelight. "You are so beautiful it's scary," he said.

"It's just the candles."

"You know that I'm in way over my head here."

"You can't be. It's too soon and I'm a really bad bet."

He smiled. "Anna, you're so sleepy I can say whatever I want and you'll forget I made a complete fool of myself."

Not bloody likely. Oh my, talk about beauty. His eyes were like jewels in that light, shimmering facets of blue and green and gold.

"Can you take me home now?"

He held me very close in the cab, and when he walked me to the apartment door, he gave me a gentle, lingering kiss on the mouth.

"Tell your mother hello for me," he said. I clung to the doorknob for support until he walked away and I could let myself in.

Ma was in bed already with her reading light on. She was always careful not to intrude on my privacy after I'd been out. If I went in to see her, that was one thing, but I could count on her to keep out of my way otherwise. I'd thought that the moment I got home, I'd collapse for ten hours of sleep. But I sat down in the dark in the living room and stared out the window. Joe was out there in some Manhattan apartment, throwing his keys down on the table, shrugging off his jacket, pouring himself a glass of water. Maybe he'd stand at the sink a minute, lost in thought, remembering the soft glow of the restaurant. I looked out at the lights in the distant buildings. They seemed magical, like Joe's eyes across the table. The fatigue crept over me again but I forced myself to stay awake. I knew the way I felt wasn't going to last for long.

4

Joe phoned Thursday night to say he'd been called out of town for a couple of weeks, but wanted to know when he could take me to the theater.

"Oh, any time," I answered, with a private nod to the little subtitle that flickers through my thoughts whenever I make plans: *Assuming I'm not in the hospital.* One of the characteristics of relapsing/remitting MS is a disconcerting element of surprise. Just when you think you're on an even keel, or maybe you've even had a day when you've forgotten you have the disease, it jumps out at you and yells "Gotcha!" Last summer, I was working out on the treadmill at the "Y." Other than a slight tingly sensation when I lifted my feet, everything seemed normal. Of course, normal doesn't mean the same thing it did when I was on the track team. Then, about ten minutes into my routine, everything simply shut down. My legs disappeared from under me and the treadmill spit me out onto the floor in a heap. I hit my head pretty hard and came to with one of the supervisors trying to lift me. I wound up in the hospital for a couple of weeks until they got me stabilized on steroids, did another series of MRI's that boasted an increase in brain lesions, and sent me home in a wheelchair. That's relapsing/remitting for you. So when I told Joe "any time," it was delivered with a certain amount of poetic license.

"Sorry I have to be away so long," he said before he hung up.

"Me, too." But I was lying. In fact, I was having too much fun savoring the afterglow. Why rush into screwing up a perfect memory? Besides, I'm a sucker for the instant replay.

In my mental video of *Joe and Anna: The First Date*, I watched the charming couple walk side by side on Madison Avenue, backlit by elegant storefront windows. Joe drapes his arm around Anna's shoulders. Hear the music swell? The shadows merge and I can almost feel the pressure of his hip against mine. Delicious. And the climactic good-night kiss is surveyed from every conceivable vantage point. The movie camera makes its slow turn around them, Joe and Anna, mouths melting together. Surely I can

48

get six months out of this before the faint taste of wine from his lips fades from memory and the video dries up into a stale rerun.

"You still awake?" Ma called.

"Sort of," I answered.

"Don't you have parent conferences tomorrow?" she asked.

"Oh. Yeah." What a jolt. Instead of lying in bed indulging my adolescent fantasies to the accompaniment of Nina Simone, I should be poring over my notes in preparation for one of the most harrowing days of the academic year. The video of *Joe and Anna* slid out of my brain, and in its place snapped the one called *Anna's First Parent Conference*. I keep it filed under *Horror and Suspense*.

At the Cameron School, it's the homeroom teacher who gathers up the academic reports and reviews them with the student and parents twice a year. It's an excellent system, but not without moments of unexpected drama. For my first conference, I had stayed up until three A.M. committing the reports to memory. I was nervous, and I guess I thought that if I didn't have to refer to the pages, I'd come off looking like a veteran instead of a scared amateur.

I congratulated myself that my earliest appointment was with the Steinbergers and their son Eric, older brother of Rudy, who at that time was still in grade school. Eric was a prodigy in mathematics, but he didn't have Rudy's gentle charm and he despised anything that required movement, like walking or breathing. It was interesting to watch Eric raise his hand, as if it were attached to a string and the puppeteer was dragging on it ever . . . so . . . slowly.

The Steinbergers had arrived promptly, carrying their copies of the reports they'd picked up in the lobby downstairs. We said our good mornings, and then I launched into my little speech about Eric's refusal to attend gym class. Mr. Steinberger promptly had a fit. I mean a real fit, where he fell out of his chair and frothed at the mouth. I remember thinking for a split second, Mr. Steinberger cares *that* much about athletics? But it turned out, of course, that the poor man was an epileptic, an affliction with which I can now easily identify. What happened as a result of this initiation rite, however, was that every time somebody mentioned Parent Conference Day, the first thing I visualized was Albert Steinberger writhing on the floor with his eyeballs popping out.

I flipped on some Vivaldi to buoy my

spirits and settled down at my desk. Joe was now safely banished from my mind, terror being a singularly effective antidote to reverie.

Our homerooms were made up of kids from all four high-school classes. I hit the ground running with a freshman whose father spent most of the conference on his cell phone arguing with the absent mother about pool repairs for the country house. Then an inspiring session with Marti Guzman who lived in the South Bronx and had been mugged four times trying to get to school on the subway. Marti had to translate everything I said into Spanish for his mother, and if she didn't like something she heard, little sparks flew out of her eyes. After that came Will Simmons, the Johnny Depp look-alike, whose parents listened to the litany of F's, D's, and Incompletes with the same charming insouciance as their son. Then a horrific half hour gnashing my teeth as I was told to arrange for Sukey's transfer out of Grant Hurst's math class or else: one, Grant would be fired; two, I'd be fired; three, the school would be brought up on charges of criminal cruelty to Sukey, who hadn't handed in a single homework assignment since September.

But at long last there were the Steinbergers, Maria and Albert (of *grand mal* fame) who were gracious enough after Eric to request me for Rudy's homeroom. The Steinbergers were what Sukey would call *nerdesque*. Maria had prominent teeth and glasses with Coke-bottle lenses. Albert's haircut was straight out of a Norman Rockwell painting, complete with cowlick. But Rudy appreciated them despite their lack of cool. I loved that he still held his mother's hand straight through his conference. Rudy got A's in my Classics and Composition class, but he had difficulty with foreign languages. The Steinbergers nodded politely at my raves, but it was the C-minus in French that elicited their unrestrained pleasure.

"Rudy's worked very hard to pass the course," Albert said. "It's wonderful to see him begin to grasp the material."

"We're so proud of him," Maria said.

No hysteria about never getting into Harvard with a C-minus on his record. It wasn't the grade, it was Rudy's self-esteem and triumph that mattered to them. When Albert in his tie clip and too-short trousers reached over to touch his son's cheek with pride, I felt my throat grow tight. Something about good parenting — it slayed me every time.

I was perhaps alone in my assessment that Rudy Steinberger had sex appeal. There was just something about his mouth, a sort of semi-dimple at the corners, that I found provocative. I predicted that one day he would break hearts. His classmates, in the manner of enlightened teen-agers the world over, called him Rootie the Cootie.

I grabbed an early dinner with Grant Hurst, my friend from the Math department. The thing about Grant was his dignity. Were he ever to slip on a banana peel, you'd want to get it on videotape and stash it alongside Nureyev and Baryshnikov. I had a crush on him a few years ago, presuming that he only *thought* he was gay and surely I could make him see the error of his ways. He discouraged me in a most tactful fashion and became a close friend. Instead of the "Smelly Deli" or the "Ill Grill" near the school, we hung out at this Mexican haunt that even the kids avoided. The thing was, I could never find a Mexican there. The owner's name was Weiner, the waiter wore a turban, and the guy who made home deliveries was Korean. New York, the great melting pot.

"Who've *you* been having sex with?" Grant boomed. The primary reason I opted for this place was that it wasn't too close to school. Any discussion with Grant was shared by everybody within a five-block radius. The Sikh waiter pricked up his ears.

"I beg your pardon," I said.

"Come off it, Bolles. You've got postcoital gratification oozing from every pore." He tipped his margarita at me and took a swallow.

"I kissed a person. Big deal."

"Must have been some kiss."

I tried for an enigmatic smile à la Mona Lisa.

"Spill," he commanded.

"He's just a guy I met last summer. I'm not going to talk about him. I might jinx it."

Grant peered at me out of close-set eyes. At such moments, you got the feeling you were being scrutinized by an extremely alert bird of prey. "Whenever you're ready," he said, a temporary reprieve. "Don't fret about Sukey," he went on. "She'll do a lot better in Frieda's section. You sailed through Report Day as is your custom?"

"Oh, sure. The usual mix of Eugene O'Neill with a soupçon of Ionesco. But thanks for the kind words re Rudy Steinberger." I accepted a second Coke. I felt I needed reviving. "His parents think his every breath is absolute perfection. I tend to agree. They brought me marmalade." Even though he was only a Sophomore, Rudy took Grant's Advanced Calculus class.

"What do you make of this?" Grant took out a pen and scribbled on a napkin: M-U-S-C-L-E-B-R-A-N.

"Musclebran," I read. "A health cereal?"

"It's a homework assignment."

"I don't get it. What're you supposed to do?"

"I didn't tell them either. Think it over."

I chewed on my burrito. I wasn't sure it was supposed to be so crunchy. "Oh," I said. *"Unscramble."*

He nodded. "Only one student figured it out."

"Had to be Rudy." I watched Grant nod and take a bite of his taco. I know it seems inconceivable, but he never lost so much as a tendril of lettuce. "Should I be worried about Michelle Cross?" I asked him.

"She's certainly acquired that lean and hungry look," Grant said.

"The mother never leaves her alone, picking lint off her sweater, dabbing at her face with a tissue." I reached across the table to demonstrate how Filona Cross, brow furrowed with disapproval, fussed compulsively with Michelle's hair. "I don't care a rat's eyelash about your education,

Michelle, dear," I mimicked. "What concerns *me* is that you're physically *defective*."

"Burn the fucking parents!" he bellowed.

"Do you always have to turn up the volume when you say things like that?"

"Did I mention names?" He scraped the last grain of rice off his scrupulously clean plate. My place setting, on the other hand, looked like roadside litter. "Teaching means you walk around with cracks in your heart," he went on. "Forgive me if I feel the need to vent."

"I know. But to my continual amazement, there's nothing else I'd rather do." I sighed. "It was just supposed to be a job."

Grant was silent for a moment, always an ominous sign. "Anna," he said, and folded his long hands, even worse.

"Uh-oh," I said.

"Somebody's been complaining again," he said.

Inside me, the half-digested burrito stood on its end as my stomach flipped over. "Now what?"

Periodically, a parent would phone our headmaster or a board member to protest that I'd been absent too many days or that I fell down in the hall and did I have a drinking problem? Once, someone took issue with my wheelchair, arguing that the sight of it was traumatic and embarrassing to their child. But up to this point I'd managed to elude serious trouble, probably because my students tended to do well in their test scores. That was the bottom line, as they say, in Manhattan private schools. But my having MS made a lot of parents queasy, and since Grant was on the administrative advisory board, he heard all about it.

"Apparently the gist of it is that your illness is becoming intrusive, as evidenced by your misplacing Jennifer's architecture project last week."

"But anybody could have done that, even you. Well, maybe not you. Anyway, I found it right away."

"Somebody ratted to her parents, who went straight to Duncan Reese. Rumor has it you've got cognitive problems."

The worst of it was, I couldn't even dispute it. Sure, anybody can misplace things, but there was that spooky sensation that accompanies such lapses, as if my mind were staring at a blank screen. I had tried to picture myself holding Jennifer's model in my hands. But when I finally found it, carefully pillowed in the spare sweater I kept in the top of my closet, I couldn't remember putting it there.

"I suppose I can take a wild guess as to

how the word got out," I said.

"The oleaginous Chubb," he said. "You knew him in his youth, Anna. Tell me he was a party animal. Tell me he's got a navel ring under all that tweed."

"Sorry." Leonard Chubb and I graduated from Cameron together. He had been the kind of kid who sneaked into the library and hid resource material so his classmates couldn't get their term papers in on time. For some reason, it had disturbed him that, like him, I'd been accepted by Harvard but was drawn instead to Brighton's unconventional, lively intellectualism and the serious commitment to athletics. "I've been trying to feel sorry for him for years," I said.

"Don't be such an asshole, Annie!" Grant boomed. "He's after your job!"

A mother with two small children glared at us. I could hardly blame her.

"He pines to be chairman of the English department and then headmaster," I said. "All I want to do is teach, so why is he always on my case?"

"First of all, he rightly judges you the biggest threat." He barreled along over my protests. "And furthermore, he's got a thing for you."

"Oh, Grant, that's absurd. What I want to know is, why didn't you tell me this before?

That I'm in trouble."

"I'm not saying you're *in* trouble. Anyhow, Report Day is stressful enough."

"Don't do that to me." I could hear the peevishness in my voice and reached out to touch his hand. "No, I appreciate the impulse, truly. But I'm not feeble and I need to know. How else can I protect myself?"

"Righto. Point well taken. Okay. No, I'm getting this one." He grabbed the bill. I didn't object because I was just too worn-out to argue. When I thought of getting fired, what came to mind were the things I'd miss the most, like the odor of the halls — sweat, feet, teen-agers. As far as I'm concerned, it's the most delicious smell this sorry world has to offer.

Outside, I leaned on Grant's arm to let him know I regretted being so snarky. "They won't fire me. They can't."

"You just watch your back, Anniekins."

"So, anybody drop dead on you today?" Ma asked first thing in the door.

"Nope." No way could I tell her about Chubb. First, she'd be on the phone with Duncan Reese demanding that the guy be canned, and next she'd be plotting out the most exquisite method of turning Chubb's life into a living hell, starting with getting him expelled from the Harvard Club.

"What about that Spanish kid from the Bronx?"

"Holding his own, but it's hard to understand how. He works two jobs after school every day." She saw I was so tired that talking was an effort. I took a quick cool shower and went straight to bed. My phone rang at ten-thirty. Joe's voice poured into my ear and down through my body like warm honey.

"Oh. Joe," I said through the fog of sleep. "I was dreaming about you." It was a wonderful dream and I almost felt it slipping out in the form of an entirely inappropriate declaration: *Joe, I love you. I do.* Instead I said to myself, What're you, crazy, woman? Get a *grip.* I sat up. "Where are you?"

"Sioux Falls."

"Idaho?"

"Iowa."

"I knew it began with an 'I.' When are you coming home?" Too grabby. He shouldn't have called me when I was asleep — no good his hearing my needs hot off the old unconscious.

"Next Thursday. I want to see you, Anna."

"Isn't that early? I thought —"

"I'm stopping in the city overnight on my

way back upstate." In my trance-like state, I could convince myself he was dropping out of the sky solely on my account, maybe with a parachute. "What was your dream?" he was asking me.

"Oh, no." In fact, we were naked. Actually, *I* was naked and standing in a frame like one of the Dutch portraits. He was looking at me with his hands on his hips, assessing. Then he gave me this huge delicious smile and reached out his arms. God, I only hoped I could step back into that one. I can do that sometimes, push the dream-video "Play" button and start it up again.

"It's lonely out here in the heartland," he was saying. "Tell me about your life."

"Today was Report Day but I don't think I can go through it again right now. What's up in the amber waves of grain?"

I could hear him smile. You can't always, like I could never hear Grant smile over the phone. "I'm working on a new airlink, but we'd have to do it jointly with another company. It's a good organization except that the CEO's a cocaine addict."

"A minor drawback?"

"I told him we'll do the deal if he checks into rehab. When can I see you?"

"The minute you get home." So much for

playing hard to get.

"My flight gets into LaGuardia at four-twenty Thursday. Have dinner with me?"

"Sure."

There was a long silence.

"I'll call you," he said. I knew he didn't want to say good-night, but he could hear I was worn out.

As soon as I closed my eyes, I slid back into another dream. There was an enchanted forest with moss hanging from the trees, and ferns and wildflowers blanketing the ground. A creature appeared, a type of wildcat only smaller. It was sleek and black, but as it slipped through the sun-dappled undergrowth, I saw it was dragging one leg. Suddenly the mood changed from a kind of magical delight to apprehension. The forest darkened and the hanging moss turned to vines, twisted and thick as snakes. Sensing danger, the creature began to run, but it was hampered by its lameness. Finally, it fell exhausted in a clearing. From above, there was a shriek and the muffled beating of enormous black wings. A giant bird swooped down, caught the helpless creature in its talons and flew off.

I woke in a sweat with my heart pounding and my left leg aching and cramped. The shadows through the window cast a sinister web against the ceiling. I lay quiet, breathing slowly. Out of predilection and habit, a teacher of literature becomes an interpreter, and it was clear that this dream was no *Finnegan's Wake*. First, the forest, a fairy-tale paradise, grew increasingly perilous. There were a couple of ways to go: my job and my attraction to Joe Malone. Both were filled with promise, but danger lurked. The animal: well, the cat not only had silky dark hair and a limp, but I also knew in the strange conviction of dreams that, like me, it had a beauty mark on its stomach. And the winged creature was Chubb, of course. As I pinned each element of the dream to something tangible in my waking life, I calmed down until my heart had settled into its normal rhythm and the shapes on my ceiling looked familiar again. Nightmares ordinarily release me once I've subjected them to scrutiny, but this time I couldn't shake it off. Something kept nagging at me. Obviously, I had been more unnerved by Grant's news than I'd imagined. I twisted and flopped around, unable to find a comfortable position. My pillow felt like a hunk of concrete. Then it hit me. The bird. It wasn't Chubb at all, it was a falcon. Lola Falcon! I laughed out loud. I felt like waking Ma to tell her what a sap her daughter was.

Instead I sat up and snapped on the light. My bed looked as if a major war had been fought in it.

When Ma trailed into the kitchen at five-thirty A.M., I was already sitting there with my herbal tea and one of her old *People* magazines, reading about a rock star who had works of art reproduced in tattoos all over his body. *The Last Supper* straight across his posterior. I swear.

"What the hell are you doing up?" she asked.

" 'Morning," I replied.

She laid her hand against my forehead. "You damn well better be in love because it's either that or you're having a relapse."

"I'm perfectly fine and I'm not in love. I barely know the man." I waved the magazine at her. "Did you see this? He's wearing *Whistler's Mother* on his pecs."

She poured water into the coffee maker. "Don't tell me. I wasn't born yesterday."

5

"I don't think I'm going to like him," I told Ma on Thursday afternoon.

She was lifting my right arm up over my head at the time. My father offered to pay for a physical therapist, but she wouldn't hear of it. "What for?" she had told him over the phone. "If I can lift a twenty-five-pound bag of flour with one hand, I can put Anna through her paces." And I have to say, of all the hands laid on me in the past five years, Ma's are the strongest and the gentlest. Furthermore, we use my exercise hour to discuss the important issues of the times, as in whether or not a certain customer of hers has had another facelift.

"We're back to Joe Malone as serial killer, are we?" Ma said.

"He doesn't want to talk about himself."

"I can't *stand* that."

"All he does is ask questions and sit there while I blab on and on. I have to drag everything out of him."

"Sounds like the perfect match to me. Him listening, you talking."

"Thank you." I was quiet for a minute while she bent my arm at the elbow. It was a little stiff.

"Having trouble with this?" she asked. She always knows.

"Not bad."

Ma raised her left eyebrow, signaling that she didn't believe me. "Maybe you'll be lucky and he'll stand you up."

"Shit," I said.

"Watch your mouth," she said.

"Oh, that's rich." I sat up and rubbed my shoulder. Everything hurt. They say weather has nothing to do with aches and pains, but they lie. Today, oozing out of a dank gray sky, there was rain just two degrees Fahrenheit short of sleet, in mid-October, no less. Whatever happened to global warming?

"I'll make a deal with you," I told her. "If you go out with Father Dewbright, I'll consider giving this guy a chance. Assuming he calls."

"Oh, thank you very much. All you have to do is stand within six feet of that old geezer and you're an alcoholic by proxy." Father Dewbright, retired from his parish on Eighty-ninth Street, was a faithful admirer of Ma's. "Anyhow, you're deflecting responsibility here."

"No, what I'm doing is blowing this whole thing out of proportion. If he calls, fine. If he doesn't, that's okay, too."

The phone chose this moment to ring. I twitched as if I'd been jabbed with a cattle prod.

Ma smiled. "Why don't you just tell him something's come up and you can't see him?"

But I was too busy lunging for the receiver. I turned my back on Ma in a vain effort at privacy, and when I hung up and turned around, she was standing there with a smirk on her face. "Is 'okay-okay-great' code for 'piss off, sucker'?"

"He wants to make dinner for me at his place. I'm supposed to bring my swimsuit."

She narrowed her eyes.

"I told him I like to swim. He's got a pool on the top floor," I explained, then looked down at my body. "You wouldn't have one of those Victorian things that covers everything?"

"Yeah, in the same drawer where I keep my bustle."

Joe's apartment turned out to be in a high rise on the West Side not far from Lincoln

Center. I stood in front of his door and stared at the "8C" for a while, imagining that stepping through was like opening the cover of a novel. I had the same anticipatory feeling. A new story is pretty thrilling but what's it going to cost me? How scared will I be? Will I cry? Will I like the ending?

The door swung open and Joe pulled me into the room and into his arms. He held me for a long moment. No kiss, but I wasn't ready for that yet. My legs felt wobbly as it was. The place smelled truly awful, like when I was nine and set my hair on fire toasting marshmallows over the stove.

"I just burned the hors d'oeuvres," Joe said.

I was busy checking the place out. It had the look of temporary occupancy. Generic furniture, everything in tans and grays, no plants, no knickknacks. But on the wall were a dozen of the most stunning photographs I had ever seen. The thought that Joe might be their originator made me catch my breath. I looked from them to him. "Yours?"

He nodded.

"I don't know what to say."

He smiled. "I have faith that if I'm very patient, you'll think of something." He took my hand and led me to the couch. There was a plate of cheese and crackers on the coffee table and two goblets of red wine. He sat down so close that our knees were nudging one another. It made me dizzy that I could be so stirred up by somebody, and I was afraid my leg was going to start bobbing up and down, like a dog's when you scratch its belly.

I stood and went to the window. "You shouldn't have fussed," I said. "You just got off a plane." The unprepossessing view of the building next door calmed me down a little. But then he was behind me.

"I felt like doing something for you," he said. Then he took my glass away and set it on the windowsill. He leaned down and gave me a long lingering kiss. Then another. Then I reached up and put my arms around his neck. Our mouths opened against one another and his hands reached behind to pull my hips against him. If he hadn't been holding me, I would have sunk straight to the floor. I stepped back a few inches and took a breath. Then we grinned at one another, big toothy smiles of complicity as if we'd done something to gloat about.

"Come," he said, and drew me into the kitchen. On the counter was a cookie sheet dotted with lumps of ash. He ignored it, and all one-handed opened the refrigerator and slid a dish with something resembling lasagne into the microwave. He had me in a death grip.

"Wouldn't it be easier if —"

"No, you might get away," he said matter-of-factly.

While we waited for the lasagne, we looked at his photographs which almost made me forget the pressure of his hip as he held me beside him. There was a dappled river scene, another print of the bridge in clouds, several of a brooding cliff veined with snow, a series of just the wing of an airplane and one shot looking down the urban wall of Park Avenue. He'd caught the shadows in such a way that if you squinted a little, you'd see a cubist construction reminiscent of Braque. Or an imposing natural formation like Monument Valley. Even soldiers standing in formation. It was a study in power and seemed very sexy to me, or maybe I was still reeling from those kisses. He was a potent magnet and I was a hapless little metal filing who had strayed into his force field. I wondered if most women responded to him that way, and I remembered the blonde jogger on Madison Avenue and the woman who'd tapped on the window at Jackson Hole.

"How come you don't photograph people?" I asked. He had pulled my hand around his waist. I liked that he was lean and muscular. I've never been attracted to bulky men.

He pointed to the photo of the rocks in the river. "That's Steve with a fly rod. Doesn't he count?"

If I squinted I could just make out the minute figure of a fisherman the size of a deer tick. I rolled my eyes.

"Well, I don't know how to do people," Joe confessed. "They confuse me."

I laughed. "Do I?"

"You most of all," he said. He was lucky the microwave timer went off, but I filed that one away for future discussion. He pointed at the table. "Sit down. I'll be right out." When he released it, my hand turned cold.

"Can't I —"

"Sit." I kind of felt like Rover, but I obeyed like a good puppy. It was touching to hear him crashing around in there as if he were cooking up a banquet for two hundred people. Pots and pans, china, doors slamming — the kitchen at the Four Seasons.

"Who's Steve?" I called.

"An old buddy. We grew up together."

I wondered if Joe had told his old buddy Steve about me. The microwave timer went off again, and Joe appeared with two plates.

He set them down, lit the candles, poured us each another glass of wine and lifted his.

"Courage," he said.

"For what?" I ticked his glass.

"For eating this stuff."

It was pretty bad. The lasagne was burnt on the bottom and gluey everywhere else. He'd made a salad out of pre-mixed pre-washed greens, but they'd passed their prime. There was something else that I think was supposed to be a kind of ratatouille. The bread was delicious, though. I filled up on that, and besides, I kept remembering his erection against my pelvic bone when we were standing by the window. The memory pretty much made dinner irrelevant.

"Why don't you ever talk about your father?" he asked, shoveling the lasagne down. He was clearly not a picky eater.

I laughed again. "How about a little chit-chat, a little how-was-your-day? First you kiss me until my legs fall off and then you want a psychological profile."

"You kissed me back. Take some responsibility." Then he just watched me, waiting.

"He left when I was sick. I mean, *six*. I haven't *seen* him since way before I was sick." Years before. I know, I know, unresolved crap. I didn't feel like talking about it. "Come to think of it, you haven't said a hell of a lot about your father either." Or your mother, or your brother, or goddamn Lola Falcon.

"It must be your fault," I said. "I never used to curse."

"What?" He watched me take a big gulp of wine. "How come this is all burnt?" he asked, poking at my lasagne.

"Did you put a layer of sauce on the bottom of the dish?"

"Oh." He grinned at me. "So how was your day?"

But the wine was kicking in at last, and besides, I was touched by his sensitivity in retreating from my boring wounds, i.e., dear old dad. Which, of course, only served to make me feel like confiding. "I suppose it sounds like a rationalization, but I don't know as I missed out. I see so much of it at school. Single-parent families or even intact families with two clueless parents. They can inflict a lot of damage. On the whole, I consider myself lucky."

"Your mother?"

I nodded. "Unconditional advocacy along the lines of Attila the Hun."

"I want to meet her."

"You've already had a lovely tête-à-tête over the phone. That'll do for now."

He was smiling. "When I couldn't reach

you at your school, I hit the yellow pages. Do you know how many bakeries there are on the Upper East Side?"

He took a swallow from his glass. I liked that he stretched it out. I was having such a good time.

"No luck," he went on. "Then finally I got to the N's. When I asked for you at Norma's Crust, this person said, 'Who wants to know?' I figured, pay dirt."

"I'm not ready to submit you to Ma yet."

"Will I need a lot of documentation? Birth certificate, tax returns, negative AIDS test?"

"Just a simple DNA evaluation will do."

"How about some dessert?" he asked.

I must have looked alarmed.

"It's from Sarabeth's," he reassured me.

I said fine. When he went to the kitchen, I took the opportunity to nose around, not that there was much to see. It was about as personal as the furniture display at Bloomingdale's. But there was a bookshelf. Some photography anthologies: Ansel Adams, Diane Arbus, Paul Strand. What surprised me were the cookbooks, three of them. I removed one called *The High-Rise Health Nut* and flipped it open. *Falcon Publishing*. There was an inscription in bold black ink: *For darling Joe — I could never have pulled it off without you! Thank you, thank you! XXXXX Lola.* Burnt lasagne couldn't have produced a more sickening jolt to my gut. First of all, I hate people who overuse exclamation points. Then I took a look at the cover flap and there was this sunny blonde smiling at me from a mountaintop. She had a backpack slung rakishly from one shoulder. The credit at the bottom read *Photograph by Joseph Malone.* I thought he didn't do people.

He emerged from the kitchen with a plateful of cakes and cookies. He saw what I was holding and his face did something I couldn't read.

"That relationship you mentioned?" I asked, tipping the book at him.

He nodded. Holding back is not the same as lying. I knew he was the reticent type, but this was different. I slid the book back into its slot on the shelf, sat down and tried to make my way through a slice of lemon cake.

"Nice thing about Sarabeth, you know you're not going to get a hunk of kumquat in your pound cake," I said.

"It really is over, Anna. She's just a very persistent woman."

"I like a girl who knows what she wants."

"You would like her, as a matter of fact," he said.

In a rat's ass, I thought. More and more,

I'm becoming my mother's daughter.

"Our parents are friends. They live fairly close to one another."

I pictured the Mothers up in the night woods, cloaked and cackling over a steaming cauldron, dropping newt's eyes into the brew to bind Joe and Lola together through eternity.

"Lola's a publisher. Well, you see that. Health-food cookbooks. She's a self-made woman, very accomplished."

You want to dig yourself in a little deeper, bub, just keep talking, I thought. I seemed to remember that summer's day we first met, a sense that Joe wasn't entirely available. There had been a gap before he'd tried to reach me. I felt myself filling up with questions. My inclination would be to ride the topic of Lola Falcon straight into a cement wall along with a perfectly respectable evening. I heard brakes squeal in my head as I reversed direction and changed the subject. To me.

"So in what way do I confuse you?" I asked him.

"You're beyond confusion," he replied. "Think seismic."

There it was again, matching metaphors. I congratulated myself on not asking where Lola Falcon registered on the Richter scale.

"How come?" I asked.

He shrugged. "I don't know if there's an answer to that."

When anybody suggests there's no answer, I open my mouth. It's Pavlovian and simply out of my control. This applies to issues ranging from Ma telling me there's no perfect way to roast a turkey to the conundrum of the Big Bang Theory. Of course there's an answer; we're just not trying hard enough. Possibilities titillated my tongue: a shared aesthetic experience, familial similarities as yet undiscovered, simple chemistry. There was nothing I enjoyed more than wrestling a mystery to the ground and beating it to death with half-baked psychology.

Joe was looking at me, waiting. "Did you bring your bathing suit?" he asked finally.

I shut my mouth. Unheard of. I like to think it was because I was learning to respect a certain fatalistic inclination in Joe, but actually I was in kind of a hurry to see him in swim trunks. "Don't we have to wait an hour?" I asked.

"That's an old wives' tale."

I got up to retrieve my bag. "Well, I'm not an old wife, so let's go. Do they have towels?"

"Everything we need."

There were small locker rooms on the top floor. I changed into my swim suit and surveyed myself in the mirror. I didn't look the same as I did before I got sick. My left leg wasn't hanging quite straight and there was a softening in my limbs, a thickening particularly in my neck and around my waist, I suppose on account of the steroids. I once had an athlete's body. I wished Joe could have seen me then. I turned my back on myself, grabbed a towel from the neat pile by the door and shoved against the heavy door that said TO THE POOL.

Joe had left the lights off, and a full moon, blurred at the edges by a film of condensation, shone through the skylight onto the water. On my way over on the bus, a cold rain was still spitting down. I felt as if Joe had banished the clouds and trotted out this glorious moon just for me.

Alone in the empty pool, he was doing laps with long slow strokes. His progress shivered the surface into a million fragments of light. Grateful for the chance to slip into the water before displaying myself so close to naked, I walked to the shallow end and gripped both sides of the ladder. When I do my pool-exercise classes at the "Y," I always wear special rubber shoes, but I was damned if I'd bring them tonight.

Better I crack my head open than look like a complete dork. This decision had prompted Ma, as I tossed the offending booties back in the closet, to point out my resemblance to the adolescents I'd presumably been providing with a sensible role model.

Oh, but the water felt good. It was cool, thank God, not that tepid brew that makes me light-headed, or worse, sometimes sends my legs into spasms. Gravity is my enemy, but in the pool I'm suspended. In time, too, as if the years of pain and disease are simply washed away.

I started for the other end where Joe had just come up. I swam toward him through liquid moonlight. I felt supple as a mermaid. He caught me as I touched the edge. It was shallow enough to stand, and with his hair slicked back and his face flickering with reflections, he looked elemental, exposed. We stood there for a moment, up to our shoulders in moonlight, staring at one another. Simultaneously, we reached out. Our kisses were long and deep. The muscles of his back slipped sleek under my fingers, and between my legs there was an urgency that seemed separate from the rest of me. As our kisses grew more demanding, he whispered, "Anna, Anna." But I had lost myself and became simply a ferocious need. He helped me pull off my suit. My breasts slid bare against his chest, my mouth was greedy on his, my legs parted for him, and when I felt him drive deep inside, I heard myself say his name in a voice I didn't recognize.

Then I was shuddering against him, and suddenly very cold. He picked me up and carried me to the edge, set me down there and retrieved my suit. He stood before me in the water for a moment, just looking up at me where I sat naked and trembling. He hoisted himself up, the sculpted planes of his face and body pale blue in the moonlight. He found our towels and wrapped us in them, leaving our feet to dangle in the water as if reluctant to make the inevitable retreat to dry land.

He got to his feet and pulled me up. With our arms around one another, we walked to the lockers, then separated to re-enter our dry clothing and perhaps some semblance of sanity.

We took the elevator in silence. Inside the apartment, Joe sat me down on his couch in the dark and went to get more towels. Then he dried my hair and watched me comb it straight.

"Mermaid," he whispered.

I gave him a tiny ironic smile. "There was so much wrong with what we just did."

He kissed me very gently.

"I have to go home," I said.

"I'll take you in a cab."

I shook my head. "No." It was my turn to kiss him. We kept our eyes open, looking into one another. "I can die now, Joe," I told him. "You understand?"

He nodded and held me for a moment. Then I slipped out of his arms. When I left the building, I stood for a moment and stared up at the moon. It was perfectly round and glassy, like the monocle of some vast intelligence peering down at me. Not with judgment, merely curiosity, as if to say, *What were you thinking?*

Well, I wasn't, and that was about the only thing that seemed clear.

6

"So how was your date?" Ma asked. She always left the bakery in her assistant's hands for an hour so she could bring me something hot from the oven for breakfast. Along with a steaming muffin, she shoved my vitamin C capsules at me. I take a thousand milligrams four times a day to keep my urine acidified. One bout with a catheter was enough to make a believer out of me, but this morning I truly almost forgot.

To my disgust and disbelief, I felt myself redden. Just like senior year in high school when I lost my virginity to Phil Massey. She'd taken one look at me the morning after the Senior Prom and said, "Anything you want to tell me?" I had tried to look baffled but my face only turned a deeper shade of crimson.

"Anna, there's nothing wrong with sex," she had said. "But there's a lot wrong with stupidity."

"I'm not in love with Phil," I said.

"I know that. Is it going to happen again?"

I was quiet. I could have denied it, I suppose, but the fact was, I had enjoyed myself with Phil and wanted more.

"We'd better make an appointment with Dr. Bernini," she said. Just a statement, no judgment.

On the day of my appointment, she asked me if I wanted her to come with me. I nodded. She sat in the waiting room while Dr. Bernini examined me, and when I came out with a six-month supply of birth control pills, her eyes welled up. I had to hand the package to her because it wouldn't fit in my little purse. In those days, we always took the bus or the subway, but that day she sprung for a cab. I clutched her hand in the backseat.

"Are you angry with me?" I asked.

She shook her head, but the tears lingered. I wanted to crawl onto her lap and shrink into the girl whose feet didn't yet touch the ground when she held me. But there was no going back and we both knew it.

"I saw your bathing suit in the john," Ma was saying. "So I guess you had a swim. Remember the pool party when you almost drowned Penny Edmonds?" She turned away, ostensibly to rinse the breakfast dishes, but in fact she was offering me some privacy.

"Penny was a brat," I answered, as I thought: (a) we could have been caught, we should have been caught, two naked lunatics in the pool. Where was everybody anyhow? (b) never a thought about condoms, and I mean, not a glimmer, not a fleeting moment after which I could at least have said to myself, Oh hell, it's worth getting some fatal STD to do it with this man; (c) there was always that faint chance I could get pregnant. Not likely two days after I'd finished my period, but nonetheless. Nonetheless. And (d) what we did to the pool environmentally is grounds for legal prosecution. One always expects those warm spots where little kids pee, but my God.

When I thought of the lectures I gave my homeroom teen-agers about safe sex, I was beyond ashamed of myself. They should revive the stocks and put me out on the traffic island, Eighty-sixth and Park, so everybody could throw rocks. Furthermore, I was so absurdly, sickeningly happy that I could have burst into song, but that would only punish everyone within earshot.

I attempted a self-possessed smile. "Are there any more muffins? I'm starving." Ma

84

loves it when I ask for seconds.

"I've always encouraged you to swim more," she said. "It loosens up your shoulders." She plunked another cranberry-banana muffin on my plate and watched as I broke it open and slathered butter on it. I took a bite and started to laugh.

"What?" she asked.

"Raindrops keep falling on my head," I warbled, giving in to song though I use the term loosely. It's the tune I always sang to myself when I flew down a ski slope. The perfect rhythm.

"I think I'd better meet this guy," she said.

So I told her the same thing I had told Joe. "Oh no. Not yet."

My unconscionably good mood came to a crashing halt when I got to school. I had an e-mail to visit the headmaster as soon as classes started, and I assumed I'd be confronted with the issue of Jennifer's lost model. Furthermore, Rudy Steinberger met me outside the entrance of my homeroom. When I put my hand on his arm, I could feel it trembling.

"Rudy, what is it?" He was scaring me.

"There's something wrong with Michelle Cross."

"Is she ill? Where is she?"

"Inside. She keeps on crying. Maybe she's sick. She got so thin lately. I don't know." The immense brown eyes were filled with pain. I saw how it was with poor Rudy and I grieved for him. He'd wisely kept his crush a secret, realizing that Sukey Marks and the other girls would have only one comment about such a match: *Puh-leeze!*

I hurried inside to find three of Michelle's friends hovering, plying her with Kleenex. Sukey was sobbing almost as loudly as Michelle and was clearly relishing the drama. My other kids hung around trying to polish off homework assignments or flipping paper clips against the chalkboard. I went over to Michelle and gestured to her friends to leave us. Then I put my arm around the weeping girl and led her to the Retreat, which is what we called the niche between some file cabinets that was just wide enough for two chairs. The bell rang and everybody else clattered out, with Sukey pausing long enough to shoot me a look of profound tragedy.

"What's going on?" I asked Michelle.

When she was upset, Michelle turned scarlet, with the exception of her nose which remained a pale chip frozen to her face. A bizarre remnant of her rhinoplasty, I suppose. She reeked of nicotine. A lot of the girls turned to smoking as a diet aid.

Michelle looked at me for a moment through swollen eyes, then buried her face in her hands. "I hate my life!" she wailed. Her rings hung loose on her fingers. What had happened to the healthy solidity of only two months ago?

"Is it the physics quiz?" She'd flunked another one yesterday, and the rest of her grades were pretty dismal.

That only set her off on another paroxysm of weeping. I handed her a bunch of tissues. "Come on, Michelle, wipe your face and take a deep breath."

I waited. She gave me a pitiful shudder, but it was a start. At least her color returned to normal.

"Okay, good girl. Want a Coke?"

She nodded.

"Don't move," I said, and fetched one from the little refrigerator I stashed under my bookcase. Then I locked the door so that nobody would interrupt us. The way Michelle was sitting, with her bony knees jammed together and her feet splayed out, she could have been ten years old, never mind the three-hundred-dollar shoes. She gulped at the soda and choked.

I patted her on the back until she stopped. "What provoked all this?"

"I can't *believe* you don't know, Ms. Bolles. *Every*body knows. The whole school's staring at me."

In my peculiar state perched halfway between guilt and ecstasy, I hadn't stopped by the teachers' lounge or even spoken to anyone on my way to homeroom. "You'd better fill me in," I said.

"My father married that person last night, that Dakota Blue. It was on TV this morning."

"Dakota Blue, the singer?"

She nodded.

"And that's how you found out, on the news?" I was incredulous.

She wiped her nose. "Mom saw it. She went ballistic and beeped my dad on his emergency cell phone and he said it was true." The tears started up again but it was hard to blame her. Dakota Blue was barely twenty, "barely" being the operative word in that the clothing she wore in any photograph I'd ever seen was comprised of two Post-Its and a cocktail napkin. Well, perhaps a slight exaggeration. So this was Michelle's new step-mom, a pseudo–Native American by way of Bayonne, New Jersey, pop singer.

"What did I do?" Michelle asked in a whisper.

"What?"

She looked at me as if I were functioning with half a brain. "Well, I must have done *something*. To make him want to leave."

I felt as though a slab of granite had just fallen on my heart. "Michelle, don't start thinking that way."

"You can say that. You don't know." And she was off again. "I thought him and Mom were going to get back together. I so feel like *killing* myself."

I wasn't one of those teachers who's pals with their students. But Michelle's anguish struck a resounding chord. I took a deep breath with shudders of its own, getting ready.

"I do know, Michelle. My father left, too."

Her head snapped up and her mouth fell open. There's misery and there's a scoop, and this was a tough contest for her. As I had hoped, the investigative reporter won out.

"Really? He left? When?" This was worth several days' rumination over frappaccinos at Starbucks.

"I was only six, but I remember how it felt. I blamed myself, too."

"Oh, Ms. Bolles, you poor *thing!* Was he having an affair?" No good deed goes unpunished, of course. I was going to have to pay with all the nitty gritty.

"Yes. With a woman much younger than my mother."

"Did he marry her?"

I nodded. "And divorced her, and married again."

"Oh my *God*. How did you ever get through it?"

I didn't want to tell her what a pillar Ma had been, given Filona Cross's dubious maternal skills. "Sometimes I think it bothered me more when I got to be your age. I felt as if I were different from everybody else. It didn't matter that half the kids I knew also had divorced parents."

She was listening attentively. Tears still oozed out, but at least she was thinking now.

"Did you hate him a lot?"

"Sure." The granite slab pressed against my lungs, making it hard to breathe. If she asked how I felt about him now, I knew I wouldn't have the faintest idea how to answer. "One of the things I learned to do was to concentrate on myself instead of him."

"I don't get it," Michelle said.

"Well, there were some things I was good at. I decided I was going to get even better at them. Not to show my father, just to make me feel better about myself." This had all been Ma's doing, of course.

"I guess you were a real brain," Michelle said wistfully.

"Actually, it was sports I loved. Tennis, especially. I started taking lessons every week and playing on weekends. And if I had a rotten day, I'd put in some extra time on the court. It was a way to balance out the bad stuff. But it could have been something academic, too, I guess. Why not?"

"Not me. I only got into Cameron because my father's donating all this money to the new science lab. I'm the stupidest person in the whole school."

"You're a wonderful dancer, Michelle." I'd seen her in the recitals and it was true. When she was moving across the stage, she shed the self-conscious concerns about her hair and her clothing and just flew, her face enraptured.

"Oh, I'm only okay. Jennifer's much better than I am."

"Just think about how you feel when you're dancing."

She was silent.

"Do you want me to talk to Mrs. Phillips?" I asked her. "I'm sure she'd let you have access to the dance studio whenever it's free."

"I guess so. Yeah, I'd like that a lot," Michelle said. We smiled at one another. There's that feeling you get when you're around a fellow foot soldier who's been wounded in the same war. Michelle and I were foxhole buddies from now on. It was going to be tough on her with such public exposure. There might even be news people and photographers outside the school today, lying in wait to capture her reaction for the gossip-hungry. I would have to talk with the headmaster.

Michelle spilled her Coke when I yelped and leaped to my feet. I had completely forgotten that I had an appointment with Duncan Reese. I glanced at my watch. Nine forty-five. I was already late.

"I'm so sorry, Michelle. I forgot I have to see Dr. Reese."

"That's okay." She stood and swiped at the drops of soda on her suede skirt. "Thanks, Ms. Bolles. Really. Thanks. God, I can't believe we share the same sorrow." I figured that had to be straight from the latest rock lyric. "God, I must look *awful,*" she went on, but before she could reach for her makeup kit and mirror, I grabbed her in a swift hug, something else I wasn't prone to do. She was a bag of bones, an issue for another day. Then I dashed off to find out if I was fired.

Duncan Reese was a large rumpled man with a ruddy face and straw-colored hair.

There was something of the aged preppy about him, and his politician's smile and wrap-around handshake inspired knee-jerk mistrust. A lot of people disliked him, but I would probably kill for the man and this is why.

Before my father made all his money out in California, I was a scholarship student at Cameron. Granted, I made straight A's, but I was also a pain in the butt, and my mother was worse. She was always protesting something — Cameron's emphasis on standardized tests, lack of support for students of color, poor nutrition in the cafeteria — the culmination being her one-woman picket line decrying the ouster of my favorite chemistry teacher. He was busted in Central Park one weekend with a couple of ounces of marijuana. Since Ma always likened the criminality of drugs to Prohibition, i.e., that such restrictions were both futile and dangerous, she crayoned a sign and paraded back and forth in front of the school. I was thirteen at the time, and let me say, those were three bad days. I've even blocked out what she wrote on that sign — I think something about gifted teachers being an endangered species. The thing was, it was late November and freezing cold. Every day that she was out there, Duncan would hand Ma a hot chocolate on his way into the building.

I've also noticed over the years that Duncan liked to promote rabble-rousers into the administration. In fact, he did it with Grant who was always running his mouth off about this or that and allying himself with the student body against the faculty. Duncan appointed him Assistant to the High School Dean. It's tough to work up a head of steam against the power structure when you're suddenly a part of it, and furthermore, Grant brought a lot of valuable new ideas and energy into the system.

Then there was the issue of my own annoying career as a Cameron student. When I got elected president of the student government, I lobbied hard for the distribution of condoms in school. Duncan didn't like it for a lot of reasons, particularly when I stole slides of venereal diseases from the Science department and exhibited them at the PTA meeting. Won over by visions of their children with green vaginas or wart-encrusted penises, not to mention languishing on their deathbeds from AIDS, the PTA proceeded to pressure the board and Duncan Reese until I got my condom machines in all the rest rooms.

Despite all this, Duncan hired me straight out of a one-year master's program with no teaching experience. Then when I got sick, he resisted considerable pressure to "retire" me. I was always wondering, though, if I was about to get the ax.

I didn't feel altogether steady on my feet, and stood in his doorway with one hand on the frame. "I'm sorry. I got involved in a crisis . . ." I never knew whether to call him Duncan or Dr. Reese. One was too familiar, the other too formal, so I just left it out. "Michelle Cross's father . . . maybe you're aware . . ."

He gestured for me to sit. "The press is swarming already," he said. "But since you're late, we're going to have to cut this short now. Anna, I've had some discussions with Jennifer Matthews's parents." He was one of those people who was always using your name when he talked to you. Another politician's trick.

"The architecture project," I said. "But I did find it."

"I'm aware of that, but nonetheless they're asking me to transfer Jennifer to another homeroom. She's building her portfolio for her college applications, and they're concerned about future problems."

"Oh," I said. Not much of a response, but this was a cruel twist. I looked forward to Jennifer's sparkly face every day. Literally sparkly — she wears a lot of glitter in her makeup.

"Was this lapse a factor of your illness, Anna?"

I had given the matter a fair amount of thought already. One does, with MS. You second-guess yourself whenever anything out of the ordinary happens, wondering if a slip of the tongue or a momentary memory loss signals a relapse with permanent and sinister consequences.

"I'm thinking of it in context with the fact that you missed two faculty meetings," Duncan went on.

I was beginning to hear those drumbeats in my head, like the ones that rattle when you're approaching the gallows.

"Those are regular weekly meetings, Anna," Reese went on. "I know perfectly well how conscientious you are, but some people interpret these oversights as indifference or carelessness. Tell me, has the MS progressed?"

What *I* wanted to know was how he'd become aware of my missing those meetings, although I could make a wild stab at it.

"It's not easy to measure," I said, "but I can tell you that I'm feeling confident about my classwork and my relationship with my homeroom students. Will Jennifer really have to move out?"

Duncan nodded. I knew there was more he wasn't telling me.

"Am I in danger of losing my job?"

There was the tiniest hesitation before the reassurance. "You're a fine teacher, Anna. I have no intention of losing you."

Well, there was a non-denial denial if I ever heard one. "I realize that there are drawbacks to having me on the faculty," I said. "But I hope I make a contribution. I think I'll know when to quit if I'm no longer effective." I guess this was probably a lie, but I was desperate.

He stood up and walked around the desk, holding out a huge paw and aiming his Cheshire cat smile at me. I stood also, taking such pains to appear in perfect control that I lunged at him. That wasn't spasticity! I wanted to say. Nerves, normal nerves!

"I'm glad you took some time with Michelle Cross," he said, ushering me to the door. "I'm sure she'll benefit by it." He slipped through ahead of me and slid off down the hall with that odd walk he had, like he was on coasters.

That was it. There was little sense of relief since I knew I'd just received a serious warning. Furthermore, I realized that I'd left some file folders in the teachers' lounge

— another lapse? I felt myself dragging my feet — incipient foot drop? And I didn't relish meeting up with anyone on the faculty. I wondered at the wisdom of teaching in a school where I'd been a student for so long. It was too easy to feel relegated back to the ranks of adolescence.

Only one of my colleagues was in the lounge: Leonard Chubb. He was coiled on the couch with his feet tucked under him, shoes on. It always irritated me when he did that. After all, who knew where those shoes had been?

Chubb had a pair of cobra eyes, small black irises that peered out from epicanthic hoods. They told me that he knew exactly where I'd been and why. " 'Morning, Anna," he said. He also licked his lips a lot, so they were always chapped.

"Don't ' 'morning' me, Leonard, you venomous snake. I know exactly what you've been up to." Actually, I just said " 'Morning."

"How are you feeling?" He swung his filthy dog-doo-covered feet to the floor.

"Great. You?" *You back-stabbing sly grub.* I picked up my notes from the coffee table.

"I wondered who'd forgotten those," he said. "I could have dropped them by your homeroom."

And then slithered right on down the hall to Reese's office to express your concern about my forgetfulness.

But Leonard was a good teacher, especially of poetry. The kids didn't like him much, but they learned the material.

One of the files fell out of my hands and slid across the floor. Leonard bolted to scoop it up. As he handed it to me he asked, "You sure you're feeling all right?" I think he'd convinced himself he was looking out for my best interests, and the school's. He'd decided that everybody, me included, would benefit by my departure.

"Never better," I said. On my way out I turned with an afterthought. "Don't forget the faculty meeting, Leonard. Monday, four o'clock."

He blinked his eyes in that slow way, waved, and tucked his feet back under him.

7

Joe had left a long distance message on the departmental machine and there was another one when I got home, just: *Why haven't you called me back?* No whine, no blame. I found his unreadable intonation both maddening and sexy. With me, the simplest "hello" waves a huge flag: *I'm happy! I'm mad! I'm tired!* The fact was, I hadn't spoken with him since our "date," which was a pretty feeble word to describe what had happened in that pool.

I dialed the number he'd left, something with a 315 area code. "I guess I've been trying to figure out what to say to you," was all I could think up. I heard moonlit pool water lapping at me, and along with it the sudden rush of excitement between my legs. "Damn nation," I muttered.

He laughed. "Well, that's a start."

"I should tell you that I don't ordinarily behave —"

"Look, Anna, there's nothing ordinary

about any of it. I'm flying in again first thing tomorrow and then I want to take you up-state."

It was difficult enough adjusting to the fact that I'd had underwater sex with this man on our second date. I wasn't ready for relatives. I could hear him smiling. "Just up the Taconic Parkway. There's something I want to photograph. There ought to be some leaves left."

"Okay," I said.

Thinking back days later, and ruminating on my resulting scars, both psychic and physical, I probably should have passed. But it seemed like a harmless enough invitation at the time, and truthfully, if he'd asked me to join him on a trek to the Staten Island landfill, I probably would have said yes.

"Excellent," he said. "I wanted to cele-brate Halloween with you." Our first hol-iday. It made me wonder if our future held a Thanksgiving or a Christmas. I forced my-self to draw the line at New Year's Eve.

Halloween is busy for Ma, and I made sure she was already at the bakery when Joe was supposed to pick me up. I waited in the lobby with the *New York Times* Saturday killer crossword. I'd pretty much decided Joe was blowing me off, and had already re-

101

sorted to magic thinking: *If I figure out the answer to 4 Across, he'll come.* After twenty minutes of mind games, he drove up. The doorman, Big Bob, flung himself at the car so he could check Joe out. Actually, it was a good thing he was there. I needed a hand getting into the front seat.

Joe made a fairly big deal about leaning across to give me a kiss. I refused to look at Big Bob but I could feel his beady eyes making a thorough scrutiny for the future police report: *The perp was wearing a yellow crew-neck sweater, blue jeans, tennis shoes. Hole in left elbow of said sweater . . .* Big Bob was always ready. He used to be a cop, but got terminated due to what he refers to as "philosophical differences" with his superiors, and subsequently went to work as a bodyguard. His boss, a "Mister G," was currently conducting business out of maximum security in Ossining, hence the doorman job. Anyhow, Big Bob made me feel very secure in contrast to Joe Malone, whose presence was already giving me *agita.* It was a damn good thing that Bob wasn't at the door when we got back, considering what I looked like. He would have rolled Joe flat as a lasagne noodle.

"Sorry I'm late," Joe said. "The garage forgot where they put my car." Big Bob backed off with a salute as Joe pulled out onto First Avenue. Standard shift. Like many Manhattanites, I find automobiles baffling, even intimidating. Most of us didn't learn to drive until we were in college, and even then we never approach a steering wheel with the same ease as our suburban contemporaries. Cars are what you rent to get someplace you can't go by subway.

"What kind of car is this?" I asked.

"A 'seventy-nine BMW."

"Is that cool?"

"Very," he said, flashing me a grin. I stared at his profile and marveled at what we had done together in the moonlight, the intimacy of it. After a few blocks, I began to feel as if there was somebody else in the car with us, somebody large and pushy. I wish I could do something about my mouth, like learn to keep it shut, but when there's something working at me like that, I become physically uncomfortable. I'm reminded of aliens who burst out of people's chests. Well, there was a beast swelling inside me, and no ignoring it.

"You're going to have to pull over," I said.

He shot me a look of alarm.

"No, I'm okay. But I need to say something."

He pulled next to a fireplug and turned off the ignition.

"What we did . . ." I started. "I mean, as mature adults we have to address —" He reached for my hand, which didn't help. "Where was everybody anyway? Up at the pool." Although the thought had occurred to me that anyone might have stepped out of the locker room, spotted us doing our moonlight water ballet, and made a hasty retreat. Some nice mommy with her little girl, no doubt. Or a nun. Probably a nun.

"Are you sorry?" he asked. "Because I'm not."

"I'm a teacher, Joe. I spend my professional life trying to train kids to . . . to construct order out of a chaotic world so they can function safely. The unexpected. So that they're prepared to handle . . ." This part I'd rehearsed, but it wasn't going well.

"You didn't answer my question."

A horn blared nearby, one of those ear-splitting truck blasts. It was an exclamation point at the end of my answer. *No, I'm not sorry!*

"I should be sorry," I said, and laid a hand to my chest where the squatter from outer space was squirming to get out. "The thing is, I could do it right here," I wailed. "I could throw you down on the backseat and jump you right here."

He laughed, but when he saw my distress he began kissing my fingers one by one. Suddenly I was disgusted with myself — for being craven, for hoping he'd explain the inexplicable, for trying to dump the responsibility on him. I didn't know what it was I wanted from him anyhow. Absolution, maybe, but more likely exactly what I'd heard, that he wasn't sorry.

"Let's just go," I said, and leaned over to give him a kiss on the cheek. Then I snapped me and my alien into our seat belt and off we went. For no discernible reason, I suddenly felt great.

I've noticed that people's driving styles elucidate their character. I'll never forget a death-defying trip with Grant Hurst to visit his mother in Connecticut. Grant is one of those drivers who strictly obeys the speed limit but insists on doing it in the left lane. Cars pile up behind him for miles as he coasts serenely along at sixty-five. I once suggested to him that perhaps he might switch lanes, but he just fixed me with his avian eyeballs and pronounced that he was observing the law and so should everyone else. Grant also tends to stray over the white lines when one engages him in conversation, so the wise thing is to keep quiet, close your eyes, and remember to take the bus next time.

Joe, on the other hand, shifted expertly through four gears while negotiating the traffic hurtling up the FDR Drive. He was confident but courteous, occasionally waving other drivers ahead and never cutting anyone off. Here was a man who knew how to take charge yet whose ego would not prevent him from delegating. Portrait of a successful executive. Encouraged to surrender my natural proclivity for backseat driving, I leaned back and watched an airplane from LaGuardia rise into the west.

"What's your biggest regret?" I asked him.

He smiled at me. "You want to tell me what prompted that?"

It was the plane, but I didn't want to say so. "You seem rueful sometimes and I can't tell why."

"I'm not right now," he said.

"But you are ducking my question."

"Give me a minute."

I'd give him hours as long as I could just sit there and look at him. The dreariness of the Bronx landscape made his beauty all the more startling. Not that there was anything conventionally pretty about Joe, not with that beak and the sheared angularity of his face. But the warmth of his eyes took my breath away. They reminded me of the water I'd once seen on vacation in Florida, when I was little and my father was still around — a mixture of improbable aqua, the pale gold of the sand, and deeper blues and greens. The darker colors seemed to predominate when he was thoughtful, like now. His hands rested comfortably on the wheel. Hands that had moved across my body with such tenderness and skill.

"I could have spent a year studying in Rome," he said.

It took me a second to haul myself up out of the pool. "During college?" I asked.

He nodded. "My father has family in Tuscany. His mother was Italian. But I was worried about screwing up my grades." His voice, ordinarily so guarded, was edgy.

"Did you ever just go for a visit?" I asked. "To see your family."

"I was supposed to, with my brother, but then something happened. I don't remember exactly what. Something about my mother, her health, though that seems strange. She's never sick." I was interpreting like crazy. Misinterpreting, more likely. "It's been a long time since I thought about that," he said, then typically threw the ball back into my lap. "What's your biggest?"

I thought for a second. Interesting that the MS didn't occur to me, though I guess that's too complicated for regret.

"When I stuffed Mr. Gross's correspondence in the wastebasket," I replied. The alien must have made me say it. I didn't feel like elaborating but it was too late now. "I had this summer secretarial job in an accounting office when I was in college," I explained. "I've never been so bored in my life. That's no excuse, I realize. But the very last day, when I was feeling so pleased with myself — a paycheck, then two weeks at the beach before school started up again — I was cleaning out my desk and here was a pile of mail all done up in a rubber band dating back to June first. I'd somehow neglected to give it to Mr. Gross. He had this terrible toupee." I glanced at Joe. "That's no excuse either. So I was petrified he'd yell at me and probably wouldn't pay me. When nobody was looking, I buried it at the bottom of my wastebasket. There. Now you know the worst."

It had been truly awful. The incident clearly indicated a fatal flaw in my character. There were times I even believed I'd gotten MS as a punishment for trashing Mr. Gross's mail. I imagined a crucial piece of correspondence: *Dear Mr. Gross: You have been selected to represent your company in Geneva at the upcoming International Association of Accountants. If you wish to accept this extraordinary honor, which is the accountants' equivalent to the Nobel Peace Prize, please answer by return mail . . .* I'd been too panicked to check. I imagined that Mr. Gross had been reprimanded or even fired on account of my cowardice. He was supporting a wife and a bald baby who looked just like him. Six months later, I'd woken Ma in the middle of the night to confess. We drank tea in bed and talked.

"So what do you want to do about it?" she had asked me.

"I don't know. Own up."

"Which would result in what?"

"I guess I'd sleep a lot better."

"What would it do for Mr. Gross?"

I thought it over. "Not a lot."

"We all screw up, babe. Sometimes badly. You'd better find a way to live with the damage because it won't be the last time."

I had toyed with the idea of converting to Catholicism — the truly appealing notion of confession and forgiveness. Obviously, Mr. Gross was still peering over my shoulder, toupee askew and reeking of breath mints.

"Does that qualify as tampering with the

109

mail?" I asked Joe. "I bet they could have sent me to jail."

Joe was driving in the fast lane now, and kept shooting glances at me.

He shook his head, absently and I could see he had something on his mind. Maybe he hadn't even heard my heart-rending confession.

"You look great," he said.

"Thanks."

"I keep thinking back to the wheelchair," he said. "It's hard to believe."

"Mm," I said, not helping him out. If he was inclined to spend time with me, he'd have to learn to ask the hard questions. Otherwise, I felt we might as well kiss the whole thing good-bye right now.

There was silence for half a mile. A sign announced that we'd entered Westchester County. I hadn't been out of the city for such a long time, not since before my last relapse. Scarsdale seemed as exotic as the Desert of the Kalahari.

"Are you pain-free?" he went on. "What I mean is, how would you know you have MS, right now?"

It was unusual for him to raise the subject, and I wanted to be careful with my response. The temptation was to lie, to tell him that if he stopped the car I could do a couple hundred push-ups. On the other hand, there was no reason to regale him with this morning's ritual, when I crawled out of bed so stiff that I had to grab on to the edge of my dresser in order to take my first steps. Then the mini-exercises to get myself limbered up enough to grip a toothbrush. This morning I'd experienced my yin and yang syndrome in the shower. As if I were split down the middle from mid-torso to knees, half of me couldn't feel the water at all and the other half seemed scalded. It doesn't happen every day, but more frequently as the months go by. Also, Joe hadn't noticed my difficulty getting into his car. My left leg wouldn't bend, so Big Bob had to sort of back me in. It was natural for Joe to have questions. Any relationship with me meant a relationship with my disease as well.

"For one thing," I said, "I feel like I'm wearing a corset around my midsection. The left side of me burns as if I've been out in the sun too long. And my feet feel as if they're tap dancing but they're not moving." I thought a minute. "I think that's all at the moment. It varies." I looked at him and saw the dismay on his face. "I'm sorry, Joe. But it's not so bad and you did ask." I let it sink in for a minute. Then I said, "Can we talk about your rear end now?"

He laughed, and some of the sun-drenched seawater flooded back into his eyes. "What about it?"

"I've been meaning to complain. It's messed up my mantra."

The traffic had thinned out and the road north stretched into a landscape of rolling hills and woods. Joe was right, that there were still some bright autumn leaves clinging to the upper branches. "When I was first diagnosed," I went on, "my neurologist suggested that I find a word or a sound to use as a response to stress. It's a relaxation technique. I chose the word 'moon.' "

Joe started a slow smile, but he still didn't exactly get it. "So for the past five years," I explained, "whenever I've been anxious or overly stressed, I could close my eyes and imagine a pale moon against a velvet sky and say the word in my mind. Moon. Slowly. M-o-o-o-o-n."

Now he was grinning.

"But ever since we went for our skinny dip on your rooftop, I can't think *moon* without conjuring up your butt, which is not designed to slow my heartbeat. I swear, I am not kidding. It's a serious problem."

He was laughing again. I hoped I'd distracted him from the litany of aches and pains.

112

"So now you have to help me find another word," I said. "Any suggestions?"

He thought a minute. "Breasts."

"Oh, that's a big help."

"They're beautiful, your breasts."

"Somehow we got off the track here," I murmured. "What about *om?* A lot of people swear by it."

But he had swerved over into the right-hand lane. He pulled straight off onto the grassy shoulder and stopped the car.

"What? What?" I thought maybe we had a flat tire.

"Emergency," he said, popped his seat belt and leaned over to kiss me. It was a long exploration. Here was a man who liked kissing. So many don't. All they're interested in is kicking the ball between the goal posts, so to speak.

I was practically panting when he released me. His eyes were scanning the woods, and I could see a golf course through the trees.

"Oh, no," I said. "We're not getting naked and having sex on the fourteenth hole. Do you think I'm completely shameless?"

He gave me a tender smile and didn't answer.

"All right. I am. I know I am. Please, Joe, let's get back on the road and roll down all the windows. I need to cool off." Heat is not good for me. Any minute now, my legs would start acting like I'd just entered the Adirondack log-roll competition.

We drove along in delicious frustration. After a while, he pulled off at a bona fide exit that said STOCKBRIDGE FALLS STATE PARK. You look back on things later and wonder how come there wasn't a sign, some warning of impending doom. But there was only Joe whistling something upbeat and jazzy. I'm too tone deaf to recognize a song without the lyrics to clue me in.

We parked in a lot that was surprisingly empty on such a crystalline day. "Everybody must be home working on their Halloween costumes," I said.

Joe reached into the backseat for his camera bag, then came around my side to help me out. I was pretty much dead weight after the long drive, and as soon as he had me out of the car, he started kissing me again. I'm tempted to blame all that kissing for my mishap, but I need to resist such puritanical rationalizations.

We only had to walk about a hundred yards along a wooded path before he stopped and pointed. Across the meadow, it appeared as if an entire section of the earth had suddenly shot up twenty stories, exposing the expanse of rock that I recognized from a photograph in his apartment. It loomed like a sublime sculpture, sheer and black above the soft maze of the autumn landscape.

"Wow," I said.

"The light in this place can fry your brain." Joe began twisting a lens onto his camera. "Can you walk over there with me, or do you want to wait here?"

The ground was level enough and it felt good to move a little. We were soon at the bottom of the cliff and I could see the natural trail that zigzagged up the face. I thought the view must be pretty staggering from up there. I said to Joe, "Have you ever climbed it?"

But he took me by the shoulders, too single-minded to answer or probably even hear me. "Stand right here," he said.

"What are you doing?"

"Taking your photograph."

"I thought you don't do people." The moment I said it, I remembered the back flap of Lola's book. I thought I might bring it up but I could see that Joe was totally absorbed. His camera was clicking, clicking, and he kept changing my position. I liked having his hands on me and gave myself over to playing Georgia O'Keeffe to his Stieglitz. Finally, he had me sit and lean against the rocks, holding my knees. The way his eyes assessed me as part of the visual field felt both impersonal and extremely intimate. He reached over to arrange my hair against my shoulders.

"I wish I could somehow reveal it, the softness," he said, more to himself than to me. "I guess it's too cold for you to take off your clothes."

"Excuse me?" I said.

"I'd like to photograph you naked against the rock."

"Oh, fine," I said. "Goose bumps should make an interesting texture." But he wasn't paying any attention and was already half kneeling to get the shot. Lola had looked so sickeningly healthy in *her* photo, all those white teeth and that blond hair blowing in the wind. It was a familiar little twisting sensation, jealousy. I couldn't see why the MS lesions didn't toast *that* ugly section of my brain instead of the part that kept me setting one foot down in front of the other. There's no justice.

"Did you ever climb up to the top?" I asked Joe again as he changed the film.

"Yes," he said absently.

I wondered if Lola had been with him. "It must be very beautiful," I said.

"Incredible."

"I'd like to do it."

He looked up.

"It doesn't seem that steep."

His dubious expression only spurred me. "No, it's okay. I'm not completely helpless, you know." I scrambled to my feet. "Come on. I'll race you to the top."

"Are you sure, Anna? I don't think —"

"It'll be good for me," I said. "I need to."

As he zipped his camera into its case, I remember thinking, Okay, Anna, there's still time to get yourself out of this. Don't be such a complete ass. But then I thought about how fit I used to be. Seven years ago, I'd gone hiking in the Sierra Nevadas with thirty pounds on my back. Those mountains made this sucker look like a road bump.

The path was well-worn and smooth at first. I suppose a lot of would-be climbers had set off with brave intentions. But soon there was a rise in the terrain and it got dramatically narrower. The footing deteriorated into loose rock and I started having trouble keeping my balance. I was also getting too warm, an almost certain recipe for leg spasms. One would think that a mature woman like myself would at this point have said, "Okay, the view's great but it's time to go down."

Joe was right behind me. "Are you okay with this, Anna? It's pretty rough." Something about the concern in his voice just made it seem impossible to stop. I was too breathless to respond so I just waved my hand at him.

I suppose I was lucky I didn't get much farther before meeting my comeuppance. As it was, I made it maybe a hundred feet up and my left leg just went out of control. It jerked off to the side in a grotesque kick and I went down hard. I remember hearing a slide of pebbles falling away beneath me as I hit, and I wondered if I was destined to be the spearhead of a spectacular avalanche. Then I guess there was a hiatus because I woke up with a man leaning over me. He looked scared and angry.

"Sorry, Dad," I murmured. "The alien made me do it."

"I should never have let you come up here," the man said. "You've cut yourself."

"But you can make it all better." I could always count on Dad. He was my hero. Never let me down in the crunch. Besides, I couldn't feel a thing. Not anywhere. That happens now and then, as if somebody slipped me a spinal. I put my hand up to my head and there was sticky stuff on my cheek and neck. "Oops," I said.

"We'd better get you to a hospital."

"Drat," I said, and started to giggle. I'd had this sudden image of myself as Icarus's sister, lying in a heap with my wings squished. " 'Drat' is short for 'dratophopoulous,' " I explained to Dad. "From the Greek." I don't know why it struck me funny, but I'd hit my head pretty hard. The world went out of focus for a moment, and when it sharpened again, Joe was helping me sit up. My father was gone, no surprise there.

"Oh. Joe. God. You must be really pissed." I got no argument. Suddenly the paralysis passed and both legs began trembling badly.

"What happened to your sneaker?" Joe asked. The laces must have loosened, and then the spasms shook it off. Joe found it nearby and put it on my foot. Not simple, since it was now uncooperatively slack and appeared to have been screwed on sideways. Clearly, there was no way I could walk.

Joe reached under me and lifted me in his arms. It was a grueling trip down, what with the loose rocks underfoot and my intermittent spasms. Blood from my face spread across the front of Joe's shirt. Neither of us spoke. I nominated myself as the world's biggest fool, and no doubt every straining muscle in Joe's body was seconding the motion.

Getting me into the car was no easy trick either. Since my left leg refused to bend at all by now, Joe finally had to install me in the backseat where I could stretch out.

"I'm sorry, Joe," I said, putting it mildly.

He didn't answer, just slid behind the wheel, tires screeching as we pulled out fast. "You didn't know the terrain," he said. But he was mad. I could see it in the set of his jaw, and those eyes could get steely.

The whole lower left side of my face had begun to throb, and it hurt to talk. Joe asked the ranger in the toll booth for directions to the nearest hospital. It was supposedly a quarter hour drive, but I'd say we made it in five.

The Stockbridge Falls Medical Center was a motel-like structure with a single vintage ambulance parked at the emergency entrance. It was beginning to strike me that I could be in serious trouble here. Joe somehow got me out of the car and through the door. I was feeling quite woozy but I remember noting that the receptionist was interestingly nonurban — a young woman with elaborately waved bangs over hair straight to the shoulders. That hairstyle always seemed the great divider between city and country folk in America. You see it on talk shows, the women in the audience, and it's one of the ways you identify tourists on Manhattan streets.

"You'll have to wait. The doctor's busy."

It turned out that the only other patient was a little boy who'd gotten his Halloween costume stuck in his bicycle spokes and gone for a header. He had gravel burns on his hands and a split lip. While he was being attended to, they put me on a bed in a cubicle and drew the curtain. Joe slumped down in a plastic chair. It was difficult to imagine that I looked bloodier or dirtier than he did. The bed was drifting. I felt that I was awash on a sea of sins, most prevalent among them Pride and Envy. Perhaps I would drown. But I was not entitled to self-pity. Joe reached out to take my hand. It hurt like everything else, but was comforting all the same.

"Joe," I said. "I screwed up. I'm sorry."

"You didn't know what was up there." It wasn't just anger in his face. Fear etched shadows in the hollows under his eyes. "I shouldn't have let you."

"*Let* me. I'm supposed to be a grown-up —" I made the mistake of shaking my head. Nausea clutched the back of my throat. I had no idea how badly I'd been hurt, and was determined to get this out before I fainted or maybe died. Joe must not be permitted to accept any responsibility here. The issue had to do with our future together, if there was to be one.

"Listen to my mind here," I began. But I was so dizzy it was a challenge to hang on to my thoughts. I was also in serious danger of vomiting and still had enough vanity left to hope I could avoid such a display. Joe gave me one of those looks people bestow on the delusional and went to demand the doctor. I could hear voices mingling in the distance, far far away:

"Where the fuck . . . multiple sclerosis . . . kind of a second-rate hospital . . . why didn't you say . . ."

I think they took an X ray. Then I dozed a little, and when I woke up, Joe was standing beside a woman with a stethoscope hanging around her neck.

"I'm Dr. Kratz," she said. "You don't have a concussion but we're going to have to close that gash."

"I have to reach my doctor," I said. "I've got MS."

"Your friend here already tried but he's not available."

I didn't remember giving Joe his number. "He's always. Reached," I said past the glue ball in my throat.

"His service says he's at a Halloween

party for his little girl," Joe said.

"Oh, how *sweet!*" It made me want to cry.

"You need stitches," Dr. Kratz said, "and you need them right away."

"Are you a plastic surgeon?"

Dr. Kratz didn't like that at all, I could see. She gave Joe a look that implied they were in this thing together, the campaign to make me act reasonable. But I was imagining a Frankenstein-like scar slicing across my cheek with pegs holding it all together.

"The wound is just under your jawline," the doctor explained. I didn't remember her examining me, but then, I'd been fading in and out. "I did my residency at Bellevue and I'm fully equipped to stitch you up good as new." She flashed me an insincere smile, but it served its purpose because I could see she'd had her teeth capped, expensively and expertly. Furthermore, I could tell that she was deft with makeup. Appearances counted with Dr. Kratz, I figured. So maybe she'd forgo the pegs.

"Okay," I said. "But no Xylocaine."

"Of course you'll get Xylocaine," she said. "And an antibiotic and a tetanus shot."

I shook my head again, forgetting what a rotten idea it was. I felt the pain roll my eyes back in my head. Dr. Kratz looked up at Joe and moved her mouth. I couldn't hear the words, but the expression on her face was eloquent enough. *This broad is a pain in the butt and what are you delicious man doing with such a pitiful specimen and can't you talk some sense into her?*

I snapped back to attention. In fact, I actually sat up halfway. By some miracle, my giant swollen head which was now the size of Utah did not roll off its pitiful stalk of a neck. I summoned my most authoritative voice, the one I always used when all hell broke out in homeroom the morning before Christmas vacation.

"Listen up," I said. "I'm not letting anybody near me with painkillers or anything that numbs. You want to give me an antibiotic, that's fine. And tetanus is okay, too, but that's it. And if it's all right with you, I'd just as soon get cracking. I'm not about to miss trick-or-treat."

Something new showed up in Dr. Kratz's eyes, which was not easy to spot since she'd narrowed them to little slits. But I now felt confident of one thing: my jaw was going to sport the tidiest little stitches of her career.

"You got a radio around here?" My dentist lets me listen to it if he has to fill a cavity. The last time he'd used novocaine, I'd had facial paralysis for two months and I learned that a person with facial paralysis drools a lot.

But there was no radio. The next half hour was a blur of what the medical community refers to as *discomfort*. Joe held my hand through it all and dried my cheeks when they got damp. I will not admit to real tears because I was not crying. I believe it's just one of those natural anatomical responses to somebody making a hem in your face — your eyes do tend to water.

The receptionist appeared briefly on some excuse, presumably because she'd never heard of anybody getting fourteen stitches without anything to kill the pain. I didn't look at Joe during the procedure. His face, so full of misery, undermined my resolve, and I needed it all. So instead I stared at the part in Dr. Kratz's hair, admired the coloring job and repeated to myself over and over: *om, om*.

8

I woke up just as we were crossing the Triborough Bridge. The sun was hanging out over New Jersey, and the Manhattan skyline was so crisply focused it made my eyes ache. The inside of my mouth felt like a subterranean cavern that was home to a million bats. I reached for the lemon lozenges in my bag. When I sat up, Joe was looking at me in the mirror. There were no smile lines now.

"How long did I sleep?" My jaw was throbbing. Talking didn't help.

"About an hour. How do you feel?"

"Not bad." Kind of like I went a few rounds with Mike Tyson and he bit my face off.

"I'll pull over and you can come up here with me."

"No. This is nice. I feel like I'm having a hot thing with the chauffeur." Much too long of a speech. I'd have to learn to keep it clipped until I healed. Tasteless to crack wise anyhow, given that Joe was probably pretty fed up with me. "Are you fed up with me?"

"I wouldn't say that."

"What would you say?"

"I wonder why you insisted on climbing up there."

My relationship with Joe up to now had been entirely unlike any other in my life. I thought back to our first meeting in the photography center, to the random or, who knows, destined reconnection at the Morgan Library, to our lovemaking suspended in sky and water. I made what I felt to be a brave decision, brave because it was difficult for me, far more difficult than enduring fourteen stitches without a painkiller.

"I was jealous of Lola Falcon."

"What are you talking about?"

He had moved into the right-hand lane, where he could slow down and hear me more easily. Traffic was heavy moving south from the bridge, maybe bringing people into the city for Halloween revelries. "I saw the photo you took for her book jacket, in the mountains. I was trying to compete. Didn't work out."

Our eyes met in the rearview mirror and held for longer than was probably safe given the vehicular insanity on the FDR Drive. I could have sworn his eyes filmed over for a second before he looked away.

"Don't ever do that, Anna," he said.

"Okay."

We didn't talk again for a while. My jaw would just as soon I never uttered another word as long as I lived. But there was just this one more thing. "We should head straight for the bakery."

"Don't you want to go home?"

"Ma will be fretting." I said *fwetting*. For some reason, it was easier on my stitches. "She'll want to see I'm alive." Joe had called her from the clinic when he was trying to track down Dr. Klewanis.

Thankfully, there was a parking space just down the block from Norma's Crust. Joe came around and extracted me. When I stood up, I almost passed out from the pain. He hung on tight. Even then, I was aware of his body, of the lean strength in his arms.

"Are you sure this is a good idea?"

"You have every right to ask," I said. It suddenly struck me that I hadn't brought a man home to my mother in a long, long time. "Ma can be cranky." Especially when she sees her daughter looking like she had her jawline restructured by a bulldozer.

I'd helped Ma decorate the bakery window in black and orange crepe paper for Halloween. There were the standard festive items: cookies in the shape of ghosts, jack-o'-lanterns, black cats, and so on. But Ma being Ma, there were also the not so standard inventions that the neighborhood had learned to expect: a severed ear that dripped raspberry sauce (she called it the Van Gogh special); the Rudy Giuliani Phantom of the Opera; and my personal, if obscure, favorite, the Leona Helmsley Lady Macbeth.

I wanted to steady myself before she saw us. I stopped Joe and sneaked a look inside. Suddenly I noticed that Ma seemed older than her age, which was fifty-two. There wasn't a lot of glamour in her tangle of curly gray hair and generous body, and I could tell by the slope of her shoulders that she was tired. She finished waiting on Father Dewbright, who only stopped by to find an excuse to grab Ma's hand and propose to her. She turned to send Carmen into the kitchen for something.

When Joe opened the door for the minister, I nodded and he gave us that smile, which I have to say was more devilish than heavenly. With his myopic eyes, he probably didn't even notice my bandages. Not so Ma. Her eyes locked on me, then on Joe, then on me and back to Joe. She looked like a spectator at Wimbledon.

"Trick or treat," I said.

"Fuck," Ma replied.

"Brought you Joe Malone," I said. It came out *Mawone*. "Joe, Ma. Norma Bolles." He held out his hand, which she didn't take. A bad sign.

"What have you done to my daughter?" she asked.

"Me," I said. "Joe told me not to. I was an idiot." The edges of her mouth began to pull downward in little twitches. During my adolescence, those ominous spasms pretty much guaranteed that I was about to be grounded. Out of the corner of my eye I saw Carmen watching from behind the kitchen door. I took note that you can see the whites of people's eyes from afar, if they open them wide enough.

"Your mother's right, Anna," Joe said. "It was unconscionable to let you go up there."

"You bet your skinny ass," Ma growled at him. She untied her apron and I knew she'd be around the counter in two seconds.

"Shut *up!* Both of you!" I said, and had to grip the counter to keep from falling over. They stared at me dumbstruck while I waited for the flashbulbs to stop going off in front of my eyes. "A short speech because this hurts. I did something stupid and I'm paying for it. You're both making it worse so cut it out."

There was a silence. Then Ma looked at

Joe. "You want to come over and get something to eat?"

"Sure," Joe said.

The apartment building was only four doors from the bakery. When I was diagnosed, we moved from a brownstone that had a lot of stairs and too many narrow doorways to a slick new boring building that made more sense.

I was torn between the desire to head straight for my mattress and a profound curiosity, not to mention anxiety, concerning Joe and Ma. Since the living area of the apartment was open, I could lie on the couch and see what was going on in the kitchen. I opted to flop down there so I could ensure that things didn't get out of hand.

In the old days Ma often had a gallery at mealtimes. Her kitchen always smelled so good, and my friends enjoyed shooting the breeze with her and serving as the tasting brigade. She was a safe adult, an emissary from the bewildering grown-up world that both fascinated and repelled us. My friend Patsy Waterman could show up smelling like an ashtray and hear from Ma, "What're you Pats, a moron, frying your lungs with that shit?" whereas the mildest rebuke from her own parents would elicit plans to run away from home. She knew that Ma adored her unconditionally, and if she should wind up in the hospital with a chest full of lung cancer, Ma would be there with containers of Patsy's favorite vegetarian chili.

Joe leaned against the bookcase in neutral territory halfway between the couch and the kitchen. He'd dipped into the giant bag of goodies for trick-or-treaters and was munching on a gooey popcorn confection Ma had made. Just watching him chew made my jaw throb.

"What can I do to help?" he asked Ma.

"Can you cook?"

He shot a look at me. "I think you'd better ask Anna."

"No," I said.

"Then you can't help," she said.

The pain in my face had taken on a life of its own by now. I tried to separate it, imagining a self-contained globe of fire that didn't quite touch me. Nobody was saying anything, and given the way Ma was beheading the broccoli, I figured I'd better make an effort.

"Father Dewbright ask you out?" I had to talk with my lips narrowed, which lent my speech a somewhat sinister quality. Ma looked up uncomprehendingly, so Joe repeated my question.

"He wanted me to go with him on a re-treat," Ma answered, resuming her executionary mission. "I have to give the old guy credit. He hangs in there."

"Father Dewbright was Ma's very first customer," I explained to Joe. Sheets of red rain poured down in front of my eyes and I knew I'd reached my Waterloo as far as conversation was concerned. They'd have to manage without me.

"He was a missionary in Kenya for fifteen years," Ma said, "and I think he figures he can convert me to his point of view if he hangs in there long enough. Oh, hell, he's a good old fart."

I wanted to tell her thank you. I knew she was angry at Joe and that it demanded heroic effort for her to behave with civility. I tried to imagine her from his fresh point of view. She had what my grandma called "peaches-and-cream" skin, and her eyes were a lively blue. Her lips had a girlish shape, but the lines on either side of them made her look older. And the gray hair, of course, which she would never consider coloring.

After that, sleep triumphed. I floated up for a moment when I heard Joe telling Ma about my stitches, that I was brave. Then they were standing over me. I felt Ma's hand on my forehead, and they were gone again. The next time I came to, they were sitting at the table drinking wine. Fragments of sound passed back and forth between them.

"How come it took you almost three months to call her?" Ma asked. Did she mean me? I swam in a helpless mixture of horror and curiosity.

"I was thinking it over," Joe said.

"Because of her illness?"

I couldn't hear the answer, but assumed he was nodding his head.

"Well, what about it?" Ma asked.

I protested, or tried, but they didn't hear me. Or maybe I only thought I was making noises.

"There was no choice," Joe said.

"There's always a choice," Ma responded.

"It was pretty simple. I just had to see her," Joe said. "The MS didn't matter."

"That's bullshit. Of course it matters."

The amazing thing was, I had the most peculiar sense of detachment. All three of us were reduced to characters in some TV drama unrelated to my life.

"*You* still love her, MS and all," Joe said.

"I'm her mother, for fuck's sake."

"Is this a test, Mrs. Bolles?"

"Strap yourself in, honey," Ma answered.

"I'm just getting started."

She appeared beside the couch out of an orange cloud and asked me if I didn't want to go to bed. I remember thinking that they wanted to get rid of me so they could beat each other up undisturbed. I don't remember if I actually said so, but she let me be. I drifted off and woke up in the hospital. At least, that's what I thought. There was a ringing sound like the bell that precedes an intercom announcement. But it didn't quit: bing, bing, bing. I saw Ma move past me to open the front door and then a shout. "Trick or treat!"

I forced myself up through the dark layers of pain, back into the living room, and blinked hard to keep my eyes from closing again. We didn't get many trick-or-treaters, I don't know why. Maybe my wheelchair scared them off.

I caught a glimpse of knee-high goblins, probably from the superintendent's family. With the exception of the baby, they all wore the map of Ireland on their faces. Dennis, however, was at seven months his mother's child. She was Neapolitan, and had bequeathed to her youngest the liquid eyes and olive skin of Italy. As soon as Dennis saw Ma, he lifted his chubby arms in the air and started shrieking at her. Meanwhile, the others kept yelling, "Trick or treat!" until the Weimaraner in 4B began to howl in protest. But Dennis knew what he wanted and wasn't about to back down.

"You kids're supposed to do the tricks, not me," Ma scolded. Dennis offered a perfect smile. "Two new teeth," Ma remarked. "Way to go, Dennis."

"Do it, Mrs. Bolles! Do it! Do it!" the children clamored. So Ma swooped Dennis up, wrapped her hand around his feet and balanced him up over the children's heads. I had been watching Ma do this for decades, and it was uncanny how the babies were never afraid. They felt completely secure, always crowed with delight and stretched out their arms like tiny acrobats.

Joe had stopped breathing beside me on the arm of the couch. At least Ma hadn't kicked him out yet.

"She's never lost one," I said. Or tried to. Nothing was working very well. And the sight of my mother balancing that child hurt my heart. I felt as if I *were* Dennis, Ma's day-to-day, hour-by-hour Dennis, whom she held aloft through her own audacity and agility. But today she seemed worn-out, and suddenly I could anticipate the time when a child would lift its arms to her and she would have to shake her head. Just like me. I will never do this, I thought. And in fact, it wasn't until this moment that I understood so clearly why I had isolated myself from Dee Sunderland these past few years.

Dee headed the Art department at Cameron and had once been my closest work friend. I had always been in the thick of her family, rolling around on the floor with the kids, playing dopey games with them, wearing babies on my shoulders and hips. It was expected from "Aunt Anna." But once I got sick, I stopped sweeping up a toddler for a ride on my knee. I no longer pressed for my turn to feed an infant its bottle so I could lay my face against the damp hair and inhale the delicious baby scent. I realized that a numb arm or a sudden spasm could make me an unreliable, even dangerous caretaker. I was no safe haven for a child and I never would be. It simply became too painful to sit and watch the youthful tumble, to shake my head when a tiny hand pressed my knee for a lift up. Perhaps I'd gravitated to Grant because he was unlikely to present me with the family scene I'd once assumed was guaranteed in my future.

The children had gone on down the hall, and Ma came out of the kitchen with a bowl of pureed broccoli. She sat down on the coffee table and started spooning it into me as Joe watched. It tasted so incredible I couldn't even be mortified at behaving like a baby bird.

"Joe's had three bowls," Ma said. I wondered if Joe had figured out that the way to Ma's heart was to ask for seconds.

"Along with curried scallops, stir-fry vegetables, and some potato thing . . ." Joe said.

"Not for you," Ma told me. "We'll stick with the goo and glue until those stitches come out."

The soup made me feel as if I might resume living someday. I wondered what had been going on here while I was down for the count.

"Have you been bonding?" I asked Joe.

He glanced at Ma. "Better ask your mother."

"We're working on it," Ma said. "But there're a few more things we need to get settled."

"Wait," I said. But of course she paid no attention.

"What does 'romantically linked' mean?" she asked Joe.

"Oh my God," I said. "You couldn't have gotten this over with while I was unconscious?" My jaw was feeling a little looser. Broccoli, the wonder drug.

"Don't make a federal case, Anna," Ma said. "It's a simple question."

"Maybe not so simple," I suggested.

"Romantically linked?" Joe asked. He was clueless, poor lamb. Well, it was still slaughter time, and at least it took my mind off my unborn babies.

"The *Crain's* article," I explained. "It said you were romantically linked with someone." As if I didn't know who.

"Oh, Lola Falcon," Joe said. "I told her publicity people they could do that. She'd just come out with a new cookbook and they wanted to get her name around." He stood up. "I'll be right back. I need some more of those scallops."

"Bring me some applesauce," Ma said. "In the fridge, the quart container. Just stick some in a bowl."

"Flee for your life," I told him. While he was in the kitchen, I whispered to Ma, "Leave him alone."

"He's tough enough," she said, spooning more soup into me.

"Promise," I said.

But when Joe came back with the applesauce, I could see by the way her eyes flickered to him that she was winding up for the kill.

"You still involved with her?" Ma asked.

He shook his head. "I haven't seen her for weeks."

"Well, that doesn't mean shit," Ma said.

The scent of the Northern Spies in Ma's homemade applesauce was too much for me. I opened my mouth for a spoonful. What the hell, Joe was a big boy, and if he was going to hang around with me, he'd better figure out how to manage Ma. Also, to be totally honest, I was pretty much dying to hear what he had to say.

"You're right," Joe said. "But I don't think about her either."

Ma nodded, but there was more. "What kind of a woman is this Lola?"

I could answer that one: accomplished, athletic, blonde, and gorgeous. You'd really like her.

"Suppose you tell me what it is you want to know, Mrs. Bolles," Joe said. Respectful but firm. He'd had enough of the game. Every now and then, I'd get this glimpse of the executive.

"Fair enough," Ma said. "Does she have a disability?"

"Hey," I protested.

"It's a reasonable question," Joe said. "Your mother wants to know if I have a thing for disabled women. And no, Lola's perfectly normal. Very athletic, actually. She wins the Glens Falls triathlon every year."

Bully for her. I opened my mouth for another spoonful. I figure you should take your gratification where you can get it.

"Nice country," Ma said. This was a peace offering. I could see she was mollified.

"You've been there?" Joe asked.

Ma nodded. "Only in the winter."

"You have?" I asked.

"One November. There was a hell of a blizzard. Took us two days to dig out and the drifts were up to our asses."

"When was this?" I asked. I thought I knew Ma's itinerary from the day she was born.

"Oh . . ." She trailed off. "I can't remember exactly." Now, I know my mother almost better than I know myself. She's a painfully truthful person. But she was lying now. Not only that — she was offering me an empty spoon.

"That's okay. I'm done," I said. She set the spoon down. "So was this before you and Dad were married?"

"Oh, no," she said. "After the divorce."

I shot Joe a whadaya-know look. Ma had gotten up and was headed for the kitchen, but not before I noticed the flush on her face. I figured she was eager enough to torture Joe, why should she get off so easily?

"So who'd you go up there with?" I called after her.

I could hear her banging pots around. She pretended not to hear me.

"Will it hurt if I kiss you?" Joe let his finger rest lightly on my lips.

"It'll hurt if you don't."

He leaned over and rested his mouth against mine. It felt as though a butterfly had landed there. The sensation coursed along an electrical circuit straight to my crotch. "You win," I murmured against his mouth. He raised his eyebrows. "In the war with pain," I explained. "Now go home. Don't forget your trick-or-treat. You've been such a good boy."

Another brush of the lips, then, "I think I love your mother."

"Why?" I asked. He hadn't said as much about me, but I wasn't about to quibble over that.

"She's a warrior."

"Torquemada of Eighty-first Street."

"I'll call from Akron."

"Thank you, Joe." I didn't know where to start, the list was so long.

He got up. I heard him say something to Ma in the kitchen, but I was asleep before he got out the door.

142

9

It must have been adrenaline that had kept me even partly conscious that Halloween night. Several days afterward I crawled out of bed, but only to collapse on the couch in front of the TV. I worried about my absence from Cameron and imagined Leonard Chubb expressing his profound concern to Duncan Reese. "Isn't it a pity about Anna?" he'd say. "Happens more and more often, but then, I suppose that's the course of her tragic disease." And all the while dabbing at his ulcerated mouth with the strawberry chapstick he stores in his breast pocket.

I slept for almost eighteen hours, a record. Of course, there were wakeful moments of pounding insistence from my wound, but Ma made certain that I had a continual flow of acetaminophen in my system. My frequent dreams were like rocks in a creek. I leapt precariously from one to the other, goaded on by the need to reach the far bank. My memory of their content was as murky as the dark water, but when I woke I had the feeling that my dream river had a name: Regret. Provoked, perhaps, by thoughts of Mr. Gross and his neglected mail, I was apparently doomed over those hours to negotiate the slippery torrents of a lifetime's supply of remorse. The last dream, the grand finale, woke me for good.

I was in a sandbox with Patsy somewhere in the country. We were naked, and although I don't recall any actual physical contact between us, there was an atmosphere of sexual exploration. It was very exciting, very pleasurable. But then I noticed that Patsy's body, which unaccountably morphed back and forth from a child's into a grown woman's, was covered with sores. Repelled yet fascinated, I touched the welts one by one, even those hidden in the tangle of her pubic hair. "You'll be sorry, Anna," Patsy said sadly. And then I was alone and filled with a sense of profound loss.

After I anchored myself back in my own room and in the present tense, I realized that I had been remembering in my sleep. Shortly before my father left, I'd contracted chicken pox from Patsy Waterman. I had a particularly disfiguring case of it, and my mother had her hands full convincing me that my father didn't abandon us out of repulsion for my ugly welts. The other element was new, that perhaps Patsy and I had been indulging in some childhood sex games. It added another dimension to the great event of my father's disappearance. It was clear that my deepest regrets, which had nothing whatever to do with Mr. Gross's mail, flowed across a rock bed of guilt.

I lay in bed for a long time fighting off another bugaboo — that if my father had stayed, I would never have contracted MS. No matter how adult I tried to be, I could never quite shake the progression which still made sense in the primitive part of me that showed up in my dreams. I was bad, Daddy left, his absence made me literally sick.

"Oh, shut up and act your age," I told myself, and pulled the pillow over my head as if that could protect me from the nightmares.

After a few days, I started to improve dramatically. The throbbing turned to a maddening itch, and instead of resembling a pelican with a pouchful of mullet, my face started to suggest the outline of a human being. The first thing I did was lie in wait for Ma when she came home from work so I could interrogate her about Joe.

"What did you talk about?" I asked her,

vaguely remembering exchanges that had to do with me.

"Feeling better, are we?" Ma unpacked the groceries. I'd tasted a vast array of liquefied food over the past few days and noticed with alarm that frozen kidneys had appeared on the counter.

"I saw you yakking away over your wine glasses," I said.

"We got along all right."

"Don't tease me. You were talking about my MS, weren't you?"

She glanced up, her face serious. "He's totally fucked, babe. You better be careful."

"How about explaining that."

"Don't go messing with his head, is all. If you want him and can stick with it, okay. Otherwise, find some way to let him down easy and do it goddamn yesterday."

It had never occurred to me until this moment to consider what Joe might be feeling. In my own movie, I was the heroine, flawed or otherwise, and up to now what had counted was Joe's effect on me. "I think I just sort of assumed it wouldn't last," I said finally. "What did he say to you anyway?"

"I can tell you he's in it for the long haul," she said.

"Joe hasn't the faintest idea what that means with somebody like me."

"Don't be so sure," Ma said. "Just because he's not a blabbermouth like we are doesn't mean he hasn't done a lot of soul-searching." She stashed the last of the groceries and slammed the refrigerator door. "You two better get yourselves on the same wavelength or somebody's gonna get mangled." She started toward the door with the kidneys.

"Where are you going?"

"Mrs. Gladstone's got a migraine and couldn't shop."

I was relieved that it was the Weimaraner who'd get the dreaded organs and not me. But Ma had succeeded in shaking me up. Over the past five years, I had obviously learned to stuff fantasies about the future in some dark closet of my brain, lock the door and throw away the key. Acceptable enough when operating solo, but now there was someone else to consider. When Ma came back from Mrs. Gladstone's, I could barely look at her. She was supposed to be on my side, after all, and here she was using truth like a saber to slash away at my self-indulgent joy.

I took a careful shower after dinner and sat at my desk to check my e-mail. Cameron was renowned for its technological sophistication, and although the faculty was still more likely to seek one another out for face-to-face conversations, most of the students tended to communicate via computer.

First, there was a query from Rudy asking me to approve his term paper topic. He ended on a plaintive note: *When are you coming back, Ms. Bolles? We're scared of the substitute.* I responded that his topic was fine, that I'd be back next week and that I hoped the class was at least a little afraid of me, too.

Then the following: *Anna: Disturbed to find you've included Morrison's* Beloved *in Amer. Lit. curriculum for spring semester. The work is overwrought and overrated, and under no circumstances will I teach it in my section. I thought we'd resolved this issue in last departmental meeting, or did you forget? Please discuss with me asap. Hope you're feeling better. Leonard.*

I felt my face grow hot. Last year when Leonard pronounced that *Shipping News* was gimmicky claptrap, I almost resorted to violence. And that little dig about my memory. I was poised to fire off an eloquent response when Ma poked her head in. I could hear the Nature Channel droning from the living room, always the same disembodied male voice that's the perfect antidote to insomnia: *"The hyenas bide their time, waiting for the lion to make a successful kill . . ."*

"Check your e-mail," Ma said.

"I am."

"Joe just phoned from Dayton. He says he wrote you a letter." I started to get up. "No," she said. "He said he'd call you tomorrow."

"He hung *up?*" But she was gone. I forgot all about Chubb and his lamentable lack of literary judgment and clicked on my mailbox where I found the following:

November 5th

Dearest Anna,

Prepare yourself. I'm making an unchar-acteristic attempt to bare my soul and it's bound to be strange. I just figured I'd do it better in writing. Hereafter the unexpur-gated Joe:

Finding you has shifted me into another place. It's both wonderful and baffling, so have patience as I try to tell you what I'm feeling. Keep in mind that for me the word "feel" has been reserved for contexts like "I feel we need a more comprehensive study of the spread sheets." I'm way out of my depth.

I haven't thought about much else since I met you at the photography center. To watch you responding to those images — well, it was the best movie I ever saw. Your remark about my bridge photo was like a physical blow. It changed everything. You changed everything. In French I think they call it a coup de coeur. A year ago I would have sworn such a thing was absolute horseshit. Shows you how much I know.

The reason you didn't hear from me until September was because I was working out how I felt about the MS. I didn't want to drop out on you. But there are couples who live with this kind of challenge. I decided that I'm strong enough. The question remained, are you? And more to the point, was I laboring under some colossal self-delusion about your feelings? By the time the leaves started to change color, I couldn't wait another week to find out.

I'm moved by everything about you. When you describe your job, it's like a great adventure, circling the globe in a hot-air balloon or exploring the moon. I'm touched by your relationship with your mother. I feel as though the two of you inhabit some interesting book while I've been living in a garage. Dickens is at work in your world — Popular Mechanics *in mine.*

And the other thing — that dimension I won't entrust to these electronic scratches. I can only tell you that the way you move your hands, the shift of your shoulders when you settle against the back of a chair, the way your eyes capture me and won't let me go. Jesus, Anna, I want you all the time. I can't concentrate on anything else.

I've never been much of a believer: not in God, mysticism, love, any of that. I've been pretty comfortable skimming the surface. But you've taken a jackhammer to everything. I'm all chopped up. Along with being scared, I'm awed. It's not that I've suddenly got religion, but I have become a believer. I believe in you.

Anyhow, I've had a glass of bourbon out here in the heartland where Miss Sue-Ann, the cocktail pianist, sings a medley that winds up with "God Bless America." I'd better say good night before I get hopelessly maudlin. I would tell you that I love you, but it seems such a pitiful offering to describe what I feel.

Your,
Joe

I read it over and over again until I could recite it by heart — which I did while lying in bed and staring sleeplessly at the shadow network on my wall. I kept asking myself: How could this be? How could I have possibly engendered this extraordinary response? Talk about ambivalence. On the one hand, I was pretty much delirious. On the other, I heard Ma with her dreaded *long haul*. It was a particularly apt phrase. I imagined Joe dragging me through our lives leaving a trail of crutches, walkers, and wheelchairs in our wake. I would think about it. I would, but first, if I could just wallow in the delicious halting poetry of his letter.

The next day, I went to have my stitches removed. I was in such a fog, I didn't even inquire about music for the pain. When the doctor asked me how I'd injured myself, I told him I'd taken this spectacular hike up the side of a cliff upstate. I knew I was gushing, but I couldn't help myself. It just seemed as if everything that had ever happened to me, good or bad, had contributed to the way Joe felt about me. I wouldn't have wanted to risk omitting any of it, not my father's leaving home, not acquiring MS, not falling on my face. It was obviously witchcraft, and you just don't tamper with the slightest detail.

I went back to Cameron after school that Friday to attend a departmental meeting I was particularly loath to miss, given Leonard Chubb's communication. Fortunately, it wasn't scheduled until four o'clock, so I had a little time to track down the other American Lit teachers and line them up on the side of righteousness and Toni Morrison. Jerry LaRosa was easy, but with Myra Zak, a testy veteran of twenty years, I had to buy *Beloved* by trading Sylvia Plath for Adrienne Rich.

When Chubb showed up, he took one look at Jerry and Myra and knew he was beaten. "Any student who graduates from this school without reading *The Last of the Mohicans* is intellectually and historically impoverished," he said, and turned to me. "Welcome back, Anna. Glad you're feeling better." His expression said *I'm gonna get you, bitch*. Then he cited an appointment and left.

On my way out I stopped at the bulletin board in the lobby. There's a certain climate about the notices: sometimes they're all about protest — last month it was gender discrimination; sometimes there's a hedonistic let's-party atmosphere. Today, amidst a festoon of New Age self-improvement advertisements, there was a crumpled scrap of notebook paper, smoothed out and suspended by one tack. It said: *"G, You'll never guess who sweats Michelle Cross. The Cootie! Is that grotesque or what? See you after practice. S."*

In teenspeak, sweating somebody means

being attracted to them. Not a bad turn of phrase, given the overactive hormones of the adolescent. Nevertheless, I snatched off the news bulletin and ripped it into shreds. Hopeless love is grim enough.

Then I remembered that Joe was flying in. I glanced at my watch and bounced out the door on little springs. He was probably already in a taxi. No doubt about it, I sweat Joe in a big way.

I cabbed to his apartment at seven o'clock. This time there was no loitering at the door. I could have blown it down with one puff, waved a finger to pulverize it into dust, or merely teleported myself through it. Inside, I looked at Joe's face and felt an overpowering sense of privilege, of gratitude. I circled his waist with my arms and laid my head against his chest. I listened to his heartbeat and realized that I was embracing the reply to questions I had thought were unanswerable. I knew that Joe Malone was exactly the man I had wanted and had believed did not exist. He was the end of a road I had not known I was traveling. I already hated death because one day it would separate me from him.

I stood that way for a long time, just holding him, feeling his breath against my hair and listening to that steady timpani that was the evidence of his being alive. Finally, I was too full of words and I had to look up at him and say, "Joe, I love you. Joe. I do."

He took my hand and drew me into his bedroom, and that's where we stayed until he had to fly away again.

Ma didn't say anything at all when I got home very late Sunday night, but I could tell by her face that there was one big question on her mind. I didn't want to think about it. I couldn't think about it. So what I did was sit at the edge of my bed in the dark and make a solemn pledge that soon I would open that forbidden door labeled *Future*. I knew it was time, but I just couldn't do it tonight.

10

I walked into homeroom Monday morning, my first full day back, to find a bouquet of flowers on my desk, precariously balanced in a jar from the chemistry lab. Some of the students were oblivious to my entrance, but three pairs of eyes — Michelle's, Sukey's, and Rudy's — zeroed in for my reaction. I was in a strange state, actually, infused with endorphins and serotonin and every other great chemical produced by nonstop sex, so what I did when I saw the flowers was burst out laughing. Michelle and Sukey gawked at me in horror and fascination but Rudy was grinning. He knew bliss when he saw it.

I said some shaky thank-you's and got down to business, which was a plan for our upcoming homeroom party. "Has anyone called Chelsea Pier to make sure we've got our lanes reserved?" The vote had been for bowling.

"Me," Michelle said. "Excuse me, but what happened to your face?"

I'd anticipated this. I was not eager for it to get out that I'd fallen, so I decided on evasive action. "Cut myself shaving," I said.

"No, *really*," Michelle pressed.

"Michelle," Sukey said. "You're so sixth grade."

"She's just concerned," Rudy said.

"Go, Cootie!" Eddie Zimmer called out. Eddie is not a subtle sort. In my Shakespeare class, I asked my students, Eddie among them, to jot down an anonymous menu for their romantic ideal and drop the papers in a hat. My hope was that from the qualities itemized, we could compose a modern love sonnet in Shakespearean style. This year the first selection I drew from the hat said: *Big Tits*. When I read it aloud, everyone immediately started throwing things at Eddie.

I tried not to resent his good-natured teasing of Rudy, but I felt like strangling him. Poor Rudy, caught out in his defense of Michelle, blushed to his roots and stared down at the floor.

I hurried on. "Thank you all for the flowers. I missed you and I'm glad to be back. The bell is going to ring . . . now." It was a joke with us. I could usually tell when the bell for class would sound. All those years at Cameron, no doubt; its rhythm was as familiar as my heartbeat.

Grant was alone in the teachers' lounge. "Jesus, Anna," he said when he saw my face.

"I confess, not one of my finest hours."

"They must have given you major morphine. You look lobotomized."

"Nope," I said with a smile.

"Oh my. Well, then, I guess we know what you've been doing when you weren't trying to decapitate yourself. Wasn't he scared off when he saw that mug?"

"I'm beginning to think he doesn't scare easily," I said. I poured us each a cup of coffee and dumped three sugars and a half 'n' half in Grant's. I like mine black, preferably with the dregs that you can chew. Grant actually spilled a little when I handed him his cup, so I knew he had something on his mind.

"Don't tell me they're firing me for falling on my face," I said.

Grant shook his head. "Reese's in deep shit." For once, he lowered his voice. "There's something going on between him and Jessica."

"Lassiter?" I was incredulous. Jessica Lassiter was the registrar, and mother of two middle-schoolers. "What do you mean, 'something going on'?"

"They were spotted at a restaurant this weekend up by Columbia looking very cozy, the report goes. Apparently, he was challenged at an emergency board meeting last night and he wouldn't deny it. Or confirm it either. Pulling a Clinton."

I sat there twisting my cardboard coffee cup around and around in my fingers. "How can this be?"

"Jessica's not a bad-looking woman." His voice had risen to its normal trumpet blast.

"But she's married."

He looked at me as if I were the village idiot. "Annie-kins."

"What's going to happen?"

Grant shrugged.

"You're on the advisory committee. They won't make him leave, will they?"

"It could happen. Sentiment is running high in some quarters."

"I can't imagine Cameron without him. He came the first year I did, first grade."

"Nobody's irreplaceable, you know that. Anyhow, it's all just grist for the rumor mill for now."

"Who saw them?"

"Nobody's saying. Look, sweetness, why don't you just daydream about your boy-toy and quit worrying in advance?" He got up and planted a kiss on the top of my head. "I'm screening a video your buddy Rudy put together for his special project. Theoretical mathematics regarding the pumpkin on the Cornell library tower. Wanna come?"

"Can't do it." I was suddenly very weary. I'd settled into a corner of the couch for a quick snooze when I sensed someone lurking at the door. I figured it was Leonard Chubb since he was always poking his head around corners to check out the territory. He was the last person I wanted to catch me literally napping, so I slapped a hyper-alert expression on my face.

Leonard was looking positively elated. For Leonard, that is. His lips glistened with saliva. "I'm delighted to find you alone, Annie," he said.

He'd heard Grant call me that and figured that as an old classmate he was entitled. It annoyed me, and also that I felt I was trespassing by taking up space on *his* couch, in *his* corner.

" 'Morning, Leonard." He sat down beside me and began picking at his fingertips. I made a serious effort to work up some sympathy. After all, what kind of childhood could this man have endured to wind up so unappetizing?

"Things may change very quickly around here," he said, his voice uncustomarily animated.

"You mean because of the rumors?"

"Oh, they're not rumors." Over the years, Reese had patronized, thwarted, and ignored Leonard. The possibility of a coup was clearly a tantalizing prospect. "I have a proposition to discuss with you," he went on. His tongue sent a fine spray into the air between us. He waited for encouragement but I just sat quietly. "You and I have divergent points of view, Anna," he continued, "but our differences can serve positive ends." He smiled as if I should understand what he was driving at.

"I'm totally clueless," I admitted. Leonard was all for reinstating the era of elitist education. More admissions testing, aggressive recruiting among the wealthy, yearly testing of the scholarship (i.e., minority) kids to ensure that they were measuring up, and he'd even once proposed that they be used for free janitorial work at the school. He had also made an unauthorized trip to Ralph Lauren to solicit a design for school uniforms. I don't know what Mr. Lauren told him, but the kids still slouched around in their eclectic attire. Since Leonard and I had often gone head-to-head over such issues, he was well aware that I stood squarely on the side of the rabble.

"What exactly are you trying to say?" I asked him.

"With Reese out, we can co-chair the department."

I burst out laughing. "You and me together?" At his wounded expression, I sobered up. "First of all, it's about ten years too early, and besides, we'd kill each other."

"On the contrary, we'd make a very effective team. I know my weaknesses, Anna. I don't have natural people skills. But you're accessible and popular. On the other hand, I'm very efficient, and with all due respect, I have a broader grasp of the curriculum."

Now I got it. I was supposed to help him achieve his goal of becoming headmaster. I had to give him credit. He knew where some of the strategic holes were and had figured out a pretty imaginative way to plug them.

"What about Mary Feeny?" I asked. She was the current head of the department. A longtime favorite of Reese's, Mary was an ex-nun who had championed American women writers back in the days when the only one anybody ever taught was Emily Dickinson. Mary had backed me up on Annie Proulx.

"Feeny's finished when Reese goes." It slipped out so gleefully that even Leonard realized he'd overstepped. "What I mean is, she'll be retiring soon anyway."

"Not for another three years at least," I said. "Mary hired you, Leonard, remember? Straight out of grad school, just like me." I stood up.

"Where are you going?" He clutched at my arm.

"It wouldn't work out." His fingers were like talons, digging. "That hurts," I said.

"Think it over, Anna," he said, letting go. "You like innovative approaches; I'm offering you one." Leonard is one of the few people I know who speaks in audible semicolons.

"You're not just talking about the department, are you?"

He didn't answer, but as I gathered up my papers, he shot a zinger at me. "If you're not a part of the solution —" he said.

I whirled around. "Don't threaten me."

"I'm merely suggesting that you be practical. Your own position could be tenuous, you know, given your disability."

"You're the one who ratted on Duncan Reese, aren't you?"

His eyelids slid closed for a second and his lips formed the saucer of a smile. As I left the room, I could see out of the corner of my eye that he'd nestled into his favorite spot on the couch with his feet tucked under him, dirty shoes and all.

I wanted to go home and complain to Ma or write Joe an e-mail decrying the Uriah Heep of the Cameron English department. But as soon as I let myself in the door and found Ma home early, I knew something was up. She was shelling peas into a saucepan and they ricocheted off the sides like buckshot.

"A little tense, are we?" I asked her.

She gave me a sphinx look that told me she intended to hang on to it, whatever it was, for a while longer. "How was your day?" she asked.

"Interesting." Two could play that game.

She shoved the saucepan aside and sat opposite me at the kitchen table. "Okay," she said. "You show me yours, I show you mine."

"Duncan Reese is supposedly having an affair with a married employee."

Ma recoiled as if I'd whacked her across the face with a wet towel.

"I know," I said. "I'm not sure I believe it."

"Who?" she asked.

"Jessica Lassiter. The registrar."

"Isn't she about your age?"

"Older. I'd say thirty-five." I waited a minute while it sunk in. "Do you think they'll fire him?" I asked her. "Maybe

164

there're extenuating circumstances. I mean, *he's* been divorced for years."

"If it's true, I'd say he's fucked."

We sat in silence for a minute. Then she got up to pour herself a drink. "Want one?"

"Sure," I said. "Just half." I still had papers to grade and I was exhausted. After she'd sat back down again, I said, "I always heard Jessica and her husband could barely manage to shake hands. Okay. Now you."

She brought herself back from someplace else. "It's your father. He's asked to see you."

"Mama mia." I held out my glass. "Maybe I'll have that other half."

I'd tried to explain it to Joe when we were lying in bed during what I recalled as the Weekend of the Thousand Orgasms. As usual, he was prodding me about my father and wouldn't say anything about his own. I remember wondering if I lifted the lid on my box of worms would Joe maybe offer me the same courtesy. It didn't work out that way, but I did unearth a few nightcrawlers of my own.

"Don't you wonder what he looks like?" Joe had asked.

"I've seen photos of him."

"Recent ones?"

"He makes it into magazines sometimes. He's the guy standing behind the person standing behind the aging television personality. I saw him twelve years ago at my high school graduation. I didn't enjoy that."

"Why not?"

"I got a lot of awards, and he acted like it was all his doing. The way he put his arm around me in front of my friends when he hadn't seen me in all those years. I couldn't wait to get rid of him."

Joe gave me a kiss between the eyebrows and worked his way down my nose to my mouth. I thought maybe he was wandering off the track but I should have known better by then.

"So didn't your mother ever talk about him?" he asked.

I rolled over onto a pretzel. We had plenty of provisions in there with us, for in between.

"From the day he left, Ma never said one negative thing about him. She used to shush her own father when he'd start up in front of me." I thought back, remembering my grandfather's angry face. It got so red I was afraid he was going to pop like a big red balloon.

"But she stays in touch with him," Joe said.

"Sure, there's financial stuff. He's very

generous about my medical bills. But she knows I'm not much interested in talking about him."

"Not interested or you don't want to?"

"Vell, Herr Doctair, a little uff both." I trailed off. In the silence, Joe leaned over and kissed me. I felt my limbs relax as the pressure of his mouth on mine set me adrift again, just Joe and me on a calm sea. It was time to toss Daddy overboard. He didn't belong in this boat.

"Maybe it's not so bad to invent your own relatives," Joe said.

I confess to dirty pool: "Sure, if the real ones are vile," I said. "But your father's not so bad, right, Joe?"

"No," he said. "Not bad, not good, not anything." Guaranteed, at the mention of his own father, that flat, undecipherable tone. He draped a leg over me and stopped my mouth. Daddy disappeared under the waves and it was just the two of us again.

This mental plunge back into bed with Joe must have taken less than a second because Ma didn't appear to have noticed. She was gazing toward the window with faraway eyes as if she, too, was floating on a memory.

"What's the occasion?" I asked her. She looked at me blankly. "For Dad's visit?"

"Oh. He's coming to New York in a couple of weeks," she said. "He phoned the bakery to ask if you'd have dinner with him." She got up and went to the kitchen counter to pound chicken cutlets with a mallet. There appeared to be a personal grudge involved, given the level of violence.

"What does he want from me?" I called. We both heard the petulant five-year-old in my voice, and when Ma turned to look at me, I gave her a rueful smile. Up to now it had been easy to avoid my father. His second wife didn't want him to have anything to do with us. By the time he'd divorced her and remarried for the third time, I had been diagnosed with MS and his rare requests to see me dwindled to none. It was only during the course of my mattress discourse with Joe that I realized my years of resentment were somewhat unjustified. I bore my own share of the responsibility for our lack of connection.

"That chicken's dead already, Ma," I observed. "He couldn't call me directly?"

She flashed me her high beams. "The second you hear his voice on the other end, you say, 'Oh-hi-Dad-Ma's-right-here-bye.' Then you bolt into your room and that's that. He was hoping I would persuade you."

"Will you?"

"Make your own decision."

There she was again, the Subtext Queen. I could see the battle going on in her face; the troops were massed. But the prospect of actually meeting up with my father made me squirm as if the kitchen chair had suddenly developed an unpleasant electrical charge. I got up and started walking around, but the annoying little zaps came along, too. I preferred to keep my father flattened out in a magazine photograph. That way he couldn't take on any unmanageable dimensions. "It's not a good time," I said. "I'm preparing for midterms, and there's Joe."

"Mm-hm," Ma said.

"What night was this, did you say?"

"Two weeks from tonight."

"Would you come, too?"

"Christ, no. Why are you twitching?"

I stopped pacing for a second. "I don't know. How about I toss a coin?"

"If that's how you want to handle it," she said.

"Don't call me an asshole."

"I didn't call you an asshole," she said.

"Yes, you did."

She closed the broiler on the paper-thin cutlets and sat down. Her eyes looked a little shiny. It suddenly occurred to me in one of those little epiphanies one has about one's parents, that the divorce had happened to Ma in ways that had nothing to do with me. For months after my father left, she used to cry in the shower. She thought I couldn't hear her.

"Make room," I said. She shoved her chair back and I sat down. Her lap was soft and still. It muted the stinging electricity in my limbs. "Pluses and minuses?" I asked. Her curly hair tickled my cheek.

"Sure," she said, "if you eat something. Your butt is getting bony again." She spilled me off her lap and went to the stove.

"Pluses," I said, then after a while, "I can't think of any."

"I'll give you one," she said, showing me a face like Margaret Thatcher in a mean mood. "You're a grown woman. It's time to quit being such a fucking wimp."

I slept on it. The next afternoon, I phoned L.A. and spoke with my father's secretary. He was male. I guess they all are out there.

"Mr. Bolles isn't in right now." If a voice can be perfectly coiffed, this one was. "May he return?"

I mulled this over. Return where? Then I realized that show-business people are presumably too busy to finish their sentences. "This is his daughter, Anna, in New York."

"Ah, yes," the voice purred. "Your father is traveling but he was expecting your call. You have a tentative reservation at Patrick's on West Fifty-fifth Street for six-thirty on November twenty-fifth. If that's acceptable to you, would you mind confirming?"

"Not at all." Sure, I thought, I'll return and confirm, I'll show and confer.

There was a moment's hesitation, then, "Mr. Bolles does have a meeting scheduled at eight P.M. that evening . . ."

I assured him that I'd not detain, then sat down with my quaking stomach and tried not to throw up.

11

I retreated to my room after dinner and distracted myself by thinking up fiendish questions for a midterm quiz. When my brain approached burnout, I checked my e-mail. Sure enough, Joe had written to me from upstate:

> *Dear Anna,*
>   *I've rearranged my calendar and as of Thursday will be in the city for ten days in a row. Count 'em: ten. I'm tempted to lure you into bed for the duration but figured we should partake of the cultural scene once in a while. I bought us some tickets. Are you game?*
>
> > *Your,*
> > *Joe.*

In my experience, guys tend to regard women as books that sit on the library shelf waiting to be lent out to them at their convenience. Joe bought tickets. Did I not have a life, a career, obligations? The thing to do was to fire back a letter listing my many engagements and how I trusted he had given some thought to the possibility that I might not be available.

So this is what I said: *Dear Joe, Absolutely.* And then, because I figured he owed me something for being so agreeable, I dashed off a carefully casual inquiry just to see what would happen: *Look, there's something I've been meaning to ask you. With all those healthy young females out there, why me? I'm not the obvious choice. Love, Anna.*

His response: *A: Because I like the way you smell. J.*

Maybe it's because of the injured circuitry in my brain, but those ten days have always felt like a shiny round ball, an ornament hanging on the intricate branches of my memory tree. More often than I like to think, I have plucked it off and held it for a moment, just for the wonder and comfort.

That Thursday, Joe surprised me by showing up outside school. Since he was incongruous there, an interloper from another part of my life, I spotted him instantly. He leaned against the wrought-iron gate in an army-green jacket, chewing on a brownie and watching the kids who were crowded around the bake-sale table on the sidewalk. He wore the intense concentration of the photographer. I was loath to interrupt but he caught sight of me, grinned and reached out, clearly intending to sweep me into his arms. I stiffened, but it was too late. I got as far as "What a nice sur—" when Joe fastened his mouth on mine. After he released me, I saw that Eddie Zimmer was standing beside us with his sneakers mere inches from my shoes. He watched us with clinical interest.

"Er," I said when I could catch my breath, and shot Eddie a get-lost look. But Eddie only stuck his hand out at Joe.

"I'm Eddie, Ms. Bolles's favorite student," he said.

Joe smiled and clasped Eddie's hand. "Pleased to meet you, Eddie, but we're out of here." Then he bent to pick up what looked like two bowling balls at his feet. They turned out to be helmets. "Put this on," he said, clipping his under his chin. Eddie hadn't shifted a millimeter. I could even see the hole in his earlobe where he'd had a pierce back in eighth grade. Joe took me by the elbow and led me across the street to an enormous black motorcycle. Eddie came along, too.

"You expect me to get on that?" I said.

"I'll go," Eddie said.

"Another time," Joe said, helping me settle on the curved leather seat. It was surprisingly comfortable. "Just hang on tight," he said superfluously, as if I wouldn't be clinging to him like lint on a lollipop.

Eddie had now been joined by what appeared to be most of the senior class and some faculty members, including Leonard Chubb. I noticed that the bake-sale table had been entirely deserted. Maybe it was the macho belch of the engine roaring into life, but I suddenly considered streaking downtown to get a Biker Chick tattoo. I waved at Eddie as we roared off.

It turned out that it wasn't Joe's bike. He had driven it down to Manhattan for his friend Steve, who was trying to sell it. We didn't go very far, just across to the West Side and down Columbus to Joe's building. But it was very sexy, having all that power vibrating between my legs. It made me think of D. H. Lawrence, and as soon as we got upstairs, we headed straight for the bedroom. It was bliss. Not big on the foreplay — we still had half our clothes on afterward — but bliss all the same.

"How come you know how to drive that thing?" I asked him. I kicked at the tangle of discarded clothing around my ankles.

"I had a Harley-Davidson in high school."

"I'm glad I wasn't your mother. I would have been freaked out all the time."

"She didn't like it much, but my grandmother did. We took a lot of trips together."

I looked at him.

"She was my first passenger the day I bought it. She especially liked the roads up in the high peaks. All those curves."

"Joe, I think you'd better tell me about this grandmother."

But he got out of bed. "I'm thirsty. You want something?" I must have fallen asleep. When I woke up, I had the quilt over me. I called for Joe but there was no answer. I got up, wrapped myself in the quilt and padded into the living room. Joe was standing against the wall in his jockey shorts, but his feet were where his head should have been. His face was deep crimson and his eyes were closed. I thought of asking *Was it something I said?* but was afraid to speak for fear of toppling him. I just sat down on the couch and watched his chest slowly expand and contract. After ten minutes or so he curled his legs and dropped soundlessly to the floor. He looked at me and raised a finger to indicate *Almost done.* He arranged his body into the most unlikely contortion, balanced on his hands with both legs tucked up next to his torso. He maintained the pose for some minutes, then lowered his feet to the floor and stood up.

"Hi," he said with a celestial smile.

"So that's how come you're so diesel," I said. He gave me that *huh?* look. "You know, buff, built, fit," I explained.

He toweled himself off. "Yoga's a portable gym. For people who travel a lot."

And for avoiding answering questions about your grandmother, I thought. "You have any other secret pastimes I should know about?" I asked.

"Mmm," he said, gulping down half a liter of Evian in one gulp. I watch the boys do that in the cafeteria at school. Men must have throats like storm drains. I glanced at my watch, which I'd never bothered to remove. "Have you got time for a quick dinner?" I asked him.

"We have a seven-thirty reservation at Café des Artistes," he said. He dropped down next to me on the couch. I stared at his bare feet propped up on the coffee table. There's something so intimate and vulnerable about toes.

"I wish," I said. "I've got midterms to correct."

"You still have to eat." He sounded amazed that I could possibly turn him down.

"Those exams are going to take me most of the night."

"How about if I help?"

"Only if I get to negotiate your next deal." I let him absorb that for a minute. "I'm not on vacation, Joe. I wasn't included in the planning stages."

"You can work over here," he said. I didn't even bother to answer that. Finally he smiled at me and scratched the soft patch of hair on his chest. "I guess I just assumed." I could see him calculating. "Does this mean you can't come to the party tomorrow night?"

I laughed.

"Michael from yoga class is having a pre-Thanksgiving blast. Oh, hell, it's all right. I don't want to share you anyway."

Fortunately, I wasn't completely wiped out when I got home. Other than the annoying sunburn sensation on my shoulders and upper arms, I felt pretty good. Ma was working late in the bakery so I was alone with my stack of exams and the persistent thoughts of Joe that at first kept intruding into the scribbled pages on my desk. Soon enough, however, I was lost in the tangle of illogic, temporizing, creative spelling, and sometimes brilliance of my students' essays.

The poetry of *Beowulf* was totally lost on Sukey, but Eddie surprised me with a sensitive analysis. He'd read the book, for a change, probably because it was short.

After a while my left leg started bobbing up and down, signaling the need for a break. I lurched around my room, then leaned over to snap on my computer. There was another e-mail message from Joe, written just after I left his apartment.

7:20 P.M.
Dear Anna,
There has been one other crucial woman in my life — Gran, my mother's mother. When I was little and broke my ankle, Gran came by every day and took me for a ride in a wheelbarrow. It was so much fun that I kept up the wounded pretense long after I was mended. She knew, but never let on. By her seventy-fifth birthday, she was pretty infirm and we celebrated at her house with champagne and cake. The next morning I dropped in to check on her and found her eating breakfast from a tray in bed — Rice Krispies and a glass of champagne. She told me that if I thought she'd be drinking orange juice when there was bubbly going to waste, I was "splashing in the wrong puddle." I had to fight my family to keep her out of the hos-

179

pital at the end. She wanted to die listening to Scott Joplin. I don't know if she could hear it, but I kept it playing nonstop for the last forty-eight hours.

Your, J.

I printed it out and slipped it in a drawer with my other Joe memorabilia. It was clear by now that Joe was most comfortable communicating his feelings electronically. I wondered about the implications. But he had made an effort, and at last I could identify one person from his history who had some substance. I was always yammering to Joe about my students, my parents, people in my apartment building, even the derelict on Eighty-fourth Street who wanted me to add *Down and Out in Paris and London* to my Twentieth Century Lit curriculum. But all inquiries to Joe about his family and friends had up to now been met with polite stonewalling. Finally, his letter gave him a new and poignant context. Joe's Gran might be dead, but she was real, and so was the sense of loss she had left behind.

For somebody as reticent as Joe, he managed in those ten days to intrude into every nook and cranny of my life. I asked him not to pick me up at work again but the damage was done. When I walked into my homeroom on Tuesday morning, there was a poster taped to the wall: Marlon Brando in *The Wild One*, straddling his motorcycle. I gazed around at the fourteen pairs of eyes. If I could only elicit this level of attentiveness in my Classics and Comp class. I removed the poster, taking care not to tear the edges.

"Thank you all so much. I'll hang it over my desk at home. Sukey, did you bring me your community service form?"

Sukey blinked sleepily. "I forgot. I didn't have coffee yet."

"Haven't had," I corrected her, and twisted a rubber band around Marlon Brando.

If it were only as easy to roll Joe up and put him away. I was always looking for an excuse to talk about him. I ran into Grant while I was reading a physical fitness notice in the teachers' lounge. That was my opening to tell him that we should all embark on a yoga program so we could be in shape just like Joe. Grant gave me that beady-eyed stare. "You're beginning to be tiresome, Annabelle," he said.

"Am I obsessed?" I asked him.

"We can test it out." He thought for a moment. "Fencing," he said finally.

"Good neighbors, Robert Frost, the

woods, the Adirondacks, Joe Malone," I said.

"Not that kind of fencing." He struck a pose. *"En garde!"*

"Zorro, movies, photography, Joe Malone."

"Turnips!" he shouted in disgust.

"I'm always hoping he'll turn up? Ohmigod. This is really scary."

Grant put an index finger to each of my temples. Steve Rosenberg, one of the Latin teachers, stopped in the doorway.

"Happening?" he asked.

"I'm giving her a lobotomy," Grant said.

"When you're finished with her, you can do me."

But the pressure of Grant's fingers made me think of the straps of my swimming goggles, which reminded me that Joe was joining me for my swim at the "Y." All rivers ran into the same ocean, it seemed, and I had no control over the floodwaters.

We sat once again with our feet dangling in the water at the pool's edge, but this time daylight streaked through the skylight as a dozen swimmers did laps, their styles varying from sea otter to water mill.

"So you'll be seeing your father in a few days," Joe said.

"You'll be gone. I don't like to think about it."

"That's the only reason?"

I kicked at the water. One ankle didn't want to bend, the other had melted and disappeared along with my foot. "I've been a little distracted," I said, giving him a nudge.

"Are you looking forward to it?"

"Yes," I said, surprising myself.

He waited. I loved that about Joe. His timing was exquisite.

"I've been unfair to hold a grudge," I said. "After all, he's been very good to me financially and I've hardly encouraged him. I think it's sweet that he wants to see me. You know, I think I dreamt about him last night."

Joe pulled a big towel around our shoulders. I imagined how we must have looked, one big lumpy body with two heads.

"I don't remember the details," I said. "He was performing some kind of mission to aid humanity. But very humbly. There was this sense of decency about him. Actually, he looked a bit like Harrison Ford. I'll bet he's a lot like Harrison Ford."

Joe leaned over and kissed me. I imagined Joe and my father meeting, having a good old macho gab, jostling each other a bit, possessive about me but respectful and liking one another. Harrison Ford was a bit young, but give him ten years, more gray in the hair. That's the guy.

My work had backed up, so we took a break while I graded papers. One night. It felt like a week. The next day we'd made plans to meet for dinner, but when I stopped by the bakery on my way home after work, Joe was leaning against the counter chatting with Father Dewbright. Ma was busy waiting on a trio of women with strollers.

"I prefer to use a mayfly myself," Father Dewbright was saying. He was an avid fisherman.

"You tie your own?" Joe asked.

"I used to, until my hands . . ." He held out his arthritic fingers, then glanced at Ma and hid them self-consciously. When Joe saw me, his face did this amazing trick, that I-just-won-the-lottery look. He stretched out an arm and drew me next to him.

"Hello, Anna," Father Dewbright said. "Joseph and I are confessing our favorite trout-fishing spots. A fisherman doesn't ever reveal them unless he gets an equal number in return."

"I used to go for trout on the Upper Eagle with my Dad," Joe said, "but I think acid rain pretty much wiped them out."

"You went fishing with your father?" I asked Joe. Suddenly this conversation had become interesting.

The tone shifted subtly. "Yeah, when I was a kid." And he turned his attention to Ma, who had finished her sale. "Norma, can you sell me a couple of these cheese things?" he asked her. I wanted to shake him and say, *"Tell me."*

Joe took to dropping by Norma's Crust every afternoon. If the store was busy, I'd find him helping out behind the counter. Otherwise, he and Ma always seemed deep in conversation. One day I lurked on the sidewalk outside where they couldn't see me and tried to read what they were saying. I felt a little stab of jealousy as I watched Joe wind up a monologue that I swore was longer than any speech he'd ever made to me. There were gestures, too, indicating profound emotional content.

"What do you and Joe talk about?" I asked Ma as I was dressing for a chamber-music concert.

"I don't know, this and that," Ma said. My zipper had stuck and there was no way I could get my clumsy fingers to release it.

"Don't be so clubby, will you?"

She raised her eyebrows at me.

"Well, I don't like it," I said.

"Is anybody bothering you?" Ma asked.

"What if it doesn't work out? It's only going to be harder on everybody if you two are such devoted pals."

"Are you thinking that it won't?"

"For about a thousand reasons," I said. It slipped out more as a testy zinger than an expression of fact. I certainly hadn't visited the matter consciously.

"If you're dumping him, do it in a hurry." She gave the zipper a violent tug. I could hear fabric tear. "Fuck," she muttered. "Guess you'd better choose another dress."

Whose side are you on, anyway? I wanted to ask, but I just slipped into another outfit and left to meet Joe.

On our last evening, a Saturday night, we went to see an off-Broadway play named *Mud Tracks*, produced by an experimental theater group Joe admired. It was playing down on Wooster Street in a loft space furnished with uncomfortable folding chairs. We sat with about fifty other people, mainly downtown types in black clothes and turbulent hair. Heretofore, Harold Pinter was about as radical as I could manage, so once the play started, I waited in pained tolerance for it to be over. In Act One the characters — presumably a family at the dinner table

— recited gibberish at one another. I half listened, shifting in my seat and hoping the sensation would eventually return to my rear end. But gradually, fragments of actual words and then bits of sentences began to rise out of the flood of syllables. I glanced at Joe. He was totally engrossed. Before long, coherent phrases stabbed like cruel beams of light, illuminating painful truths. I found myself wincing with each revelation. By the end, the dialogue had become entirely straightforward and almost unbearable to hear. The audience left looking shell-shocked.

We were mostly silent walking to the restaurant around the corner. There was a clammy breeze and I wished I'd worn an extra layer. Over sushi I asked Joe what he thought. As usual, he took his time answering. Finally he said, "Sometimes I don't understand what my photographs are about until they take form in the chemical bath. Once they're not contained in the parameter of the lens, they get away from me." He paused again, drank some sake and went on. "Sometimes they're not easy to look at. I'm being informed about myself whether I like it or not."

I was moved by his poetic and intensely personal association to the drama. "Is that why you like plays?" I asked him. He looked baffled. "To inform yourself about your-self." I thought that was pretty clear, but his confusion began to look more like discomfort. I could feel him retreat. It was almost a physical sensation, as if he'd backed a few inches away from his side of the table.

"You sound like Steve," he said. "Don't you want a *toro* hand-roll? They're amazing here."

"What does Steve say?"

"That I'm a chronic spectator. He calls me 'the drama critic.' "

"When do I meet him?" I asked.

That brought a laugh. But I was thinking, Okay, you'll open up on e-mail when we're safely encapsulated from one another, you'll give me cryptic hints into your psychology if there's a metaphor to hide behind. But those photographs are emotionally loaded. *You* are emotionally loaded.

"Where's the guy who photographed that bridge in the fog?" I asked. "I get glimpses and then you hide under a rock."

Joe had stopped eating and was making circles in the soy sauce with a chopstick. Then he looked up at me. His voice was quiet but his face wasn't. "I'm trying, okay, Anna? You scare the shit out of me." He gestured with the chopstick, moving it back and forth between us. "This scares the shit out of me."

Why are you torturing the man, Bolles? I asked myself. If it turned out the only way he could reveal himself was by bouncing electronic signals off a satellite, that should be okay with me. Shut *up*.

I got out of my chair and went around to his side of the table. "Give me room," I said. He slid his chair back and I sat down in his lap. I wrapped my arms around his neck and gave him a big kiss, one of those long juicy ones that make you think you'll suffocate to death before it's over. Then I got up and went back where I belonged. The chefs behind the sushi bar looked a bit startled. I guess people don't do that sort of thing in Japan. But this was downtown and I figured what the hell.

That night, I slept in Joe's arms and dreamed once more about my father. He rode a horse and wore a battered felt hat — Harrison Ford again — and somehow before the end of the dream, a small child appeared behind him in the saddle. I woke up with the feeling that nothing bad could ever happen to me. It lasted until I sat up and saw Joe's open suitcase at the end of the bed.

12

I battled nausea all day Tuesday, telling myself I was merely somewhat nervous due to my dinner date that night. Furthermore, the numbness in my hands had flared up again. So far today, I'd dropped my toothbrush, a bus token, a file folder, two pens, and a Life Saver. Once I got home from work, the notion of changing clothes for the restaurant overwhelmed me — a daunting prospect of zippers, laces, panty hose, and buttons. Also, I needed a shower. I swallowed hard against the half-digested lunch in my throat and started painstakingly unbuttoning my blouse. Since I couldn't feel anything, I used my eyes to guide my fingers.

I heard the front door slam, Ma's quick steps, and she was framed in my doorway. She made the instant Anna-status assessment that reminded me of my software's virus check when I booted up my computer. Only Ma was a lot more thorough.

"Hands?" she said.

I nodded.

"Shoulder, too."

"Oh," I said, and tried to stretch the muscle there. I hadn't noticed that it had locked tight.

"We'll work on it when you get back," she said, and had me out of my clothes in seconds. "You could wear your one-zip special. You want something for the nausea?"

"I'm okay, thanks. But just out of curiosity, how can you tell?"

"Color around your mouth." She laid my A-line black wool with the single zipper up the front beside me on the bed. "Let me know when you're ready."

"I think I can manage. Thanks, Ma."

"Okey-dokey." She started out.

But I caught her hand. "No, I mean, *thanks*."

She turned around and I knew she understood the volumes I was trying to say. She smiled. "No fucking problayma, dahlink."

I got to Patrick's ten minutes early, stood outside and debated with myself whether to waste some time before going in. I wasn't feeling exactly rock solid in the balance department, and a trip around the block without my cane could easily wind up in a pratfall on the sidewalk. On the other hand, I disliked the prospect of my father finding me lying in wait like some eager groupie.

191

But the numbness was creeping up my foot. I went inside.

They seated me at a table with a view of the entrance. People with theater reservations were trooping in, and I studied each lone male who seemed even faintly similar to the last photo I'd seen, reminding myself that the dashing figure of my dreams was hardly likely. Here was a candidate: balding, a bit paunchy, but a certain gravity of expression, a certain dignity — not so bad. But he strode past me. Next a retro-bopper, slicked-back hair with ponytail, deep tan, heavy gold necklace — please God, not him. It wasn't, though he shot me one of those I-might-have-time-for-you-later-doll smiles. But then I knew. He was coming straight at me. The irony of it — after all these years, I was going to be reintroduced to my father by a waiter.

"Your usual table, Mr. Bolles," the waiter said, and pulled out the chair opposite me. So he was a regular.

But my father came to give me a kiss on the cheek. He was nice-looking and appeared at least ten years younger than Ma. He wore a dark gray silk shirt without a jacket. When he sat down we stared at each other intently, then started to laugh. It seemed auspicious enough. It suddenly flashed through my mind: *Maybe he'll join us for Thanksgiving. We'll be a family.*

"You look so much like my mother," he said. "Only prettier. God, you're gorgeous. Those eyes could get you a film contract."

That felt good. But now that I had a closer look at him, I could see that he was no stranger to the hair dye, and the skin around his eyes was suspiciously wrinkle-free.

"What happened there?" He pointed to the scar along my jawline.

"A little hiking accident."

"You can get that fixed," he said. "I'll give you the name of a good man on Seventy-first. So how long's it been? Nine, ten years?"

"Twelve."

"That long," he said absently, and hailed our waiter. "We should order. I have to be crosstown by seven-fifty. The halibut's excellent. Also the risotto."

There was pleasure in allowing him to order for me and hearing him say, "My daughter will have . . ." I looked around at the other patrons, savoring the unfamiliar sensation: *I'm with my dad,* I told them all silently. *This here's my dad. We're doing a father-daughter thing.*

When he folded his hands on the table, I noticed that his nails glistened with polish.

I'm not crazy about that, so I did an instant rationalization. In his business, one had to follow the protocol. Surely, if given his druthers, he would never *opt* for a manicure.

"So how's your mother?" he asked.

"The bakery's busy. She needs to hire another assistant."

I was surprised that this didn't go over well. "The whole thing's ridiculous. What does she need the aggravation for?"

"She likes it," I said.

"The trouble with your mother is, she can't accept help. She knows I'd send her anything she needs. Stubborn woman."

I felt this guilty urge to fall in with him in a little minor dishing of Ma, so I probably overcompensated in my tone. "Maybe she just likes being independent." I could feel my chin thrust out the way it does when I get annoyed.

He didn't react, just slid into another subject. "I was so glad you decided to come, Anna." He reached across the table to take my hand in his soft palm. I'd imagined just such a moment a few thousand times over the years. My eyes began to sting. I commanded myself, oh *no,* under no circumstances.

"So tell me all about yourself, Anna. You teach up at the Dalton School?"

"Cameron," I said. "But same idea."

"History, right?"

"Well, no, English."

"Must be rewarding." He had spotted someone he knew and hailed him over. This fellow, a sturdy rooster in jeans and a polo shirt, smelled of expensive aftershave. I assumed he was important if he felt comfortable in that getup. "Ron, this is my daughter, Anna Bolles, teaches history to rich brats."

Ron bent over my hand and kissed it. "You're wasting your time. We need a face like that in the business."

I shifted my head a little farther aside to conceal my scarred jawline, although I was thinking that I should be shot as a traitor to my gender. I was so busy preening under all the male attention it momentarily escaped me that my father had gotten my job description wrong.

He and Ron traded show business news for a moment while I tried to look calm and self-assured. In fact, I could smell wet wool from where I was sweating under the arms of my dress, and the numbness had now achieved the unprecedented heights of my left hip. I felt precarious, as if I were perched on the edge of the chair. I reached down with my hands to make sure I was centered and wondered if half of my brain would soon turn numb as well. If I had only half a brain, which functions would still remain operative? Perhaps I would lose my sense of color to a black-and-white world. The restaurant would assume the romantic atmosphere of Rick's in *Casablanca*. And what about my auditory sense, if perhaps only articles and prepositions would register, reducing conversations to *in the an a out?*

But soon Ron, with another gallant kiss, disappeared into the power room at the rear of the restaurant. You could see through the glass doors that there wasn't even a token woman back there.

"Is Ron someone you work with often?" I asked. In fact, if my father was in total ignorance about my career, I was quite the clandestine expert on his. He and two other entrepreneurial types had recognized fifteen years ago that the cultural appetite of the American public was becoming ever more banal. They joined forces in founding something called Straight to the Slot, a video production company of films marketed strictly for VCRs across America. I had watched dozens of them, hoping to detect a hint of originality, of challenge to my intellect, some spark of creativity. Ma finally explained that I was missing the point, that the productions were created specifically to avoid such tiresome qualities. Viewers found it comforting to pop one of those stories into their TV, then sit back and predict every line of dialogue. The end result was that my father could divorce and remarry a dozen more times without worrying about coughing up the alimony.

"I think you've got my nose," my father was saying. "Ginnie's got it. My youngest. She's a dynamo. What an athlete. She already serves tennis balls at sixty miles an hour and she's only eight."

Where were you when I won the Best Athlete Award my junior year of high school, the first female in twenty-two years to do it? But he was off on another tack altogether.

"So is there a man in your life? A beautiful girl like you . . . Oh." He caught himself. "I guess . . . I guess maybe that's. . . ." I gathered he'd remembered the MS.

"Actually, there is," I said, trying not to sound defiant.

"That's great! Is he . . . ? I mean, does he also . . . ?"

I shook my head. "No, he's perfectly normal."

"What's he do, a teacher at your school?"

"No, he's a businessman. He was in *Crain's." He's beautiful and honest and tal-*

ented, daddy, I wanted to say. But I had the feeling I could have explained that Joe trains boa constrictors to squeeze film executives to death and my father would have responded, *Great, that's great.*

"Think you'll marry him?"

"No." It slipped right out with such confidence it was almost as if someone else had uttered the word. *What?* I wanted to ask myself. *What did you say?!*

"Too bad," he muttered. He suddenly shoved his plate aside. The mood shifted so fast I felt as if the overhead lightbulbs had blown out, and it wasn't because my father was concerned about my future with Joe.

"You know, Anna," he said, "there was a particular reason I wanted to get together with you. Well, of course, I wanted very much to see you. Didn't want to force you, of course."

I had very quickly dismissed from my mind the prognosis regarding my future with Joe. It was far too complex and disturbing to contemplate here. So I just sat and waited for my father to spit it out. There didn't seem much point in my mentioning that a little tenacity on his part would surely have convinced me to see him long ago. I began to suspect that I could get through the rest of the evening uttering ten words or less. I resolved to count. Maybe six.

"I've had some bad news." And he did, in fact, look shaken all of a sudden. "It's my prostate. Cancer. They're treating it with a combination of chemo and radiation. I've never been sick a day in my life. I'm a mess, can't go to the gym, haven't got energy for anything, sex life's blown to hell. Oh, sorry, but we may as well be frank with one another."

Speak for yourself, I thought, but he just kept on. "Anna, you've had your illness for so long you don't think about it anymore. It's better when you get hit young because you can adjust so much more easily. But a guy like me, I don't have to tell you, it's been hell. With a gorgeous young wife and all . . . Obviously, you've already come to terms with the fact that you're not going to have a full life span. God, honey, I've tried Prozac and every other damn thing, but I'm still scared shitless. Can you give your old dad a hand?"

I stared at my father across the snowfield of white linen. The man was clearly in terrible distress. His forehead was pebbled with sweat, he had turned an unsavory taupe that clashed with the expensive shirt. His eyes were watering with self-pity. I thanked my lucky stars that I was half numb. If one hundred percent of me had to take this all in, I don't think I could have borne up. I said to myself: *Forget that this is your father. It's just some pathetic person who has nothing to do with you.*

"You've raised a number of issues here," I began, amazing myself at my measured, unemotional tone. Maybe Joe was rubbing off on me. "For one thing, you seem to be laboring under the misapprehension that multiple sclerosis is a fatal disease." Actually, I sounded like a prig, but I was so outraged, so wounded, that inflated language seemed preferable to the only alternative, which was flipping the table onto his lap.

"It isn't?" He was truly surprised.

I shook my head.

"But a colleague of mine, his wife had it and she just died, fifty-three years old."

"MS can cause life-threatening complications on occasion," I lectured, "but with competent medical care, there's every reason to expect a normal life span."

"Oh." He was deflated for a moment, then made the giant mental leap and managed a half-hearted smile. "Well, that's great news. I wish I'd known that earlier."

I was Ma's child, too, so I figured what the hell, go for it. "So you would have done what?" I asked him.

He looked at me as if I wasn't all that

bright. "Well, it's pretty self-defeating to invest your emotions in someone who's terminal, wouldn't you say?"

"You mean you stayed away all this time because you thought I was dying?"

"That was part of it, sure. Who wouldn't? Plus you weren't much interested in getting together."

"It wasn't up to me. I was a *child*." People at the nearby tables turned to stare at us.

After a moment of chilly silence, I could see that my father had come to a decision: I would be of little use to him in his health crisis. He raised a hand to call for the check. "Sorry we don't have time for dessert or coffee." He must have been a good tipper because the waiter appeared before he got to the last syllable. He signed the bill as I struggled to control myself. In addition, I was worried about logistics. If my legs wouldn't hold me up, I might have to ask for help from my father. At the moment, that notion made me feel like gagging.

Thankfully, I was only numb, not weak. As we walked to the door, my father put his hand on my elbow. "It's nice that you keep slim," he said. "Is your mother still so heavy?"

"Ma looks just fine." He was oblivious to the ominous quaver in my voice.

"Norma had some figure," he went on.

"Especially her legs. Outstanding. The last time I saw her, she must have hit a size twelve, maybe even fourteen. No self-discipline, to let herself go like that." We were out on the pavement. He waved for a cab as I extracted my elbow from his grip.

"Don't you dare criticize my mother, you ignorant, self-absorbed man," I said. "It was nice meeting you. Thanks for dinner."

I half fell, half lunged into the back of the taxi. I didn't even cry. Maybe I was so hot with fury that the water evaporated into steam before it got past my tear ducts. And it wasn't until we got nearly home that I remembered the money. All that cash he sent year after year, without any questions. Of course, he'd apparently been thinking I would drop dead soon enough, but still. So much for Harrison Ford.

Ma was pretending to watch TV when I dragged my left leg through the door. I wanted more than anything to head straight for my room and hide under the bed, but that didn't seem too awfully mature.

"Hi," I said, and flopped down at the other end of the couch.

"Uh-oh," she said, and snapped the Off button on the remote.

"Didn't you tell me you could never get

him to talk about his feelings?"

"Blood from a stone."

"Well, he's learned to vent." I rubbed my toes, a peculiar exercise since I had no feeling in either my fingers or my foot.

"Are you gonna be cryptic or are you going to tell me what happened? And how about some Lioresal? You're walking like fucking Quasimodo."

I shook my head. Lioresal makes my ears ring, and I had enough shouting going on in there at the moment.

"So is he bald?" she asked me.

"I think he's had implants. His head looks like a vineyard."

"I knew it. God, he had the most gorgeous head of hair, but his mother's father was a cue ball."

"Ma, can I ask you a personal question?"

She didn't have to hear it. "He was *very* good-looking," she explained.

It felt good to laugh.

"Oh, and that doesn't count when you're eighteen?" she said. "Not only that, he was clever and funny and my parents couldn't stand him. What more could a girl want?"

"Well, what happened to him? Was he hit by lightning or something?"

"Now there's a thought," she said. "And all this time I figured he just got stuck in adolescence. It's not so unusual, you know. And then they head for L.A. That town is full of men in a state of arrested development."

I told her about his prostate. She was quiet a moment. Actually, I think she was a little choked up. Then she recovered and said something about how if he had to get cancer, it was only fitting it should strike a territory that had caused the most grief to the greatest number of people.

"He thinks MS is fatal," I said. "He wanted me to counsel him on facing premature death."

"I told him a thousand times," Ma said. "He's on the MS Society mailing list, for God's sake."

"Well, the man's not a great listener."

It was her turn to laugh. "I get the feeling you're not likely to make this a regular thing."

"Not only that, I doubt if we'll ever see another nickel out of him."

"That bad."

"I got pissed."

She raised one eyebrow.

"Maybe I can get a raise," I said. "I'll talk to Duncan Reese."

"We'll manage. But your father can't help himself. He'll keep sending cash until he drops."

"Now I understand why you got migraines."

"Not until after he left. There *were* some good years, Anna Marie. And don't look at me like you don't want to hear about it."

"I hate him," I said. I heard my voice sounding like a small child's.

She took my hand, and I thought about my father's similar gesture at the dinner table. But his hand was empty, not like hers. I lifted it up and laid it gently against my sore jaw. A healing hand, a making, doing, fixing, loving hand.

"I'll take a pill now, if you don't mind." The cramps in my legs were pretty excruciating. When she came back with the medication, I swallowed it and said, "I heard you talking to Hannah once, and I quote: 'Jamie could never learn to keep his dick in his Jockey shorts.' Do you care to elaborate?" Hannah was my godmother and Ma's best friend for thirty-five years. I was sort of named for her. Unfortunately, she'd moved to Europe right about the time I got sick.

"When was this?" she asked.

"You were talking to her on the phone. I was maybe ten."

"Okay," she said. "But you're only getting one side of it."

"Would you *please* stop trying to be fair?"

She brought us some cocoa and a chocolate carrot-and-banana cake that was a lot better than it sounded.

"It's pretty simple. He started fooling around with the secretaries at his father's insurance company, then more serious affairs."

"Was this after I was born?"

"Oh, from the beginning, except I didn't know about it then."

"God," I said.

"You asked for the whole scoop, you're getting it, babe," she said. "I wanted him out, but I was scared to death. No job, no training for anything. I couldn't imagine how I'd cope."

We sat in silence. It seemed like a lot to absorb.

"This is not an original tale, Anna," she said quietly. "It happens all the time."

"Now I can see why you were so upset about Duncan Reese," I said. She didn't respond. "Did he take off or did you kick him out?" I asked.

"A little of both, I'd say."

"Ma."

She sighed. "Okay, he promised he'd quit messing with other women, but at my next checkup it turned out I had syphilis. Sure, he would have stuck around. Why not? It was the best of both worlds. I had to wave a bread knife at him to get him to leave."

Well, I'd asked for it, hadn't I? Surprisingly, it was almost a relief. Some of the stories I'd made up in my head were even worse. "But how about you?" I asked her. "Was there anybody else in your life?"

She hesitated for just a second, then shook her head.

"Ma?"

"No. There wasn't. Look, Anna, your father acted like a jerk, but he was never malicious, he never drank or hit either of us, and he's been true-blue financially all these years. That's a hell of a lot more than I can say for the rest of the divorced male population."

"I shouldn't have yelled at him."

She smiled and cut me another slice of cake. "Aw shit, honey, I'm sure he deserved it."

13

Ma and I had a Thanksgiving celebration with neighbors, an event memorable only for the raucous dogfight that ensued under the table. AirMalone was extra busy with the holiday so there was little hope of seeing Joe over the next couple of weeks — fortuitously, since I had begun to have trouble sleeping and needed every scrap of energy for end-of-term work. Most nights, there were bouts with *nocturia,* which loosely translated means "once in a while you lie there and you *don't* have to pee." Then there was PLMS, or "periodic limb movements in sleep." In addition to the twitching and urinating, I was experiencing what can only be described as waking nightmares. A presence had taken to visiting my room, something so real I once actually spoke to it. Several times I reached to turn on the light in hopes of getting a look. It wasn't menacing. Quite the opposite, in fact. A wise, protective soul for whom I felt overwhelming love materialized about two A.M. to envelop me in a benevolent capsule of warmth. I would bask in the joy of it, feeling so cherished, so safe, and then, suddenly, it was wrenched away, abandoning me to isolation and fear. It was as if someone dear to me kept dying over and over again. And when morning finally arrived, so would my conviction that the emptiness would ever heal.

I dragged myself dazed and haunted through the days that followed these anguished episodes. On the last morning, Ma gave me one of her long, scrutinizing appraisals and then wordlessly handed me the Metro section of the *Times* with my coffee. The article was headlined: CAMERON SCHOOL SCANDAL. *Headmaster Duncan Reese,* it said, quoting an "anonymous source on the faculty," *has created a tempest in the prestigious Upper East Side school by carrying on a liaison with a female member of the administration. At a second emergency meeting of the Board of Directors, a letter of resignation was drafted and Mr. Reese will reportedly be asked to sign it. According to the same source, many members of the faculty have been dissatisfied of late with Mr. Reese's tenure and believe this relationship to be representative of his behavior over several years.*

I looked up at Ma. My mouth was

hanging open, and not just because I was too tired to close it.

"Your buddy Leonard Chubb?" she asked.

"Has to be." I skimmed it again. "Leonard must have put his cousin on to this. Vernon Chubb writes for the Science section."

"I think they're gonna boot him out," Ma said.

"If he's out, I'll be next." My mysterious nighttime struggles suddenly seemed inconsequential. I could be out of a job.

Ma went to the kitchen and turned off the coffee maker. "You can't assume that," she said, but then she missed the garbage can and dumped coffee grounds all over the kitchen floor. I was just too exhausted to help her out.

There was an undercurrent of strain at Cameron, what with the photographers loitering across the street and clusters of teachers and students arguing in the halls. Duncan Reese's door remained closed and Jessica Lassiter didn't show up, but truthfully, I was waging my own battle against fatigue and kept out of the fray. I was relieved to step out onto Eighty-seventh Street at four o'clock. That is, until I realized that the snow had begun to fall.

When I was small, I looked forward to

those first flakes as if they were gifts especially for me. I imagined that angels were shredding the clouds against a golden grater and sending the icy fragments spinning down, down into the city streets where I could examine them on my mittens or catch them on my tongue. Then as I grew older and became an expert skier, I followed the snow from mountain to mountain, cadging rides to Stowe or Sugarloaf or out West, or wherever there was enough of a base to send me flying down the slopes with billows up around my knees as if the snow were nothing more than frozen air.

But now snow is my dreaded enemy and commands a kind of wartime mentality. It slicks the steps, the sidewalks, and the streets. It camouflages treacherous patches of ice. All winter I study the weather reports, and if there's even the faintest possibility of snow, I take my cane. But this morning, I'd been too distracted by that article to flip on the TV. So, caneless on my way home at Lexington and Eighty-fifth, I lost my footing on the manhole cover in the crosswalk and went flat on my behind. I knew the damn thing was there. I knew the placement of every manhole cover on the route from Cameron to my apartment. They're lethal when they've got snow or even rain on them, and why the city insists on sticking them in the middle of the crosswalks, I'll never understand.

I lay there waiting for my legs to act as if they were attached to the rest of me, but every time I made an attempt to get up, they told me they were on sabbatical. Meanwhile, the traffic had begun to back up and the horns were blasting. Ordinarily, I find New Yorkers to be enormously helpful in such situations, but today the street was filled with grade-school kids who, embarrassed, gave me a wide berth.

Then the most peculiar thing happened. There I was, like a pile of rags about to be crushed under the wheels of an oncoming car, and I was struck instead by a conviction. I saw myself telling my father over dinner that I would never marry Joe. There it was: it wasn't going to work out. The simplicity of it astonished me. I faced a lifetime of episodes in which my body betrayed me. They would be embarrassing, comic, dangerous, perhaps ultimately even fatal, but they would be private. I would not share them with Joe. I would not endure a relationship that required my significant other to be my nurse. I did not want Joe wheeling me around in my chair, helping me out of bed, buttoning my clothes, feeding me. It was simply too degrading. I suppose this entire mental exercise transpired in a matter of seconds but it felt as if I had been lying there for hours staring up at the sky as it hurled fat globs of snow into my face.

A large hand appeared in my line of vision. I took it without looking to see who was at the other end. It turned out to be Duncan Reese.

"Are you on your way home, Anna?" he asked once I was standing.

I nodded. The landscape, the planet, seemed to have altered. I forced myself to connect with my life prior to the epiphany about Joe. Pain was a help. I could tell I'd bruised my backside pretty thoroughly. I concentrated on that and on the humiliation of being rescued from an undignified skid by my beleaguered boss.

"I'll walk with you," he offered.

"Oh, that's not necessary," I said, at which point both feet went out from under me again.

Duncan, holding me firmly upright, had the grace to point to his giant rubber galoshes. "Pure luck I happened to have these stashed in my office. Treads like snow tires."

As we walked, I ferreted around for something clever to say. "I'm sorry about the *Times*," I managed finally. "I thought the tone was inexcusable."

"Thank you, Anna. No one else has had the courage to mention it."

As if it could be ignored. I remembered a summer job interview where my prospective employer wore a stuffed parrot on his shoulder. Was I supposed to pretend it wasn't there?

Duncan deposited me at the bench just inside my lobby. I sat there for a few seconds, catching my breath and watching Big Bob sling suitcases into somebody's trunk. When I got up, I glanced down the street, thinking that if the sidewalk had been thoroughly sanded, I'd stop in at the bakery. I felt like looking at Ma for a few minutes. I was just in time to see the back of Duncan Reese disappearing into Norma's Crust.

Joe had planned to fly in just for the night so we could celebrate a private Christmas together. The glut of holiday travelers assured a hectic schedule for him, and he'd otherwise be away from the city until early January. But now I wished I could cancel our date. I needed time to absorb the assault of my street acrobatics, both physical and mental. I felt that a feather touch anywhere on my body would produce another bruise, and furthermore, I had no idea how to confront Joe with my certainty that our relationship was doomed.

In the shower, I aimed the shower head at the wall, scooped the water in my hands and poured it gently over my battered body. That helped a little. Then I dressed, grabbed my Santa satchel and started for the door. I knew I should take my cane. I stood looking at the umbrella stand where I kept it handy. I could smell peppermint and chocolate wafting from the kitchen, where Ma was experimenting with cookies. She poked her head out and saw me contemplating the cane.

"Better take it, babe," she said. "You're looking a tad feeble."

"Mm."

She was familiar with that noncommittal *Mm,* so she just gave me a look and retreated to the kitchen. It was on account of not wanting to look infirm in front of Joe that I left without it. Big Bob found me a cab and Mr. Singh and I slid across to the West Side on bald tires.

Joe opened the door. He was wearing a Santa hat and Mel Torme was singing "Chestnuts roasting on an open fire." I promptly burst into tears. Joe was sympathetic, but totally confused. He led me to the couch and made me sip some eggnog. Store bought. He, for one, had learned his strengths.

"Don't be alarmed," I sobbed. "I think it's my pseudo . . . pseudo . . . pseudobulbar palsy."

"You want to hand me that one again?" Joe asked.

"Produces weird mood swings . . . and other stuff." It wasn't easy explaining through a torrent of tears. I mopped at my face with a napkin. "I'm pretty sure that's what it is." Looking back, of course, it was a combination of neurological freakout and the fact that I was already grieving.

"What can I do?"

"Put up with me until it passes."

"Is there a medication?"

"Thor— Thor— Thorazine."

He looked horrified.

"I'm kidding." I took a long raggedy breath. It was starting to ease. Strange, as if the devil has hold of you and his talons suddenly loosen and slide away. "The medication has side effects worse than the symptoms, at least for me. Uh-oh. Here we go." I ducked my head into Joe's chest and wailed. I think I even said *Wah!*

"Listen to the music," Joe said. Mel had quit with the chestnuts and we were on to the *Messiah*. It was a gorgeous rendition with period instruments and boy sopranos. The devil couldn't possibly hold out against

216

it, and by the time we got through the first chorus, I had stopped carrying on. Joe's shirt was drenched. He held me away from him to check me out, and when he stared at my nose, I knew it was blotched on the end with those unsightly red dots I get after I've been crying for a while.

"Maybe I was Rudolph's older sister in a former life," I said. Talking gave me a trembling feeling in my chest as if I were going to weep again, but I steeled myself against it.

"Better?" Joe said.

"The rough places are plain. Thanks."

He kissed me, another one of those long sweet ones that are my favorites. You could count to thirty slowly and he'd still be there. I was thinking, is this the last one? Finally, he broke away.

"Not such a gala Christmas party," I said. "Sorry."

"Blow your nose," he said. "We're hitting the bedroom." He got up. "I'm just taking a leak."

That was another thing about Joe. I knew he'd leave the john door open, and wouldn't care if I dropped by to comb my hair while he was peeing. He was totally open about such things. The last time I stayed overnight, he had barged right in while I was sitting on the toilet and seemed startled when I yelped.

217

I waited, in conflict about my ethical obligations here. If it was over, shouldn't I just tell him so and go home? But I wanted one last time when I really paid attention, to store up sense memories that I could carry with me into the lonely future.

I wandered into the bedroom with my bag of gifts. Joe had put a Christmas tree in the corner. Other than a red gym sock tied to the top and a single string of lights, it was unadorned. The smell was wonderful and poignant. I supposed that the lump that had lodged in my throat would remain there for the rest of my life.

Joe came in and settled cross-legged on the bed. He reached under his pillow and pulled out a package wrapped in tinfoil and tied with red and green ribbon.

I sat and unloaded my three gifts. "You first," I said. "That's from Ma." I could see there was just the one for me, and I liked that he didn't go into an apology about it. He shot me a smile and started unwrapping. It was a pleasure to watch the way his fingers moved — deliberately, no fumbling, getting the job done. He could undo me with the same expertise.

Ma had baked him this year's version of a Christmas cake. It looked traditional enough, like the typical dark spice variety, but I happened to know that she'd buried pieces of candy cane inside. I'd advised her that she was treading on litigious territory, maybe from some unsuspecting soul with brand-new dentures. But I also had to admit that it tasted surprisingly good.

"That was nice of her," Joe said. He made like he was bowling for a spare. "Substantial."

Next there was the chocolate airplane I'd special-ordered from Bloomingdale's. It said *AirMalone* on it.

"I can't eat this," he said. "I'm keeping it on my desk."

"It'll melt," I said. "Anyway, instead of being consumed by your work, you have to consume *it*."

The last was a volume of Stieglitz photos of Georgia O'Keeffe. After he opened it, he gave me a penetrating look and handed me my gift. He sat very quietly while I undid the ribbons.

It, too, was a book, but a handmade compilation of photographs. Instead of Stieglitz on O'Keeffe, it was Malone on Bolles. Joe had developed the photos from the cliff upstate and also a few indoor shots. One memorable night the month before, he had asked if he could photograph me naked. We'd been watching the video of *Tootsie* so I'm not certain what prompted the notion and it took some persuading on his part. I was secretly self-conscious about a close scrutiny of what to me seemed the ravages of too many steroids. He made me strip and then draped a bed sheet around me. Sometimes I was mostly covered, sometimes totally revealed. I think we only made it through half a roll of film before we abandoned the effort to a night of wild lovemaking. Now I stared at the woman in the pictures and thought that two things were very clear: there was too much pain in her eyes, and she was profoundly in love with the photographer.

"They're wonderful, Joe. Thank you."

"Merry Christmas," he said, and leaned over for a kiss. "They're a work in progress," he murmured against my mouth. Then when he held me away from him, I could tell he was looking straight through my clothing, imagining how the texture of my skin would photograph in the soft light from the Christmas tree. He ran his hands down my shoulders and across my breasts. I closed my eyes. I would just feel, that's all. No thought. I could do this. But then, to my surprise, it was painful when he came inside, as if I were being seared by a hot poker. Joe felt me pull back.

"What is it? Your fall?" he asked. He had seen the bruises.

"Nothing. No, it's okay." I couldn't tell him that my insides were on fire. I wrapped my legs around his back and let the tears run into my hair.

"What happened, Anna?" he asked me afterward. He knew that I hadn't come.

"I don't know," I said. "It was a little uncomfortable inside."

"I'm sorry. I don't ever want to hurt you."

I was silent. The words *IT'S OVER* were hovering above the bed, so bright that they dulled the Christmas lights.

"Where have you gone, Anna?"

My heart was thumping. I didn't feel ready to get into this. "Oh, Joe." That's all I could think of to say.

He raised himself up on his elbow and stared down into my face. "You'd better tell me."

I gazed back into those jeweled eyes, which were dark now, chips of midnight-blue. "I don't think it's going to work out."

There was a moment of disbelieving silence, then, "How can it not work out?" As if he was asking how the sun wasn't going to come up in the morning. As if it were some kind of natural law, the two of us together.

"I can't do it."

"What is there to do, Anna? There's nothing to do."

I sat up against the cold wall and was grateful for the pain the movement caused me. I was hurting him and I wanted to be hurt back. "I don't know if I can make you understand."

"Try me," he said. There was more than a little anger in his voice. It helped to keep me from crying.

"It's my illness."

"I don't care about your illness," he said.

"But I do. It's going to get worse and I don't want you in it with me."

"Isn't that for me to decide?"

"No," I said.

"You mind telling me what brought this on?"

"When I fell. Maybe it shook some sense into me, except I think it's been brewing for a while."

"Let me get this straight," he said. "You're going to trash what we've got so you can walk off into the sunset, just you and your fucking MS? How cozy."

"Tripping all the way," I said. I was getting pissed now, too. But then he sat up and swung his legs over the edge of the bed. With his back turned to me, I could see the way his hair curled at the back of his neck, and it broke my heart. I loved him so much it was like a taste in my mouth. He was in my veins — red corpuscles, white corpuscles, Joe corpuscles.

"How am I supposed to get you out of me?" he asked. "You're in my blood." The prickles stood up on the back of my neck. "We always knew you were sick," he went on. "We came to grips with it."

When was that? I wanted to ask him. But it seemed irrelevant now. "I wasn't thinking ahead. Today I finally did and I see I can't do it. Not with you, not with anybody." I wondered how long I'd been leaning all my weight against that closet door in my head, trying to keep the monster from jumping out. Maybe all the way back to my Halloween nosedive.

"You think it might be wise to sleep on it?" he asked.

"It won't change anything."

He dropped his head into his hands.

"I want to ask you a favor," he said after I'd sat for a while listening to somebody's heartbeats thundering in my ears. "Come upstate with me." I took a breath in preparation to saying no, but Joe shoved in ahead of me. "I need you to share that part of my life," he went on, "even if it's just for a few days."

"I guess I don't understand," I said.

"Well, I don't understand *you*."

223

"I don't expect you to. You're not the sick one."

"It's like MS is some exclusive club you belong to," he said.

"In a way." I hunkered over to sit beside him, careful not to intrude by touching him. The pillows were heaped on the floor at our feet. When Joe was in the throes of love-making, he always jettisoned them, as if he couldn't bear to have anything else in the bed except us. The Christmas lights reflected off our bodies, little piercing pin-pricks. I half expected to see blood.

"I love you, Anna," he said. It was the first time he'd actually said it straight out, un-adorned and direct.

I should have responded in kind, even given my decision, which in no way altered my feelings for him. But did I tell him how much he meant to me, what a rare and incredible human being he was? How grateful I felt that he tread the same planet?

"Yes, but would you love me if I didn't have MS?" That's what I said.

He was quiet for a long time while I sat there wondering if it was possible to drown oneself in a glass of eggnog like the one sitting on the bedside table. If you were determined, that is, and inhaled the entire contents into your lungs with one cosmic snort.

"I'm sorry, Joe," I said. "I love you, too." But he didn't appear to hear me. I'd only told him once before, but God knows I'd said it in my head a hundred times and, to my embarrassment, had once even written it down the way schoolgirls do: *I love Joe. Anna Bolles Malone. Mrs. Joseph DeLand Malone.*

I had always prided myself on not having told any man that I loved him, not even Bobby Zaklow. Well, with two exceptions. The first was my fifth grade math teacher, and I didn't say it, I wrote it in an anonymous letter which turned up on that same Cameron bulletin board, the dirty rat fink. No wonder I wasn't so quick to make that particular declaration again in a hurry. And the second time I was drunk at a fraternity party, and I think I said it to a gorgeous, narcissistic theater major. But I didn't mean it and I never saw him again so that didn't count. My pledge was that I would go to my grave without saying it to anyone unless I was truly sincere. But it had crept up on me with Joe . . . crept up with enormous thundering Godzilla feet. I loved him, that's all. I wasn't sure I wanted to, especially now, but it was a bald fact. What a fiasco. Meanwhile, he hadn't said anything at all for a very long time. Neither of us had moved, two statues with goose bumps at the edge of the bed. "Joe?"

"I'm thinking."

"What about?"

"You asked me a question."

"You mean you've never fantasized about me being well?"

"Do I hope they find a cure? Of course. I don't want you to suffer."

"Picture me as a healthy individual, no wheelchair, no tumbling over, no aches and pains." Like lovely Lola, I thought. "Would you love her, too?"

"How would I know? You're not that person and it's not your disease I'm in love with." He got up, tossed me my clothes and pulled on his pants. "I can fly you up for New Year's."

"I don't think it's a good idea."

He leaned down to the bed, a hand at either side of me on the mattress, his face three inches from mine. "I don't give a shit if it's a good idea or not," he said. "I want your imprint on my life up there. I want you to meet the people close to me so you're not just a phantom when I mention your name."

"Won't that make it harder?"

"I don't know. I don't care. I feel that you owe me this."

I thought about that. It seemed like the truth. "All right."

"Thanks."

He rose, lifted me up and took me in his arms. Both of us were breathing in that unnatural way that signifies tears. "Do you hate me, Joe?" I asked with my head against his chest. Stupid, selfish girl, I thought.

"I'm working on it," he said. "It's snowing. Shall I cab you across town?"

"No," I said.

So he released me. I grabbed my clothes and fled.

In the taxi, I had this bleak sensation of freedom. I wondered if prisoners facing execution felt something similar: The decision has been made, it's all out of your hands and absolutely nothing matters anymore. I went straight to my room when I got home, and the next morning Ma gave me one of those looks that she shoots the VCR when it misbehaves, as in: something's wrong with you and you'd damn well better tell me what it is or I'll make you wish you had. She tends to get physical with the VCR, and I half wondered if she was going to give me a swift kick. I ignored her, and my muffin, and sipped coffee in silence.

"Can I tell you something, Anna?" she said.

"No," I answered, realizing it was fruitless.

"You've been acting weird ever since you saw your father."

"How so?"

"Not talking enough."

"Or thinking more," I said. Maybe that would be the end of it.

"All men are not assholes, you know."

"I fail to follow," I said. "And please, don't elucidate. It's too early in the morning."

"Everything all right with you and Joe?"

"Depends on what you mean by all right," I said.

"Don't be coy." She slid the muffin a couple of inches closer to me.

"I'm just not ready to talk about it." One of Ma's more surprising qualities is that despite her bulldozer style, she can be exquisitely sensitive. She's like those ballet dancers, the hippopotamuses in *Fantasia*. All that hulking power poised delicately on one toe. She backed off instantly, and I knew she would not say a word about it again unless I raised the issue myself.

"You never told me what you and Duncan Reese talked about yesterday," I said.

"What do you mean?" I took minor satisfaction in so easily diverting her from my state of mind.

"I saw him go into the bakery," I said.

I don't know what I expected, but not what I saw on her face, the sadness.

"He's firing me, isn't he?" A justifiable conclusion, given her expression.

"I don't think so," Ma said. She got up, went to the sink and began washing dishes much too thoroughly before dropping them into the dishwasher. "He didn't say."

"Then what was he doing in your store?"

"He told me that you'd fallen on the street and that you were all right, that I shouldn't worry."

I couldn't read her voice, the one thing I felt I could always count on.

"What is it you're not telling me?" But the fact was, I barely cared.

14

Dear Anna,
    This is the way I want to play this out. I figure I'll have plenty of time to be pissed and miserable and I'd rather not waste our last days together in that state of mind. I can see that you mean what you say and I'm going to try to honor your decision and focus my attention on the good stuff. I want you to meet my family and Steve, the speck in the photograph. I want to make love and laugh (impossible maybe) so that when it's over I'll have that much more to remember. I realize it's a tall order but we're going to pull it off.
                                                    Yours,
                                                    Joe

"Yours," not "Your." What a difference an *s* makes. I e-mailed him back that I agreed it was worth a try. We spoke several times by telephone after that and adopted this kind of wartime mentality of cheer in the face of impending catastrophe. I was just so grateful that he wasn't trying to dissuade me, which would have been more painful than I could bear.

I had agonized over clothes, not having a clue what people wore in the hinterlands over the holidays. Given the size of my suitcase, you'd think I was going for three months.

"Will there be parties?" I had asked him over the phone. He was snowed in up in Bangor, Maine, waiting for a blizzard to peter out so he could fly down and fetch me.

"New Year's Eve at the club, probably. That's it."

"Ah, the club," I echoed casually. There was a time when I would have approached a black-tie affair at the White House with total confidence, and relished the job of officiating. But when you wonder if you can pronounce the name of the President of the United States, or suspect you might splash cabernet down the front of the First Lady's dress, the fantasy dims.

I hadn't had a serious relapse in a while, and had asked Joe to not tell his family that I had MS. I could see no reason to and I just wanted to be a regular person for the few days of my visit. Then my MS and I could slink off together just as Joe had said. Real cozy. I still had only the haziest concept of what life would be like after parting from Joe other than the fact that despite the terrible loss, I was acting out of some basic and critical need.

I threw every medication I had on hand into my suitcase, including some that produced pretty heinous side effects. I wanted the widest array of choices. For my swan song, I didn't want to be waddling like a guinea hen.

Joe picked me up wearing an open topcoat with a dark navy uniform underneath. There was a name tag on his lapel that said: JOSEPH MALONE, AIRMALONE.

"What's this?" I asked him. "Some promotional thing?"

He reached for my bag. "Passengers like their pilots to wear uniforms. It makes them feel more confident."

"What?" I said.

"Marty's stuck in Pittsburgh with equipment trouble so I'm filling in." Joe had his pilot's license but I thought that was merely a formality. It had never occurred to me that he actually flew anything.

"We'll take a cab to the Marine Terminal," he said. "It costs a fortune to leave the car."

Big Bob was profoundly impressed by Joe's getup and even saluted when we pulled away from the building. The fact was, he looked very sexy. What is that anyway? Why should a pilot's uniform be so much more dashing than, say, a state trooper's? I had a boyfriend in high school who once showed up at my apartment in his Eagle Scout attire. It was the beginning of the end, but back in those days I had my superficial side.

"I wish you'd tell me something about your family before we get up there," I said.

"Just ordinary," he said. "Nothing special. Not like yours."

"I only have Ma."

He gave me a wistful smile. I could see his point. "But there must be stories. Every family has some, specific moments . . ."

"Okay, here's one," he said. "My brother pushed me out of a tree when I was seven. You must have noticed the scar?"

"No," I said, vaguely remembering something about a broken ankle. But I'd thought I knew every detail of his body. It seemed a failing on my part that I had missed it.

"We climbed the oak in the backyard so we could jump into a leaf pile we'd made underneath. The branch was really high. I got scared and couldn't get myself to jump. So Frank pushed me. I cracked a bone and they had to operate on it."

I was silent for a moment, thinking that

Frank would have been fourteen at the time, old enough to know better. "I think I hate Frank," I said.

"Oh, Frank's all right," he assured me. "You'll see."

At the AirMalone gate most of the preflight routine had been accomplished. But there was another pilot poring over some computer printouts.

" 'Morning, Sam. Sam Barney," Joe said by way of introduction. Joe took a pair of earphones out of his canvas bag. I later learned that pilots carry their own personal headset. They have microphones in them for listening to the tower.

" 'Morning, Joe," Sam said. "Whoa, she *is* gorgeous. Hi, Anna." He held out his hand.

This was interesting. Up until this moment I had never met anyone acquainted with Joe. Other than the two women who had spoken to him on the street last summer, it was as if he existed in a vacuum. All the fragments of his life had been outside my experience. It produced a little frisson of jealousy that Sam Barney had a past with Joe, too, and I suddenly realized that I was about to be jettisoned from the protected cocoon we'd inhabited together. Good, I told myself. This would be a halfway station for the ultimate letting go.

"What've we got?" Joe asked, leaning over Sam's shoulder.

"Not bad. A few flurries just north of the Coate intersection."

"How many on board?"

"Six. We picked up a couple of casino guys."

"We're twenty miles from the largest casino in the state," Joe explained to me. "The management are good customers of ours."

"Thanks to Joe here," Sam said. "He worked hard on that one."

I was intrigued, but Joe said, "Later. We'd better boogie."

AirMalone had the best safety and on-time record of any charter its size. This proclamation, straight from the radio ads, was a line I repeated to anybody who asked me what my boyfriend did for a living. When Joe and Sam ushered me through the gate and out onto the tarmac, I began thinking about the safety part of that slogan. It was a nice-looking airplane as toys go, but I had never flown in anything smaller than a Boeing 737 in my life. Joe looked at my face.

"What were you expecting, the Concorde?"

"What is that?" I shouted. There was a lot of noise.

"Kingair."

Joe went off somewhere while Sam preceded me up the aluminum stairway into the cockpit. I didn't like the rickety way it swayed with each step. Then Sam stashed my luggage and installed me in a seat directly behind him. He began doing undecipherable things with the instrument panel, and since he'd put his headset on there was no point asking him any questions. I craned my neck around the cabin to see if there was a special rack that held the parachutes.

Pretty soon Joe showed up with the casino executives, who turned out to be Native Americans from the Oneida tribe — a fellow named Roy and his nephew. Roy and Joe seemed quite chummy and had a brief but technical conversation about airport expansion. Joe slipped into the right-hand seat beside Sam, put his headset on, and within a few minutes we were taxiing out onto the runway. I looked at the back of Joe's head and remembered that I had in fact been in bed with this man not long ago. I wanted to touch him, to make a physical connection while I still could. But in the meantime we were careening across the ground, bobbing a little from side to side. When we lifted off, the roaring sound relented with a sigh and we were soaring up over the bay with Manhattan spread out in splendor to the west. It was thrilling, far more intimate than the gigantic impersonality of the planes I was accustomed to. Joe turned around and raised his eyebrows at me in that look he had that said, *Is this cool or what? Am I cool or what?*

I liked it up there where the air felt muscular and solid, flexing for sixteen thousand feet beneath us as the earth fell away. I also found out how much Joe loved to fly. When he turned to talk to Sam, there was an expression I'd never seen on his face before, a kind of rapture. It surprised me and produced an ache in my chest. There was so much about this man that I would never learn.

About an hour later the plane came to a stop in the middle of the sky, or at least it felt that way. We hung in the air for a long moment and then began to drop down, down, to the snow-covered patches of Andrew Wyeth winter below.

I had imagined some sweet little log cabin of an airport alongside a single landing strip, maybe with a wind sock at the end. I was certainly not prepared for a hotel-sized facility crowned with a glass control tower. There were eight runways and two more under construction. Signs outside the terminal warned against smuggling. That seemed romantic, but it turned out that what people smuggled were not stolen jewels but drugs, particularly into smaller airports that had loose security. You could hop out of the plane with a couple of kilos of heroin in your bags, get picked up by the local dealer in his SUV, and you were in business.

We had to stop at the terminal office for debriefing. When Joe disappeared with Sam into the back, I looked around. First of all, there was country music playing. It seemed exotic to my urban ears and reminded me of backpacking trips I used to take along the Appalachian trail. There was a wall full of what looked like shreds of old T-shirts. Each piece had a name, a date, and "First Solo Flight" scribbled on it with Magic Marker. I knew that AirMalone ran a flight-training school, and supposed that these were the students' graduation certificates.

Joe emerged a few minutes later. He had in tow a large dour-looking man whose features were Joe's, inflated with a bicycle pump; same idea but bloated into the giant economy size.

"Anna, this is my brother, Frank. Franklin, this is Anna Bolles." We gripped hands and tried not to stare too rudely at one another. Frank had dark thinning hair, I saw now, and his eyes were not as complex as Joe's, just ordinary blue.

"Brave of you to risk your life with little brother at the controls," he said.

"That's pretty hostile, first thing out of your mouth," I said. Well, no, I didn't. I only thought it and gave Frank my most deceitful smile. I wasn't forgetting that he had shoved Joe out of that oak tree.

"I'll be back as soon as I get Anna settled in," Joe said. I'd known that he would be spending a lot of time working, but it hadn't occurred to me that without Joe I would be pretty much stranded. As we walked away, Joe had me by the arm, for which I was grateful since I felt Frank's eyes on us. I knew I was favoring my left leg.

Outside, the air was frigid but crisp, without the damp cruelty of a Manhattan winter. We were in snowbelt country. A recent blizzard had left waist-high drifts beside the parking lot, and there was that clean bite with every breath, which made me yearn for a pair of skis. We stopped beside a pickup truck that was buried under eight inches of new snow. The door handle had iced over so it took a minute for Joe to release it.

"Can you manage with your suitcase under your feet for a few minutes?" he asked, helping me in. Actually, it was easier for me to step up into the truck than to back into his low-slung BMW in New York.

"Sure." Joe had to coax the engine a little but eventually it burst into life with a throaty rumble.

"We'll let her warm up a minute." He pushed a button, and a spurt of heat wheezed out from under the dashboard. We sat there with the windshield frosted over, back in the cocoon again, just Joe and me. He leaned over and gave me a kiss. I suppose it created the same confusing response of pain and pleasure for him as it did for me because he backed off with eyes averted. I felt like asking him if he was sorry he insisted on this trip. Maybe he was beginning to realize how excruciating it might be. On the other hand, I could imagine us frozen here together, the truck sealed by a thick layer of ice. They'd find us in the spring, entwined in one another's arms, solid as a couple of Popsicles. There was a certain appeal.

"You like to fly, don't you, Joe?" I asked, grasping for a distraction.

"I'd forgotten, but yes," he said.

"Why?"

"When I was a kid, it was the freedom," he said. "I liked escaping from the ground and everything on it."

Maybe every*one*, I was thinking, but let him go on.

"Now, it's more complicated. The release when the wheels leave the ground, but there's also a visual element. The sky is never the same. Did you ever see the film, *The English Patient*?"

"The opening sequence, that little plane over the desert."

"It's probably my favorite image from any movie." He looked like he wanted to kiss me again, but instead he put the truck in gear. As we started off, the chains on the tires slapped musically against the road.

"I've never been in one of these before," I said. Riding so high off the road rendered an altered perspective on the passing scene and the vast open sky. There was a physical sensation to escaping the urban warren, a stretching of muscles and expansion of organs. It was also scary. There's something comforting in containment, particularly if you don't trust your own body.

It was a fifteen-minute drive from the airport to North Lockville. "They were supposed to build an offshoot of the Erie Canal up this way," Joe explained. "With a lock on account of the rapids. We got the name, but not the canal."

I guess I had been expecting terrain similar to the landscape around Brighton University, but these sweeping hills made that part of Connecticut seem lumpy. We drove up a winding road past farms with their fields buried under snow. As we slowed around a bend, I could see into a barn where the dairy cows stood in long rows, breathing steam. We turned at the top of the rise and drove along a ridge with a view across the valley to the Adirondack Mountains.

"Oh," was all I could say.

"I took the scenic route," he confessed. He pulled over and helped me down onto the icy road. "These hills were scooped out by the glacier. All across upstate New York. See down there? That's the airport."

This was a new note. He loves this, I realized, and I appreciated that he didn't make some apologetic remark about how I should see it in the springtime when everything was green. He loved it now and all the time. I leaned back against him and watched the dark gray clouds. They were moving fast along the opposite ridge, chased by an unruly winter wind.

"Beethoven's Fifth," I murmured.

"What?" Joe asked. It was hard to speak when every word was snatched out of our mouths and flung all the way to Canada.

"If I were orchestrating that." I gestured

at the sky. "Beethoven's Fifth."

He turned me to him and held me against his chest. There have been so many times that I've remembered that moment and clung to it for comfort. I can still taste the wind.

The Malones lived at the edge of one of those small villages that have a town square with a gazebo for summertime band concerts. Colgate and Hamilton were only a few miles down the road, and there was the feel of a college town, with a bookstore and a coffee shop that advertised cappuccino. We pulled into the driveway of a white colonial set back from the street. There were several towering old trees on the front lawn and I could imagine how impressive they must be with their summer foliage. Instead of pulling up in front, we circled around behind the house. There was a barn at the far end of the property, with fields and wooded hills beyond.

When I got out of the car I could see that the main house had been expanded in the rear. There was a stairway leading to a separate entrance.

"My apartment," Joe said. "It's a little strange being so close to my family, but I'm not here much and it makes those midnight crisis sessions more convenient."

"Do Frank and Eva live here, too?" I had managed to extract from Joe that his brother had a wife who was "nice enough." No kids. The fact was, Joe never said much of anything about these people. For all I knew, the dinner table could be populated by Addams family caricatures.

Joe's apartment was a lot more lived in than the New York place. Someone had laid a fire in the fireplace, and it smelled like the woods, with raw pine walls and a table and chairs of Adirondack "twig" style. The bedroom had red and black plaid blankets and old kerosene lamps that had been converted to electricity. There were bookshelves filled with collections of plays, and the walls were covered with framed photos of airplanes. I heard a distant clatter from somewhere below.

"Who's home?" I asked. The only vehicle, another pickup truck, had been parked down near the barn.

"You'll meet everybody at dinner." He threw my bag on his bed. "I figured you'd be glad for a rest while I'm at the airport. And there's plenty of stuff in the refrigerator. I got you ice cream, cheese doodles, and Granny Smiths. Poke around." He stood for a second, watching me sit there next to my suitcase. I knew what he was doing — photographing me with his eyes. When he blinked, I could almost hear the snap of the lens.

"It's good to have you here, Anna," he said. "Thanks." Then he gave me a kiss and was out the door. I pictured the quick easy grace of him going down the stairs.

For the first time since my icy sprawl on Lexington Avenue, I felt a trace of doubt about ending it with Joe. Perhaps because my real life seemed so far off, the day had taken on a dreamlike quality and, like Dorothy, I had flown through the sky into another dimension. "Don't be stupid," I said out loud. I forced myself to remember the indignity of my Halloween nosedive. That was our future, an endless cartoon of pratfalls with Joe the beleaguered crutch. I sobered up in a hurry.

I had thought I would begin my inspection of the place the moment Joe drove off, but instead I lay back on the bed. My head was aching and my eyes had the dry, popped-out feeling they get from being overtired. The next thing I knew, the phone was ringing. For a moment I had no idea where I was, and then I couldn't find the phone. I tracked it to the shelf under the bedside table and said "Hi," figuring it would be Joe.

"Hello?" It was an older woman's voice, pausing, then, "Oh. You must be Anna. This is Celeste Malone."

"And were blurp do sing ner mada," I said. When I first wake up I sometimes have a difficult time articulating.

"Excuse me?" she said.

I shook my head hard, hoping to rattle my synapses into submission. "How do?" I said.

Another pause. She must have thought I'd gotten into Joe's liquor supply. "Fine," she replied, all business. "I just wanted to make sure you'd arrived safely and to let you know that dinner will be at seven-thirty. Joe tends to be late, as I'm sure you've noticed."

No, I haven't, I wanted to say, but there were a lot of reasons I thought better of it, the main one being that I'd never get my tongue around it. "Gord," I said. One-syllable words usually came out all right, so I knew I was in big trouble.

"Looking forward to meeting you," she said with the tone of someone expecting the Bearded Lady. She hung up before I had to squeeze out any more grunts.

The first thing I did was laugh in a hysterical mirthless sort of way. I felt like calling Ma because I knew she'd appreciate the comic element. Instead, I dug into my vast supply of drugs — one of these, a couple of those — I swallowed an arsenal, and then stepped carefully into the other room, turned on the television and sat in Joe's big worn-out leather chair. It was the E! channel, and who was plastered all over the screen but Michelle's father, Deke Cross, with his child bride Dakota Blue tastefully attired in fringed bandeau and skintight capri pants. Even on the small screen I could make out three navel rings. The commentator adopted the slightly ironic tone that was supposed to signal her superiority to celebrity mania:

"And who made a last minute appearance at Elton's concert but everyone's favorite Native American pop star, Dakota Blue, and her multi-billion-dollar groom, Deke Cross. Elton tried to persuade Dakota to join him in an impromptu duet but she turned him down. Too shy, Dakota, or was it simply impossible to unlock your lips from your new hubby's? One trendy restaurateur tells us he considered phoning the vice squad when this pair recently went a bit over the limit in demonstrating their devotion."

I hoped Michelle had missed that one, but even so, the media was full of the newlyweds. In the divorce papers, which had leaked into the tabloids, Deke Cross had accused Michelle's mother of a fondness for young boys. Filona counterclaimed that

Deke enjoyed being spanked with wet panty hose. All of it was excruciating for Michelle, especially when some clever classmate hung a pair of damp panty hose from her locker. But I'd arranged to free up the dance studio two afternoons a week, and Michelle had taken advantage of the opportunity. I'd stopped by one day to find Rudy Steinberger standing outside the door. There was a small pane for viewing what was going on inside. I put my face to the glass to see Michelle spin across the room in a spectacular demonstration of flight.

"Wouldn't it be wonderful to be able to do that?" I'd said to Rudy.

He nodded, and I could see he couldn't talk around the lump in his throat. My heart broke for him as he headed off down the hall, his shoulders drooping, one sneaker untied.

I snapped off Joe's television and went to the window. The snow was coming down in fat dollops. It had piled up on the window-sill and framed the pine trees on the distant hillside. The scene reminded me of a calendar that hung in the teachers' lounge at Cameron. I wasn't having much success at leaving the city behind. I stood there gazing, unmoved by the breathtaking view, instead fretting about the meeting of the board of trustees that might be transpiring at that very moment. It seemed unimaginable that they'd fire Duncan Reese halfway through the school year but he had been too unrepentant about his relationship with Jessica Lassiter. I wondered just how closely my own professional future was yoked to Reese's.

This train of thought was hardly soothing. I turned away from the Grandma Moses view with intent to distract myself by some serious snooping. My Stieglitz gift lay prominently on Joe's coffee table along with a pile of *Playbill* magazines and a Nestlé's chocolate bar. Joe was a serious chocoholic. A detective could easily track him down by following the wrapper trail: M&M's, Clark Bars, Snickers. I'd seen him eat a tablespoon of raw cocoa once when he'd run out of everything else.

I walked over to a wall of photographs that was a series of a man and two boys standing beside an airplane in various stages of construction. One of the boys was clearly Joe, with rounder cheeks and white-blond hair. Frank was beefy even then, and wore glasses. The man's face was shaded by a felt hat. None of the shots were particularly well composed and some were actually blurred. It surprised me a little that Joe would display such inexpert photographs.

I turned to Joe's desk next, practically rubbing my hands together with guilty anticipation. Desks are a treasure trove for the seriously inquisitive. The first thing I noticed was the row of framed photos, mostly of me, across the top of the desk. But one, larger than the others, was lying facedown. I turned it over and looked into the eyes of an old woman. As the only smooth surface in a topography of wrinkles, they startled me. The portrait invited, demanded, study. I was so lost in it that I didn't even hear Joe's car door slam. He burst in, covered with snow, threw off his jacket and swooped me up in his arms. He had been so tentative with me lately that I was surprised by the extravagance.

"You smell wonderful," he said, "wood smoke and shampoo."

I shook the snow out of his hair and handed him the photo. "Is this your Gran?"

He nodded and replaced it on the desk. Facedown. "It's still too hard to look at it."

I thought he had told me her death was four years ago. "Did you take the photograph?"

"Yes, not long before she died. I see it there in her face, that she's leaving." He went over to the fireplace and dumped a log on top of the coals. It was clear that the subject of his grandmother had been dismissed for now. He poked at the fire and when he turned to me again, he was smiling.

"I like this," he said. "The little woman waiting by the hearth."

"Oh, yeah, the little woman," I said. "You can move me around, you know. Park me by the fire, or stand me up by the stove. I come with accessories, a set of bellows and an apron."

He opened his mouth to make a wisecrack and thought better of it. I figured he was thinking about sex, but that topic was just a little too fraught for levity. Under the circumstances, making love seemed out of the question.

"Your mother called," I said. "She woke me up from a nap and I wasn't very coherent."

"She got me at the office. We're supposed to join her for a drink. You ready?"

That was an easy one. "No," I said.

But as soon as Joe went to the bathroom — with the door open, of course — and changed out of his wet slacks, he announced that Happy Hour at the Malones' was a command performance.

There was a door through Joe's kitchen that led down a flight of stairs into the foyer of the main house. Since I got sick, I've learned to make an instant assessment of the disabled-friendliness of an environment. Just standing in the hallway, I could already tell that this place was a nightmare. To begin with, the foyer had two loose rugs for catapulting me into the Flying Starfish, which is what I call the spectacular fall when all parts of me are off the ground simultaneously. In the living room beyond, the pile of the wall-to-wall carpet rose to a height that was only appropriate if you happened to be a lion on the prowl for wildebeest. For those of us who have trouble lifting our feet, it spelled certain disaster. So having determined that I'd need a four-wheel drive to get to the living room sofa, it was additionally daunting to note that every square inch of surface visible through the doorway was covered with pricey little knickknacks. Just the sight of all that porcelain produced spasms in my fingertips.

Standing there beside Joe, I began flicking my wrists violently. Sometimes that helps ward off spasms, but of course, this was the precise moment Celeste Malone chose to enter the foyer from the kitchen. She had started toward us with her hand extended but stopped in her tracks as I flapped at her like some hyperactive hummingbird.

252

"It's MS, actually," I said. "I have multiple sclerosis. How do you do?" Mrs. Malone looked like she'd just jammed her finger in a lightbulb socket. Her mouth made a perfect little O while her hand remained extended, stiff enough for chin-ups.

"Mother, this is Anna Bolles," Joe said. "She wanted to tell you herself."

"I'm sorry to be so abrupt," I said. Joe's arm around my waist was a help. "I'm afraid I was a bit nervous." Break it to them gently, was what I had counseled myself, and even then, only if you have to. Kind of like I'd dropped a Toyota on her head from ten stories up.

I had to give her credit. She was nothing if not poised, just shook my hand and gave me a ghastly smile. She was very well dressed, I noticed, in a designer pantsuit and a cashmere cowl-neck sweater.

"Let's have a drink," she said, turning on her heels in a crisp military maneuver. "Joseph, the usual? And what can I get for you, Anna?" Joseph? Who was Joseph, the butler?

"A glass of wine would be lovely," I said, figuring it out.

"Red or white?" Her voice made it sound like a test.

"Either is fine," I answered. A woman of undiscriminating tastes, that's me, as long as it does the job and renders me totally unconscious in a big hurry. Well, at least the cat was out of the bag, so to speak. A cat with a serious limp and memory lapses like you wouldn't believe. I reminded myself that since these were my last few days with Joe, it didn't matter. But pride is a potent vice, and I sure would have liked to leave a decent impression in my wake.

"Come sit by the fire," Joe said, and led me through the shoulder-high pile toward the sofa. He sat me down and went to help his mother. I took the opportunity to look around. The room was done in off-white, beige, and taupe, with a few accents of Chinese red here and there. You'd think with all those figurines, there'd be some sense of personality, but it was instead handsome and completely without character. Even the leftover Christmas decorations were stark — a creepy white branch on the mantelpiece reminded me of Boris, the skeleton that hung in the corner of our freshman biology class. There was a grand piano in one corner, however, that did add a touch of humanity, though its lid was down and there was no evidence of music anywhere. Silenced, perhaps, by the intimidating severity of the room.

Joe handed me my drink and sat beside

me, or almost on me as was his wont, despite the fact that his mother took a seat directly opposite. The fire made a loud pop and I nearly spilled my drink. She'd brought me red wine, which I realized too late was a mistake. I decided that the thing to do was gulp it down fast. I did so, and studied Joe's mother while the two of them chatted about equipment, by which Joe means airplanes.

Celeste had a striking face that, feature by feature, was similar to Joe's. Same bony nose, same spare angularity. The startling exception was her mouth, which was full and sensuous and painted Chinese red to match the living room accessories. A handsome woman in a handsome home. She scared the hell out of me.

"Joseph tells me you're a teacher," she said, turning her attention to me.

"Yes, in a private school in Manhattan."

"A noble profession," she said. Kind of like cleaning toilets, was the message, but hey, somebody's got to do it. "What exactly do you teach?"

"Literature." I'd had enough wine to feel like saying LIT-tra-choor à la Lady Supercilious La Snoot, but I tried to behave like the piano and kept the lid on.

"I find I never have time to read anymore," she said, "other than business periodicals and that sort of thing." She said it the way some people tell you they never watch television.

"Anna's mother owns a bakery," Joe said. I guess he figured it would help to change the subject, but it turned out to be another dud.

"How interesting. French?"

"Icelandic," I answered. Not really. "Actually, she has her own eclectic style." I had considered bringing an assortment of items from Norma's Crust as a gift but thought better of it and opted, thankfully, for a simple glass bowl. "She likes to experiment with unusual ingredients."

"It's the piñata school of cooking," Joe said. "You never know what you'll get in a muffin until you crack one open."

"How interesting," Celeste murmured, yet again. I had already learned one important fact: Joe's mother always said *how interesting* when she was stupefied with boredom. "Joseph's grandmother on the DeLand side was a talented chef," Celeste said. "Cordon Bleu and so on." So much for Ma's muffins, the Cordon Bleu-Cheese school. Celeste tossed back the rest of her high-ball and got up. "I'll just see what's happening to dinner." And maybe skim a couple of articles in *Forbes* to break the monotony, I figured.

"Aren't Frank and Eva coming?" Joe asked. I thought I detected a wee hint of desperation.

"Oh, they'll be along at the last possible minute, as usual."

Damn clever of them, I thought.

As soon as she was out of hearing, I held out my empty glass. "Bring me another one, quick. But white this time."

"Didn't you tell me you took some medication?" he asked.

"Not half enough."

He brought my glass back with about an inch of wine in it. I made a face at him but he was right. I was beginning to hear John Philip Sousa in my head, a dangerous sign. "So what's with the DeLand side?"

" 'De' as in 'of' and 'land' as in 'land.' Mother likes to think of her family as aristocrats, but in fact they were peasants. Her grandfather got lucky investing in fabric mills, but before that they were all dirt-poor farmers. What do you think of her?"

"You couldn't have warned me?"

"You make her a little nervous," Joe said.

"Oh, *that's* funny." I considered taking Celeste aside and putting her out of her misery. *"Joe and I don't have a future,"* I'd tell her. *"You can quit working your jaw like you've got ten packs of Juicy Fruit back there."*

But dinner was ready and we trooped into the formal dining room, me lifting my knees chin-high to negotiate the carpet. Frank and his wife, Eva, must have been lurking outside until they saw the roast come out of the oven because, as predicted, they showed up just as dinner was served. Eva was round and lumbering and completely cowed by everybody, not just Celeste. She looked like the kind of woman who used to be referred to as a "vessel," i.e., the ideal producer of children. But Joe had told me that, ironically, she'd never managed to support a pregnancy. As we ate I watched the way she snuck adoring looks at Frank and wondered what their sex life was like. It pleased me to sit there listening to Celeste drone on about something called the Airline Service Improvement Act and imagine Eva and Frank having steamy, preferably kinky, sex in the privacy of their own home or maybe right out on their front lawn when the weather was better.

"Sam says the Oneidas have plans to build their own airport," Frank was saying.

"Where?" Joe asked with interest.

"Clinton Center."

"That's nonsense," Celeste said. Frank reddened like a ten-year-old who'd been rapped on the hand. He fell silent and

258

reached into his pocket for a magazine which he slipped under his plate. I could tell he was dying to read it. "Put that away, Frank," Celeste said. "It's a very uncivilized habit, reading at the table."

"I wasn't, Mother," Frank protested. "I just wanted to show something to Joe later."

But Celeste ignored him. "Joseph, the Oneidas have no complaints about us, do they?" she was asking, looking at Joe as if he were the world's greatest authority on Indian Affairs.

"That's not the issue," Joe said. "Why should they hire us to squire them around when they can afford to buy the entire U.S. Air Force if they feel like it?" He turned to me. "This must be a very boring conversation for you."

"All anybody ever talks about around here is business," Eva blurted, then ducked her head in fear.

I shot a quick look at Celeste, as did everybody else. Her eyes flashed ominously but my presence was enough to keep her in line. She raised the corners of her lips and aimed a sort of smile at me. "I'm afraid it's the family curse, the passion we feel about AirMalone. Joseph in particular has always been possessed, just like me. We've always been like two peas in a pod."

Wow. Where was Ma when we needed her? Someone to say, "Actually, Celeste babe, you're about as similar to your boy here as chicken shit to chicken salad." I was in serious danger of giggling. When Frank put his magazine away, I could see it was about fly fishing. Out in the middle of a stream in his waders where he wouldn't have to listen to this woman rant on about his perfect little brother. As a serious student of families, I've seen it happen over and over again. The good-looking child is almost always favored, and the homely one — poor Frank — gets screwed over.

I looked at Joe to check out his reaction to Celeste's fawning. He caught my eye and smiled, entirely oblivious. I got the impression his mother had said it so many times that everybody just accepted as gospel that Joe and his mother were alike in so many, many ways.

But by far the most astonishing thing about that meal was that Joe's father was missing. Opposite Celeste was an empty seat and a place setting but nobody referred to it, or even seemed to notice it. I could hardly wait to get Joe alone.

Celeste pushed her chair back from the table and stood up. "Why don't you all just sit and enjoy your coffee? I have to get over to the club to see about the decorations for the New Year's gala. Oh, and Joseph, I don't think I mentioned to you that Lola called this morning. She'll be in town New Year's Eve so I asked her to join our table." She turned to me. "An old family friend, Anna. I know you'll like her."

Oh . . . My . . . God. . . . I have to say that even Joe blinked at this, and he wasn't easy to rattle. In response to this bulletin, I was prepared to produce a grand mal seizure worthy of Rudy Steinberger's father, but I restrained myself. For the first time, Eva stopped looking bored. She had her eyes drilled on Joe's face to see how he'd react.

"Fine," Joe replied. After all, what was he going to say?

Celeste Malone's behavior was looking as if it might earn her a spot in that dark corner of my psyche reserved for heinous offenders. I keep them caged back there: Patsy Waterman's father, who ruined Patsy's life by making her renounce Rock Bulfomante, her one true love; the camp counselor named "Vi" — for Vile — who because I was homesick called me a baby and made me suck my thumb in front of my entire bunk; occasionally my father, though he's allowed out once in a while on account of Ma's intervention; Leonard Chubb, for obvious reasons; and finally that woman I met during a relapse who looked at my crutches and told me I reminded her of Itzhak Perlman. Now, if I'd been brandishing a violin at the time, I might have been delighted. As it was, I opened my mouth and out hopped my observation that she was a dead ringer for Luciano Pavarotti. I could hardly wait to report this one to the MS website, but to my amazement, it turned out that there were a lot of Itzhak clones out there. At least a dozen MS people, two of them female, reported the same phenomenon. We could start a whole string section.

Granted, Celeste Malone's hauteur didn't sink to such idiocy, but I could tell already that she was capable of dastardly deeds. Yes, I could definitely see Celeste Malone incarcerated in my cerebral dungeon with that villainous lot.

But at least the dinner ordeal was over. Frank and Eva slunk off into the night, and Joe and I beat it up to his room. There were embers glowing in the fireplace and it smelled good. The atmosphere of the place wrapped its arms around me and so did Joe. I was so loaded up on medication and wine that I didn't have the brains to decide once and for all whether sex was a morally righteous alternative. *But, your honor, I was too stoned to act in a responsible fashion.* It didn't wash, I realized.

Then Joe made it even harder by saying, "Come in here. I have something to show you." He drew me off the couch and into the bedroom.

"I think I've heard that one before," I commented, but you didn't see me protesting.

Joe reached to the bedside table and produced what looked like a tube of toothpaste. "Ready for a cosmic journey?" he asked. I saw that the label read *Astroglide*. I knew that it was a lubricant for alleviating painful intercourse. And I thought I'd been so discreet with my discomfort last time around. "The thing is," he said, "now what do we do? Is it for you or for me?"

We sort of went for the democratic approach — he put a little on me and I put a little on him, and the next thing, he was inside me and it didn't hurt at all. The dying fire in the other room cast the only light, and Joe's hair was like threads of gold. I didn't care that my stomach hurt from too much medication nor that I hated Joe's mother, and Lola Falcon, and that it was the beginning of the end. As long as Joe and I lay tangled together in the firelight, the future could just damn well wait.

15

It was a restless night. Once, I dreamt that I was pinned under a fallen tree, and woke up to find Joe's leg draped over me. Then I lay there worrying about who did the laundry. I'd forgotten to urinate before sex and had leaked a little. It was one thing to pee in Joe's bed in the city, but I could imagine Celeste Malone examining the sheets and maybe casting some kind of evil spell over my dried body fluids. There in the upstate darkness where there were no friendly lights pouring out of neighboring buildings, it was easy to lose myself in weird fantasies. But then Joe rolled over in his sleep, warming my shoulder with his breath. I curled into him, drifted to sleep again and didn't wake up until he was standing at the bottom of the bed, dressed and ready to leave for work. I sat up with a start.

"Where are you going?" I was panicked at the thought of being left alone with his mother and the dirty laundry. It seemed to me that the sheets reeked of urine.

"I'll be back by two. I'm just making a run down to Ithaca and back."

"Where's your mother?"

"At the office, I'm sure."

I tried not to look too relieved, but Joe saw it and smiled. "She'll be away all day. What will you do while I'm gone?"

"Fix myself some coffee, read, watch the soaps." He gave me a kiss. Among Joe's many virtues is that he couldn't care less about morning mouth. "Do me a favor and don't crash," I told him.

"Okay. If you can wait, I'll bring lunch."

Then he was gone and it was suddenly so quiet that I could hear the refrigerator humming from his kitchen. I rolled over to check the sheets for stains — they weren't as bad as I'd feared — when there was a loud bang outside that propelled me straight out of bed. I creaked to the window on my drowsy limbs and looked out. A row of gigantic icicles had simultaneously lost their grip on the eaves and plummeted to the ground. I wondered how many people lost their lives each year by having their brains impaled by these hypothyroidal stalactites. You never read about it.

I switched on the TV for company and went to the kitchen. There was a banana peel and a Mounds wrapper on the counter, relics from Joe's breakfast. I'm so addicted to my daily dose of caffeine that I brought my own coffee in case Joe's wasn't ferocious enough. I sat in the living room with my mug watching Katie Couric and wondering what Ma was up to. I imagined how I'd tell her about last night's dinner and about that empty chair nobody mentioned. As soon as my mind wandered to the number of days that were left to Joe and me, I got up and headed for the shower.

I was dressed by ten o'clock. For some reason, I felt better than usual. Not as stiff, no blasts of pins and needles radiating down my legs. Nothing was twitching and I had some energy. I wandered to the window. It was one of those winter days where the palette is limited to soft grays and whites, with the bare trees in stark contrast. Below me, the wind shook a dusting of snow from the branches. There was no way I could stay inside.

I'd packed boots and an aluminum fold-up cane just in case. I figured I'd be all right once I got down the steps to the driveway. Then I'd just make my way carefully to the barn at the end, rest a minute, and come back. I'd got myself all suited up, gloves, hat, a scarf, and opened the door. The frozen air was like a slap across the face. Tears sprang to my eyes and I slammed the door, leaned my head against it and tried to collect myself. It's such a surprise, sometimes, the grief. I've learned not to watch the winter Olympics, for instance. The sight of those athletes careening down the slopes is simply too painful. But I wasn't prepared this morning. Merely standing in the doorway with the bite of cold air in my nostrils was enough to remind me.

I had never taken a run down a slope without pausing for a moment at the summit, looking down to breathe in the beauty and the challenge of it. I had enjoyed teasing myself, postponing the inevitable rush. Skis together, knees cocked, upper body quiet, the plunge and then the nearest thing to pure flight I would ever know. It hurt, and right now it didn't help me to remind myself how lucky I was to have experienced it at all.

I indulged myself in a few major sobs, the wracking type that sound like faulty plumbing in a prewar apartment building. Then I chased after the blessings. First I thought about Ma. How many people in my condition had a Norma Bolles to kick their butt? And my job, which to my great surprise I believed I was born for, and then Joe, who'd provided me with enough memories for a lifetime. So what if I could no longer risk life and limb by sliding downhill on a couple of pieces of wood? Furthermore, I knew how much worse it could be — and probably would be soon enough. I told myself to just shut up and go for a walk.

I stuffed some Kleenex in my pocket and started off with my cane. The steps were icy but there was a sturdy railing, and once I got to the bottom I felt pleased with myself and ready to stretch my legs. It was probably a thousand feet or so to the barn, but the drive was thoroughly sanded. I wondered why they bothered since Joe hadn't mentioned that the barn was used for anything. But when I got closer, I noticed a plume of smoke emerging from a tin chimney. Now I was curious, so I picked up my pace. It felt so good to move, even with a cane. I knew my stride was stiff, that my left leg had a quirky kick with each step, but I was energized and, at least for the moment, past the twist of old psychic pain.

The barn was one of those weathered structures that people try to simulate in the New York suburbs. Over the door was a hand-painted sign advertising *Kielbasa Airlines* with a logo of a sausage with wings. There was a snowdrift pressed against the entrance, as if nobody had been in or out for some time. But the door hung slightly off kilter and I was able to prod it open with my cane.

Junk was piled floor-to-ceiling in a display that would have inspired Louise Nevelson. The scrap that littered the floor appeared to consist mainly of airplane parts — wheels, tailpieces, wings, propellers. Shelves crammed with mysterious gadgets lined the walls, and in the shadows were half a dozen airplanes covered with tarpaulins. One area to the right had been sectioned off and I headed for it. I was freezing and I could see the chimney of a stove rising to the ceiling behind low walls. Faint country western music accompanied the hammering of metal on metal.

I rapped on the swing door and waited. Nothing. I knocked again, louder this time. There was a brief hesitation in the pounding, but then it resumed as rigorously as ever. I gave a shove with my shoulder and stepped inside.

It was difficult to believe that a person could actually stand in there. The worktable left barely ten inches of margin, and the pot-belly stove was crowded by piles of uniden-tifiable stuff including signs that said *Whatever we've got you'll never find* and

Lasciate ogni speranza, voi ch'entrate. The precarious shelving overflowed, and who knew where the music was coming from? Leaning over the worktable was a man in denim overalls. He looked up and took in the whole picture: woman dressed for a Himalayan expedition, red nose, cane.

"You Joe's girlfriend?"

I nodded. "You Joe's dad?"

He nodded. He had brown eyes and dark whisker-stubbled skin. His hair was dark, too, and salted with gray. He was slim and stooped, maybe from a lifetime of workshop labor.

"What's that?" I asked. I already had the feeling that verbal economy counted so I decided against an apology for barging in.

"Tailpiece, 1929 Kittyhawk." The lettering on the object said VIKING AIRBOAT CO.

"Airboat," I said. "Nice."

He shot me another quick glance. "What's that for?" He meant the cane.

"Multiple sclerosis."

He didn't say anything, but reached into a pile of junk and lowered the volume on the radio. "Guess you'd like to sit."

At least he wasn't throwing me out. "I wouldn't mind," I said.

He retrieved a stool from under the table, wiped it off with his sleeve and set it near the

270

stove. I sat. And waited. I liked watching him work. Under all that grease, he had the same elegant hands as Joe. He was sure-fingered, and if it's not a word, it ought to be.

"Joe at work?" he asked.

"Yes. Flying to Ithaca."

"Good pilot, Joe. Always was."

I wasn't quite sure how to keep things rolling, but I was determined to try. "Joe tells me you started the airline."

"I just like planes. Building them, flying them. I leave the business to the rest. You a businesswoman?"

"No. English teacher."

He nodded at the quotation from Dante. "You teach the classics?"

"We do the *Inferno*, yes."

He smiled at me, the first one. If my extremities hadn't warmed up already, that smile would have done it. I wondered how I could get him to do it again.

"Want me to show you around?"

"Yes, please."

We skirted the outside of the mechanical maze, with Joe's father taking my elbow to be sure I didn't trip over anything. He mostly wanted to lead me to the tarpaulins at the rear of the building. On our way I heard fluttering sounds and looked up to see birds swooping in the rafters. That seemed appropriate in a place dedicated to the construction of flying machines.

One by one he hauled the covers off his planes and introduced them as if they were old friends. There were two Cessnas, a Fleet, and a Tigermoth, which was a British plane from World War Two. I remembered a series of photographs on Joe's wall, a man and two boys standing beside an airplane in various stages of construction. "Did you build a plane with Joe and Frank?"

His face took on the identical closed-for-business look that Joe's did when I poked into forbidden territory. "I keep it out at the airport. The boys don't bother with it anymore." But we'd moved on to the last plane which he revealed with some ceremony.

"Oh my," I said.

Pleased at my obvious admiration, he allowed himself to run his hand along the wing in a caress. "Stearman. She's a beauty."

It was a yellow and black bi-plane, larger than the others. "I'm trying to finish her before next summer's fly-in out West."

"What's a fly-in?"

"A couple hundred of us Stearman nuts get together and fly around all day. Then we drink a lot of beer and tell each other lies about flying."

"How long have you been working on this one?"

"A few years."

"Can I . . . is it possible to sit in there?"

He looked pleased. "Sure. Wish I could take you up, but she's not ready yet." He helped me into the rear seat. There was a heady smell of leather and paint. I sat there and closed my eyes, imagining myself on a summer's day, open to the cloudless sky, soaring. I get it, I thought. I can see why a person would do this.

But then I couldn't come back down to earth. Literally. My legs just refused to bend in a direction to permit egress. "I hope you don't mind if I go with you to your fly-in," I said. "I don't think I'm ever getting out."

But he stepped up onto the wing, grabbed me under the arms and lifted me out. Like Joe, he was much stronger than he looked. I landed awkwardly on the ground and twisted my foot a bit. He saw my grimace.

"You all right?"

"Fine."

"Cup of tea help?"

"Sure."

When we got back to his work area, he plugged in a teakettle and rummaged around until he found two mugs. "Not used to company," he explained. "How long you been sick?"

"Five years."

"You on Betaseron?" He saw I was surprised. "Lawyer friend of mine comes in here to tinker. He's had MS twenty, thirty years."

"I haven't had much luck with the medications. They make me feel sicker than the disease."

"Stuff's held off his relapses, he says. We went skiing together last week."

"Oh!" It came out unbidden, a pathetic cry. He shot me a sharp look over the teakettle.

"You a skier?" he asked.

"Was." I stared down into my cup and told myself, *Anna, if you cry, I'm writing you off. You will not.*

"This is for the Stearman," Joe's father said, holding up a curved piece of metal that looked as if it might cover a wheel. "Had a hell of a time locating it. I finally found it through the Internet, out in L.A. Friend of mine drives a tractor-trailer. He went out on a job, brought this back with a truckload of broccoli." Some speech for such a laconic individual, but I realized that he was offering me time to collect myself.

We talked through two cups of tea. It turned out that Gus — whose name Joe had never mentioned — was an avid reader of adventure stories, especially people like Joseph Conrad, Melville, and now Patrick O'Brian. But then I was suddenly seriously fatigued.

Gus set down his mug. "You're looking a little worn-out. It's time you got back." I didn't argue as he helped me into my coat, but then he shrugged on his own jacket and started out with me.

"You don't have to come. I'll be fine," I said.

"I left something up at the house," he said, but I knew he was inventing a reason to keep me company. Snow had started to drift down, dusting the road. I was too tired to make the effort to keep my balance and was grateful for Gus's arm to lean on.

Joe drove up just as we got to the house. He peered at us through the snow, and when he got out of the car he seemed almost angry. I glanced at Gus and the only thing on his face was naked love. It's funny, the first thing I thought was that I hoped Gus looked at Frank in the same way.

"Your father's been giving me a tour of his workshop," I said.

Joe stuck his hand out and Gus shook it. "Dad," Joe said, as if I'd just introduced them.

"We had tea," I explained. Gus smiled at me but Joe looked confused. "I thought you were coming home at two," I said.

"Weather," Joe said. "It's a lot worse down toward Ithaca so we couldn't fly."

We stood in silence for a moment. I wanted to ask Gus if he'd join us for lunch but I figured Joe might kill me.

"Well," Gus said, and started back toward the barn.

"You forgot your . . . whatever it was," I said. But he just waved and kept going.

"Come on," Joe said. "I brought some stuff for lunch. In the car."

I vowed not to talk about it until we actually sat down to eat. The fire was crackling, the sandwiches were lying in wait, and I had found a bottle of seltzer in the cupboard. I poured us both a glass. He sat, took a swallow, and said, "You two sure got cozy in a hurry." There was an edge to his voice.

"Huh?" I said. Clever, but I was tired and not tracking well.

"Never mind," he said.

"What the fuck, Joe?" I said. Now *I* was feeling edgy.

"You sound just like your mother."

I ignored that. "Did you not want me to meet him?"

He shrugged and took a giant bite of his

276

sandwich so he wouldn't have to answer.

"First of all," I went on, "it didn't take you long to get chummy with my mother. She probably knows a hell of a lot more about you than I do. Second, what's the story between you and Gus?"

"No story."

"You act like he's a stranger."

"We just don't have much in common, that's all," he said mildly. "How's your sandwich? It's a new place, some couple from Boston. They spell mozzarella wrong but their intentions are honorable."

So here was an interesting situation. Clearly, Joe had been laboring under a misapprehension, a skewed family myth. For years he'd been brainwashed to believe that he was Celeste's clone when in fact he was nothing like her. Does one tamper with such basic psychic stuff or is it wiser to keep one's mouth shut, particularly when one will soon be out of the picture anyway?

"You're exactly like your father, Joe," I said. So much for self-restraint. "And what's more, you're not even remotely like Celeste."

He stopped in mid-chew. "Well, that was quick. Instant psychoanalysis."

"I'll bet she's been doing it forever, just like at dinner, all that expounding about

277

how you two are identical. Joe, you're not even from the same planet."

"Hey. Anna. Go easy, will you? You just got here. You don't know these people."

"Well, I know *you*, and it pisses me off. I like your father. A lot. And he's crazy about *you*."

Joe dropped his sandwich on his plate and got up. "All he ever does is lock himself away so he can play with his toys. He doesn't participate."

"I doubt that he feels welcomed." I could imagine Celeste trying to dude him up for cocktail parties. "Why don't you try visiting him on his territory?"

"You know, for somebody who has a rotten relationship with her own father, you've got a lot of moxie starting in on me."

"Moxie?" For some reason, the expression struck me funny. Coming out of Joe's mouth, it seemed totally incongruous. I started laughing, and then so did Joe.

"That's why I've got such a big mouth," I said, getting up to loop my arm through his. "To let the moxie out."

We were quiet for a moment. Then he said, "So how do you think I'm like him?"

"Can we sit back down and eat if I tell you?"

First he stoked the fire. It was a real

278

healthy blaze. I imagined it cauterizing the misconceptions stretched like cobwebs across Joe's mind.

I listed the qualities I'd noticed in Gus Malone: the conversational economy, the body type, the movements of his hands, the sensitivity and generosity, and finally the creativity, the need to build something, make something.

The phone rang. Joe didn't reach for it, but I can't tolerate an unanswered phone. I picked up the receiver and was rewarded by a female voice. "Hi, is Joe there?"

"Right here."

I handed it to him and he half growled hello. "Sorry," he went on. "I'm in the middle of something . . . Yes . . . Sure . . . Yeah, great . . . I will. 'Bye." He looked a little odd when he hung up. "I don't see why that makes us similar," he said.

Not on your life, I thought. I mean, there are priorities. "Who was that?" As if I didn't half know.

"Lola Falcon."

"What kind of phony name is that anyway?" I asked. No, I didn't. I just waited until Joe decided what to tell me.

"She's looking forward to meeting you tomorrow night."

"That's it?"

"And just that she wants to see me for lunch next week to discuss a new venture she's involved in."

"How nice," I said, as my back teeth ground together. This was good: a reality check. Did I think his life wasn't going to continue when I stepped aside? I guess I'd just never considered the probability that he'd wind up with her.

"I'll grant you a couple of superficial similarities," Joe was saying. "But I don't see why you say my father and I are creatively alike."

I took a breath. I'd see Lola Falcon soon enough and there'd be something repulsive about her to give me comfort. Maybe she'd have her hair sprayed into curls you could hang your coat off. Joe hated hair spray. That's probably why he broke up with her.

"Okay," I said. "Your photography. Even the business. You both love airplanes. Making them."

"My mother's responsible for the charter. Dad bowed out of it as soon as we bought a plane with plastic seats. It was the same thing with the club. Once he disapproved of something, he wrote the whole enterprise off and never showed up there again. He's very dogmatic."

Or maybe uncompromising, I was thinking, which is not necessarily a bad thing. "I don't know anything about the club, but as far as airplanes are concerned, it's a passion with him. Planes represent a certain integrity that he can't betray. Celeste may be a wonderful business-woman, but she wouldn't care if you sold washing machines as long as you made money. It's you and Gus who love air-planes." I gestured at the photographs on the wall, almost all of them of aircraft.

"Planes are what I know about, that's all," Joe said. But he leaned his chair back on two legs and locked his hands behind his head. It's a habit he has when he's ruminating over something.

"Have you ever tipped over backward?" I asked him.

"Once," he said, but didn't elaborate. "I'm trying not to be defensive."

"Of whom?"

"I don't know. Me. My mother. It seems like a radical idea."

"Could you just live with it a little?" Give Gus a chance, I wanted to say. But amaz-ingly, I kept quiet. I figured I'd laid enough on him for now. And furthermore, I had to leave the room in a hurry. Leaking again. I'd planned to wear an expensive dress on New Year's Eve. Was I supposed to ask Joe to buy me diapers?

Fortunately, Joe was deep in thought. I admired how he processed information, even when it was unpleasant or difficult. He was a problem solver, whereas I was strictly from the hand-wringing school.

Joe went back to the office after lunch and I slept most of the day, buttressed with minipads and dreaming of Chopin and George Sand. Talk about a dysfunctional pair. There was a moment in my dream when Sand said, "Play our song, Fred," and Chopin obligingly sat down and rattled off an étude. Joe and I didn't have a song and now it was too late. That seemed tragic.

When I woke up it was dark and I was late with my vitamin C. Ascorbic acid, in my experience, requires simultaneous food or you wind up with a wicked bellyache. I checked out our leftover lunch, which I'd been too tired to tidy up. The bread had curled up on the edges and the mayonnaise glowed with botulism. There was nothing left in the fridge except half a lime. I knew I had to find something in a hurry so I crept down the stairway to Celeste's house — funny, I didn't think of it as Gus's — and headed for the kitchen.

Then I heard the music, a Chopin nocturne. It was so lovely that I forgot all about food and went to search out the CD player. I wanted that recording. In the doorway to the living room, I stopped short. Celeste was at the piano, in near darkness, playing from memory. It had been her sweet, sad sounds that had floated up through the walls and into my dreams. I stood there listening for a while but she never saw me. Sometimes when I get to thinking I'm pretty damn clever, a moment like this comes along to remind me that I don't have a clue.

16

The next morning, New Year's Eve day, Joe left to fly people to their party destinations around the state. I didn't mind because I just wanted to lie around. I felt a peculiar ache, as if someone had tied a band around my head and was squeezing tight. I popped some Tylenol and at eleven o'clock I finally managed to make myself some coffee. I was curled up in front of the TV watching *Roman Holiday* and getting ready for a good cry when the telephone rang. I hoped it was Ma. I missed her, and had actually restrained myself from calling her by remembering that I was twenty-nine years old. But it was Gus Malone.

"You busy?" he asked.

"Just being lazy," I said.

"I've got something to show you. Want some help getting down here?"

"No, but can you give me half an hour?"

"Yup," he said, and hung up.

Curiosity helped to distract me from my

discomfort, though in addition my balance seemed compromised. The room was tipped like it was in that Fred Astaire movie where he dances on the walls and ceilings. And since I wasn't quite as nimble as Fred, I had to grab furniture all the way to the bathroom.

But the icy air outside shocked my headache into submission and seemed to level the horizon out again. By the time I reached the barn, I was feeling alert and excited. Even the latch on the door pleased me. There's nothing more frustrating than a doorknob when your fingers won't work. I let myself in and headed for Gus's workshop. He was bending over an odd contraption that looked like crutches with slats on the bottom. He gave me a nod and checked to see what I was wearing on my feet.

"Those'll work," he said. "Nice day for skiing. Want to give it a whirl?"

I realized now that the slats were in fact cross-country skis with runners attached on both sides. I must have looked dubious.

"Planes have stabilizers," he said. "Why shouldn't you?" He secured one last screw and we went outside. I followed him past the barn, where a snow-covered track bordered the meadow. We stopped at the edge and Gus helped me slip my snow boots into the straps. My heart was beating so hard I could barely hear his instructions.

"Just lean your weight on one foot and then the other," he was telling me. "Don't go anywhere yet." As *if*, I thought. Once I'd gotten my balance, more or less, Gus did a preflight check. "Try sliding your right foot," he suggested finally. "Just an inch or two."

I took a breath and did it, teetering, but the odd-looking aluminum crutches were adroitly positioned to support me. I slid the left foot. Same thing. Then both again, this time a little farther. I felt totally secure. Wow. I grinned at Gus but he was focused on the process, what worked, what didn't, though as far as I was concerned, this thing already deserved to be enshrined alongside the other two greatest inventions of the twentieth century — contact lenses and tampons.

I worked my way along the edge of the meadow, and after a quarter of a mile or so was proficient enough to make my strides a little longer. At the end of the track there was a gentle slope. Gus stood beside me at the top of it.

"What do you think?" he asked.

"Oh, I think definitely," I said, and gave a shove. Granted, it wasn't much of a hill, but it was enough to give me some momentum, enough to make the cold air slip past my face and to make me sway just a little, right, then left — *Rain-drops-keep-fall-ing-on-my-head* . . .

I tipped over at the bottom and Gus came running, but I was happy to just sit there in the snow laughing like a lunatic. Gus stood grinning down at me. With the snow reflecting light onto his face, I got a vision of what Joe was going to look like in a couple of decades. I've never stopped being grateful for that image.

When we got back to the barn I asked Gus if he was coming to the New Year's Eve party.

"No," he said, and started tinkering with the skis.

"How come?" I knew it was nervy of me to ask, but I would have liked him to be there, given the formidable alliance of Lola Falcon and Celeste.

"Don't have much use for the club." He twisted one of the crutches. "There. That'll work better next time." He looked up and said, "I'll take you home."

On the way up to the house I asked him how many hours it took him to build the skis.

"A few," which I took to mean, Don't ask. At the bottom of the steps I told him I could make it the rest of the way. He turned to go but I put my hand on his arm.

"Gus," I said. "I don't know how to thank you."

But he gave me that dismissive wave and trudged off down the driveway. I knew he'd be tinkering with his new invention until he was satisfied. As far as I was concerned, it was absolutely perfect.

I wished Ma had been there to see me fly up those steps. My adventure on the skis had pumped me so full of adrenaline I was ready to tackle the giant slalom. How far was it to Lake Placid, anyhow? It should be just down the road.

And so I proceeded to slip into one of those delicious but idiotic states of denial that happen every now and then. I was strong, almost like the old days. I'd been in remission for such a long time I was obviously healed. Some people with MS go for years without a relapse. By the time it struck again, they would have a cure. Hell, they were closing in fast. The ABC drugs — Avonex, Betaseron, and Copaxone — were a giant step forward. All they had to do was beef them up a little and iron out the side effects. Etcetera, etcetera. I was on a delirious internal rant. When Joe came in, I nearly toppled him over.

"Joe, it's going to be okay," I said after planting a marathon kiss on him. "I take back everything I said. Do you still want me?"

"What have you been smoking?" he wanted to know. But the smile lines were back, if warily.

"I've been skiing with your dad."

"Excuse me?"

"He built me some skis. I skied down a hill. It was a molehill, but it wasn't flat. It was definitely not flat. God, Joe, I haven't felt this good in five years."

He took me by the hand and drew me over to the couch. The fire was dead but I couldn't have cared less. "I think you'd better calm down."

"Our future was just snatched from the jaws of death and you expect me to be calm?"

Joe got up and poured himself a stiff one. He raised the bottle by way of inquiry.

"Sure, it's New Year's," I said.

Then he came and sat down. His face was still red from the cold. "The fact that you went skiing means we can stay together," Joe said slowly.

"I know it sounds crazy, but don't you

see? It's a symbol. I'm not going to be some horrid shut-in burden. We can have a life." He still didn't look cheery enough to suit me. "Do you want me back, Joe?" I asked. Suddenly I was afraid he'd already let me go, that it was too late.

"Look, Anna, you should know me well enough to understand I wasn't going to give you up without a fight."

"You seemed so stoic," I said. Almost passive, even. I should have known better. You don't get into *Crain's* by being a wimp.

"I hoped that if you came up here with me, you'd get some perspective."

"Well, you were right. That's exactly right. I've got perspective." I knew I might be raving a bit, but it felt so good to regain my confidence in the future. "You know," I went on, "it's possible I could never have another attack."

His face darkened a little but I ignored it. I didn't feel like being gloomy. "Really," I went on. "Something's lifted. Physiologically. It's quite remarkable."

"I'm glad."

His smile was strictly a lip job now. The eyes remained sober.

I got up without gripping the arm of the couch. "You'll get used to it, Joe. As for tonight, look out. I'm in a partying mood. Are we seeing your old fishing buddy Steve?"

"He'll be there."

"Excuse me. I'm going to make myself into a simply stunning example of New York womanhood."

I had brought a silk dress, black with silver threads and three pairs of shoes with heels of varying heights. I figured I could leave the decision to the last moment, allowing the condition of my muscles to choose. Even in my towering stilettos, my legs felt strong, no twitches. I watched Joe put on his tuxedo. It was a pleasure to watch him move around the room with that loose-limbed style. I'd had trouble imagining him in formal attire, but he looked breathtaking in his tuxedo with that pale hair curling over the collar.

"To the manor born," I said. He gave me a look. "The aristocratic you," I explained.

He smiled at me and offered his arm.

In the car I asked Joe why his father didn't like the club. "I'm surprised he even mentioned it," Joe said.

"Well, he didn't elaborate."

"When I was a kid, my father was instrumental in building the place," Joe said. "North Lockville needed someplace for families to hang out. A pool, a small golf course, a tennis court. With access for everyone in the area."

291

We drove up a steep rise and suddenly the entire valley was spread out below us with the lights of the little towns sprinkled into the distance like stars in the galaxy. "Dad was concerned about the water table. He rigged up a system to use water from the creek. I guess it was pretty innovative. Engineers from around the country still come to look at it."

"Wouldn't you think he'd be proud of it?"

"Well, the place changed, and Dad didn't approve. At first, everybody used the club, from the sanitation workers to the corporate types. I have some great memories of those years, games in the pool and Halloween parties. It was a terrific place for kids."

"So what happened?" The car hit an icy patch. I could feel the rear end fishtail, but Joe gave the wheel a twist and we caught the road again.

"Some of the wealthy people decided they wanted a more exclusive atmosphere. They got themselves a majority on the board, raised the dues, and gave it a new name — Highgate. Started keeping people out if they weren't the right sort. That's when Dad quit showing up."

"Joe, I wish you were closer with him. I wonder why not."

There was one of those long meditative silences that meant he wasn't offended, just thoughtful.

"I don't know, Anna," he answered finally. "I've been thinking maybe I got you up here partly to answer that question. Or at least to ask it."

We pulled up to a two-story building with columns on either side of the door. A valet helped me out and took Joe's keys. There were Christmas bulbs strung around the trees and bushes. Inside, the place was ablaze with lights. There was an almost celestial glow surrounding the building. I held back for a moment, gazing at it.

"That's amazing," I said to Joe. "How do they get that effect?"

"By flipping the light switch," Joe said. For a photographer, I felt he was surprisingly unappreciative of visual phenomenon. It didn't register with me at the time that there could be something sinister about that heavenly radiance.

After we got rid of our coats, Joe led me into the grand lounge which was decorated with streamers and balloons and lit with a rotating disco ball. A band was playing loud seventies music. Everyone there knew Joe. The men stopped to shake his hand, the women kissed him. People were openly curious about me. Some maybe a little hostile, especially the women, but I was a city girl, after all, and I'd usurped their local star. By the time we got to our table, Joe's cheeks were covered with red smears. He leaned down to greet Celeste and another woman who was flashing me a killer smile, teeth clenched, cheek muscles hard as fists. "Anna, this is Barbara Falcon."

I smiled back, noting with guilty satisfaction that Barbara's teeth were goppy with lipstick. Mercifully, Joe sat us one empty seat away. Lola's, I supposed. There were two more vacancies beside Celeste.

"Frank's not here yet?" Joe asked his mother.

"They seem to have joined the Polaskis," Celeste said.

"Eva's family," Joe explained, craning his neck to look for them.

"The Mortons could have sat with us after all," Celeste complained. "It's very thoughtless of Frank." We all knew she meant Eva.

"Maybe we can snag Steve and Darwina. They've got another party but they'll be here later. Let's dance," Joe said, pulling me to my feet.

I gave the women a little apologetic smile as if to say I would much prefer to chat, but what, after all, could one do with a man who can't sit still? I'd never danced with Joe before, other than a turn around his bedroom when we were both naked and a little drunk, which was no preparation for this rowdy rendition of "Twist and Shout." I did a little discreet shuffling but Joe grabbed me around the waist and began hot-footing it around the dance floor. He seemed to know precisely where he was going, and by God I was coming along whether I liked it or not. And I liked it. I didn't know if I'd be breathing after five minutes but we'd sure as hell given my new high heels a workout.

I made it through "Blue Suede Shoes" and "Celebrate" before I collapsed against him. "Enough, Joe. Where did you learn to dance like that? You're wonderful."

"Practicing with Frank. Look, same footwork."

Indeed, Frank flung his wife around the periphery of the floor with a similar take-no-prisoners style. Eva was red-faced and laughing. I wondered if they'd ever show up at our table.

Joe poured me a glass of wine as I tried to be ladylike about mopping my face with the table napkin. The music was too loud to permit small talk with Celeste and Barbara so I just kept smiling at them like a Stepford

Wife. Joe leaned close to my ear. "Check out the hierarchy."

I noticed that the guests at the tables close to the dance floor were opulently dressed, with lots of expensive jewelry. Farther back, polyester proliferated, as did the cheaper haircuts and some chewing gum.

"See the guy in the blue suit? He's got a plumbing supply store. One time a bunch of us jumped off the bridge into the creek. I hit my head on a rock and would've drowned if Gino hadn't pulled me out."

There was a stir by the doorway. Guests began turning their heads as the band suddenly switched into "Whatever Lola Wants" from *Damn Yankees*. A tall blond beauty swept through the entrance. She was wearing ice-blue satin and her hair swung shiny and free to her shoulders. No fucking hair spray, excuse the French. Barbara Falcon and Celeste were beaming with pride.

"Lola," Joe explained needlessly, getting to his feet. Every eyeball in the place was trained on her, waiting to see what she'd do when she reached Joe. What she did was give him a kiss on the mouth. It was only slightly more than a peck, but still. Then she turned to me with a knockoff of her mother's toothy greeting except no stains on those perfect ivories. We shook hands, and to my satisfaction she was wearing a ring. My athletic squeeze had to dent that ring finger just a little. The thought struck me that maybe I hung out with teenagers too much. Clearly, I hadn't matured. But she could have kissed him on the cheek like everybody else.

Lola sat down between Joe and her mother. She made a big deal about leaning all over Joe in order to talk to me. "I'm so happy to meet you finally," Lola said. She barely moved her lips when she spoke, making it difficult to figure out what she was saying. But it was also sexy in a maddening kind of way. Anyone would have to move in close to get the drift. "Joe has told me all about you."

I never know how to respond to that remark. First of all, Joe doesn't know all about me. Nobody knows all about anyone. "That's odd, he hasn't told me a bloody thing about you, doll," I replied. Well, no, but it was annoying to imagine Joe talking to her about me. I noticed that Lola's champagne glass was empty already. She must have tossed it back in about four seconds.

"I admire you so much," Lola gushed, if you can gush through lips parted a mere quarter of an inch. "All you people with MS have such amazing attitudes. I know three MS people now, and every single one of you is so upbeat. Maybe it has something to do with the nerve damage in your brain. Do you think?"

My homeroom students tell me that when their parents lecture them on schoolwork, sex, or drugs, the rule is: *nod and smile*. I was making good use of that technique tonight. Meanwhile, Lola was pressing her breasts, which were ample, against Joe's side as she leaned across him. I looked for telltale signs of silicone but they looked bona fide to me. Her navel did, too. Actually, I couldn't see *that* far down, but damn close. She handed her glass to Joe. "Joe, would you be an angel and get me a refill? And for Anna, too?" It occurred to me that she was quite drunk, and no wonder. I was ashamed that jealousy had blinded me to the painfulness of her situation.

"I read your cookbook," I said.

"Which one?" She seemed surprised.

"*High-Rise Health Nut*. It was wonderful. Very smart and funny." I hadn't wanted to be impressed, but there it was. She was a good writer, clever, literate, and entertaining.

But my praise, in combination with half a gallon of champagne, had apparently flipped a switch. She took my hand in hers and gazed at me with beautiful if slightly unfocused eyes. "Anna. Anna. If you'd been a bitch, I wouldn't be telling you this. But you're obviously a special person . . ." She looked around for Joe who was nowhere in sight. "He's a bad bet, Anna. I know him better than anybody, so I can say with complete authority that he's fucked up. Closed off. Intimacy? Forget it." She glanced around again, hair swinging like a sheet of gold, and moved in even closer. "Last summer, we go on this hiking trip in the Adirondacks, four days back in the brush. Fantastic. Campfires, shared a sleeping bag, watched meteor showers all night. Talk about bonding. Then we get home and I don't hear from him for a month. Not a call, nothing. Dropped out. When I confronted him, guess what he said . . ."

She paused as if actually waiting for me to conjecture. I opened my mouth, but she went on before I could tell her that I was sorry but I thought that this conversation was somewhat inappropriate.

"He forgot about me," she said. "Those were his very words. He'd been really busy with work and he *forgot me*." She released my hand and tugged at her dress, which had slipped precariously low. "There's something seriously wrong with a man like that, and believe me, it's only one example. A year ago I would have kept my mouth shut, but lately I've come to believe that we women have to protect one another."

I grasped at a response but the vivid image of Joe and Lola cocooned in a sleeping bag together under the starry sky crowded everything out of my mind. The only thing I could think of was to reach for her hand again and give it a sympathetic squeeze. Fortunately at that very moment Joe came to the rescue.

"Let's get something to eat," he said. It was difficult not to smile — so primitive and male after Lola's tortured, emotional narrative. I imagined Joe in his bearskin with a club in one hand while Lola and I sat huddled in the cave complaining about how the menfolk only cared about sex and hunting for dinosaurs.

"Go ahead," Lola said with a brave and tremulous smile. What if, given half a chance, I really would like her?

Joe steered me to the line that snaked along the buffet table. "You two seemed to have a lot to say to one another."

I was glad not to have to shout. The band had taken it down a notch so that people wouldn't get *agita* from eating with Jerry

Lee Lewis singing. "She was just filling me in," I said.

"On what?"

There was nothing to be gained by elucidating, so I opted for evasionary tactics. "I have to say I'm impressed," I said. "No band ever played 'Anna Banana' when I walked into the room."

"Only because nobody ever heard of it. Anyway, it's just a hokey tradition. Lola's kind of a favorite around here."

"I noticed," I said. "What were you, the king and queen of the ball?"

"Actually, yes, they used to do that." My face must have revealed that I'd only been kidding. Joe looked sheepish. "They made us wear these corny crowns," he went on, "and they took photos for the local newspaper. It was so ridiculous we made them stop."

"When was that?"

"Last year."

"On the D.L., Joe, I don't think she's quite over you."

"D.L?" he asked.

"The *down low*. Sorry, teenspeak. Confidentially. Lola sweats you, big-time."

"Don't be silly," Joe said, spearing a hunk of roast beef. There wasn't a vegetable in sight unless you counted the peppers stuffed with hamburger. "We're friends now, that's all."

As I scanned the table looking for something appetizing, like maybe a slice of smoked salmon or a shrimp, it all turned sparkly, kind of the way water looks in the moonlight. It was beautiful but peculiar for sure. A pot of Hungarian goulash, even when it's *really* good, doesn't customarily glitter like diamonds. I looked up at the lights to see what accounted for the extraordinary display dazzling before me, but just as suddenly, all returned to normal — macaroni salad and baked ham. By then I should have gotten the message that all was not well inside my brain, but I was taking such a soothing warm bath in a tubful of denial.

"Okay, Anna?" Joe asked. He'd begun to sense when I was checking myself out for trouble.

"Sure," I said. "I think I could use the ladies' room. Can you manage two plates?"

"It's past the entrance on the right," he said. "You need any help?" He was giving me that penetrating look that Ma had.

"I'm fine." But I guess I wasn't too fine because I headed left instead of right, and rather than finding the ladies' room, I wound up outside a small game room with card tables. I stood in the doorway for a moment trying to get my bearings when I heard a woman's sobs coming from inside. I should have turned away immediately, I suppose, but the sound was so heart-wrenching it brought out the Samaritan in me. Perhaps there was something I could do. Then I heard the words through the sobs, in Celeste's unmistakably deep voice, "If she really loved him, she'd leave him alone. What kind of future does she think he'll have with *her?*"

I stood rooted on my dead legs as she wept on. "You know how I've always felt about physical deformity, Barbara," she sobbed. "I know it's not kind of me, but my God, she's just another of his strays." A break to blow the nose, and then, "Remember how he was always bringing home wounded animals when he was little? I knew I should have sent him to a therapist."

That was enough. I forgot that I had to pee and wandered in a kind of trance back to the ballroom. Joe and Lola were dancing. What a couple. They looked perfect together, and I wasn't the only person who'd noticed. A few of the women were downright misty-eyed. When Joe and Lola left the dance floor, they seemed to be wearing halos around their heads. I squinted, wondering if somebody had revived the crown ritual. Was God trying to tell me something? Like how we'd all be better off if I slipped into the night? A lady with tight curls touched my arm and told me what a lucky girl I was to have captured the heart of North Lockville's favorite son. She actually said *captured the heart*. I hope I smiled at her.

By the time I groped my way back to the table, Joe had grown another head. It turned out to be the best friend, Steve, embracing Joe from behind. Steve's head studied me with its chin resting on Joe's shoulder. I noted idly that he was handsome in a careless, androgynous way, with blue eyes that seemed to penetrate to your underwear. Joe had told me that Steve was a computer genius, a musician, and the best fisherman on the Little Moose River. He was often unreliable but was much forgiven on account of his self-reproach and genuine good nature. I think ordinarily I might have been unnerved by the scrutiny of those eyes, but I just stared back in a daze.

"Get out of my way," Steve said to Joe, shoving him unceremoniously out of his seat. "I have to talk to this woman."

"Go easy on her," Joe said. "Where the hell's the chocolate? What kind of a party is this anyway?" He went off to forage the dessert table. Beside me, Lola was pretending to listen to an aging admirer, but I could feel her half leaning into my lap as she tried to overhear what was going on between me and Steve.

"He's hooked, you know that," Steve said. "First time for old Joe. I never thought I'd live to see the day."

"I think I shouldn't have come up here," I said. Whatever zone I was in did not allow for temporizing.

"He counted on persuading you not to cut him loose," Steve said.

"That wasn't the deal." I knew I should be telling him to butt out, but there was no resisting Steve's eyes. The government could use this guy for getting secrets out of terrorists. "But I guess if I'd truly believed it was over, I wouldn't have put us through this." Whatever *this* was. "I'm so confused," I finished lamely.

"Let's start with what *you* want, lovely Anna."

"If things were different, I'd want Joe. I *do* want Joe, but I can't be happy with him." Then I closed my mouth. Was I obligated to share my deepest conflicts with this person? It was beginning to feel as if everybody in upstate New York had lined up to get a shot at me. But Steve took my hand and kissed it. The gesture was compassionate, not flirtatious, and disarmed me completely. Then Joe arrived with a plateful of brownies and elbowed Steve out of the way. The masculine physicality of their interaction seemed like a poignant parody of the lunchroom at Cameron. I squinted at them, but they had blurred. I blinked hard, trying to clear the windshield, but it didn't help.

Somehow we all got through until midnight. Steve went off to find his girlfriend. Celeste and Barbara returned to the table. Lola flashed her cleavage at Joe and complicitous looks at me, but my resentment had melted away. She almost seemed like someone I could be friends with under different circumstances. Then suddenly it was only ten seconds to a new year. The bandleader started counting down as guests cleared the dance floor. "Where's everybody going?" I asked Joe.

"Tradition," he answered.

"Four-three-two-one-midnight! Happy New Year!" To the strains of "Auld Lang Syne," Joe kissed me, then Lola kissed both me and Joe on the lips, Celeste and Barbara hugged tearily. Then the bandleader shouted, "First dance of the new year! First dance!" Everyone quieted more or less, waiting, as he announced with a drumroll, "Our own Joe Malone and his lovely friend from New York City, Annette Bolles!" Instead of the correct "bowls" pronunciation, he said "bolls" as in "dolls."

I averted my eyes from our table as Joe led me to the dance floor amid shouts and rowdy applause. I didn't want to see Celeste's expression, or Lola's either.

"Sorry," he murmured in my ear. "It never occurred to me they'd do this again."

The bandleader was having a field day with "You Are the Sunshine of My Life." There was nothing to do but go with it. I melted into Joe, leaned my head against his shoulder and closed my eyes.

The trouble was, when I opened them again, it was still dark.

"Joe," I said.

"Mm," he murmured against my hair.

"How literal is it when they say that love is blind?"

He heard it in my voice. He stopped dancing and held me away so he could look into my face, at least I guess that's what he was doing. Everything was pitch-black, as if I had suddenly plunged to the center of the earth where no sunlight could ever penetrate.

"Tell me what's happening," he said.

"I can't see. Everything's gone black."

He hugged me to his side and walked me

off the dance floor. I remember his hip moving against mine and the sound of the music faltering and dying away. Then it was the confusion of being handled and half carried and stuffed into a car. I heard Steve's voice, low and calm, asking Joe if we needed an ambulance.

"I want to go home," I kept saying. "Please, can you take me home?" I've turned into one of Joe's strays now, I thought. If I was ever anything else.

Joe had to pack my things and arrange for a plane. On account of the holiday, Air-Malone was short staffed, and there would be a scramble to find equipment. "I won't be long," Joe said, settling me on the couch in the Malone house. "My mother will stay with you."

"Please, where's Gus?" I said.

After a while I felt a callused hand take mine. "What's going on?" he asked. I tried to picture him in that austere room, perched in his coveralls on one of Celeste's ivory brocade chairs. He must have dragged it next to the couch. She wouldn't like the tracks in the carpet.

"I can't see," I explained. I wondered what it was about Gus that made the panic retreat.

"Ever happen before?"

"No."

"What can I do?"

"Tell me a story." It just fell out of my mouth, I don't know why.

I could hear him smile, just like Joe. "I was never much good at that," he said. "There's that one about the three pigs but I don't remember the end."

"Just talk about planes. Tell me about the plane you built with the boys."

Gus covered my fingers with his other hand. I wanted to creep into that sheltered space.

"We chose her from a catalog," Gus began. "Built her from a kit. It took us five years, but we had a lot of fun."

"How old was Joe?"

"Must have been no more than eight when we started, and Frank in high school. The plans were pretty much a muddle, but Frank could always figure them out. And Joe, it's all he ever wanted to do was work on that plane. Cut school half the time and caught hell from his mother."

So he could be with his dad, I was thinking. I was starting to drift. I don't know how much I missed but I remember hearing something about crashing the plane, which roused me enough to ask if anybody got hurt.

"Nah, it's just the metal struts on the landing gear were too lightweight."

"Gus, this means something, my going blind. About Joe and me." I struggled as my brain was squeezed into a tiny black ball. But I clung to consciousness so I could stay with Gus.

I heard him say "Don't go getting mystical on me," and then I couldn't fight it anymore. I slept. At one point, I think Celeste came into the room. There was muted conversation, but I was unable to snap out of my semiconscious state. Through it all, Gus's presence warded off the terror, suspending reality enough so that I could rest for the battle I knew was coming.

Joe and Gus sat beside me in the ambulance, and Steve rode up front with the driver. When we pulled away from the house with a lurch, I must have protested. It felt terrifyingly perilous, sliding along the road without my sight, as if it were my eyes that kept us on the road. Joe took one hand and Gus the other, what a comfort.

"I'm so lucky," I said. They laughed just a little, identical sounds back in their throats that said *this woman is nuts*. Two peas in a pod.

17

When you can't see, movement is a strange and frightening experience. It's as if sight is the anchor and without it you're cast adrift. Flying south, with Gus and Sam Barney at the controls, I felt the earth turning on its axis beneath me. There was no gravity. I wanted to be in a bed where I could grip the sides and hang on tight.

"Do you have any pain?" Joe asked above the howl of the engine.

I shook my head.

"Can I get you something? Is there any medication?"

"No. Thanks. I'm okay." I just couldn't see anymore, that was all. And I didn't want to talk, couldn't seem to talk. As if the power of speech were somehow connected to my optic nerve. Shutdown. Meltdown. Anna's seen it all, said it all. It's over.

At the hospital I think they must have given me a shot, because I barely remember any of it. I slept through strange dreams and when I woke up there was the familiar scent of fresh-baked bread.

"Hi, babe," Ma said beside me. "What's new?"

I opened my eyes slowly, hoping against hope, but all was dark. The tears came then. At least that part worked.

"Go ahead," she said. "You're entitled."

There was a catch in her voice, but she started rummaging around beside the bed and it was business as usual. "Where the fuck do they hide the Kleenex in this place? It's a hospital, for Christ's sake. Okay, this'll do."

I heard her running water at the sink. After a moment, she came back and wiped my face with a warm washcloth. It felt good. I slipped into another doze. At some point there were footsteps that stopped in the doorway. There was a subtle rustle of fabric as Ma got up, and I wanted to say *don't leave me*. But I couldn't talk through my drowsiness and that resistance seemed tied to the blindness was there.

I heard a strangled cough, then Joe's voice, soothing. "Norma. It's all right. It'll be all right . . ." And I faded again.

When I woke up the next time, I was still blind but had regained my mental clarity. The first thing I realized was that it was finished with Joe, once and for all. No more excursions into denial for either of us. Ironic that it took blindness to reveal the truth. I listened carefully for evidence of someone else in the room. Nothing.

"Hello?" I tried. It was difficult to push the word out. No one answered. As the reality of my isolation began to sink in, I started to panic. I may never see again, I thought. How could I live, how could I work, what would happen to me? I started searching for the buzzer to summon a nurse. I tried to get up but the rails of the bed were raised and I had an IV in my arm.

"Help me!" I yelled. "Help!"

Within seconds, I heard footsteps and that swooshing sound that only accompanies a starched uniform on the move.

"What is it, honey?" A sweet voice, a compassionate voice.

I wanted to tell her, *I'm scared. I'm so scared.* But the words wouldn't come. She put her hand on my forehead.

"Do you want a pill to help you sleep? Dr. Klewanis ordered you a little something."

Oblivion. Yes, that was just what I wanted. I nodded, and soon I was back in a place of faces and colors. I dreamed of the Prince and Cinderella from my favorite Walt Disney movie, waltzing together in the grand ballroom, only it was Joe and Lola. I was there, too, watching with the others, only the others were all me as well. I stood apart from the elegant pair, swaying with the music and believing with all my heart that this was exactly the way it was supposed to be.

I lay there like a hollow jar, the passive recipient of medication, food, the laying on of hands, some gentle, some not. Dr. Klewanis had the kind of clout to install me close to the nurses' station. It was an advantage medically, but a little noisier. I heard him the first morning, inquiring in that mild midwestern style as to why my blood workup results had been misplaced.

"Any theories?" I heard him asking the nurse supervisor. "Nothing more stimulating first thing in the morning than hypotheticals. Better than caffeine. How about you just find them for me, nurse, and then we can have a chat about procedure. Nothing physically punitive. Psychological intimidation's more up my alley."

I heard the nurse's murmured reply, respectful but not cowed. My neurologist rarely allowed the smile to slip off his face, and an undercurrent of humor ran deep with him. I suppose it kept him afloat when forced to confront the inevitable deterioration of so many of his patients. I heard his footsteps approaching my room and pictured his stocky form, white coat askew, looking more like a TV repairman than a world-class physician. Other footsteps clattered in his wake, the omnipresent students.

He stood at the foot of my bed, studying the chart, I presumed.

" 'Morning, Bolles. Private plane, eh? Not too tacky. How're you feeling?"

"Peachy."

He spoke to his students, who were mouse-quiet. "Patient twenty-nine-year-old female Caucasian, diagnosed with relapsing-remitting MS approximately five years ago. This is her first episode of retrobulbar neuritis, resulting in total blindness. What's in that IV, Johnson?"

"Corticosteroids?" answered a head cold.

"And?"

Much shuffling of feet.

"We're playing hardball with Ms. Bolles here, people. What else?"

"A.C.T.H.?" A female voice. I tried to smile in gender support but it was too much effort.

"Hang out your shingle, Finnegan," the doctor said. "In my opinion, the whammo jolt is the only way to go. Close monitoring and ease her off gently. I'm going to persuade Ms. Bolles here to indulge me when we get her out of here. The ABC's. Benillo, what do I mean by that?"

"Avonex, Betaseron, or Copaxone?" I heard the tremor of anxiety in the voice, wondering if he got it right.

"Exactimento." He came over and picked up my wrist. "Whadaya think, Bolles, you finally ready to play on my team?"

"The injections?" What an effort. It seemed like a hundred words.

"Bingo."

"Mixing metaphors," I said, and figured that was about it for talking.

"English teacher," he explained to the troops.

I remembered the misery of the last attempt at drug therapy, the shakes, the aches, the joint pain. It doesn't happen to everybody and sometimes it goes away after a while. One of those concoctions sent visions of nooses and razor blades dancing in my head like sugarplums. Odd that a drug can produce such a specific ideology — in my case, fantasies of suicide, and I wasn't even all that depressed. But right now I was more interested in the short term.

"Get my sight back?" I asked.

"Hope so. How's your speech?"

"You noticed."

"That's why they let me work here." He bent over me and lifted my eyelids. I assumed he was shining his penlight in there.

"Words are lead," I told him. "Not slurred."

"A bit, actually," he said. That was news. I had thought my enunciation was pretty clear. He stood up. "Ms. Bolles here is scheduled for an MRI later on." A hand on my shoulder. "Okay, slugger. I'll stop by tonight. Your ma can catch me about seven, and tell her I want some of that cranberry nut bread." The sound of receding footsteps made me frantic.

Don't go. Fix me. Heal me. Help me.

I didn't say any of it. It was too hard to spit it out, and besides, what was the point?

Since I was unaware of the brightening and dimming of the sunlight outside my window, I became dependent upon certain events as markers in my day. The doctors' morning rounds, the meals that I found difficult to choke down — though Grant later pointed out that I was not entirely at a disadvantage by being unable to see what I was eating. The pop-ins from Ma — brief, but several a day — the phone calls from Joe, who was undergoing a business crisis and was thankfully not in the city. I needed time to formulate the words to explain myself, an impossibility when my tongue had collapsed like an old rug onto the floor of my mouth. Joe didn't press me over the phone. We just left it that I was medically unable to communicate.

But after a week of Dr. Klewanis's radical treatment, my speech began to improve. Grant had been badgering me about visiting and it was getting difficult to put him off.

"Lookit, Annie," he explained. "You're blind as a bat. You won't see the lugubrious pity on my face anyhow so why not let me come? I've got gossip."

"You can tell me over the phone," I said.

"Ah, but I won't."

"You bastard."

"Four o'clock?"

"Oh, all right."

It's not easy to participate in a serious hug when you're loaded down with IV tubes but somehow we managed. He smelled wonderful as always, the morning shave's cologne faintly mingled with the merest hint of tobacco from an occasional furtive cigarette.

"What are you wearing?" I asked.

"What is this, an obscene phone call in person?"

"The gray herringbone, I bet."

"Nope, brown and green plaid." I felt him sit on the edge of the bed.

"With the tan slacks?"

"And the taupe tie with the creepy millipedes."

"I love that tie."

"Wore it just for you, darling. I brought you something." I heard a paper bag rustle and was suddenly transported to our Mexican restaurant. Tacos! It was the first laugh I'd had in a while. I sat up in bed, presumably dribbling hot sauce all over my sheets, while he filled me in.

"Duncan Reese is out. Did you get your Duke of Windsor letter?"

I shook my head, too stymied by taco to speak.

"The board hinted around that he could keep his job if he acted *really* contrite and got rid of Jessica. Reese composed a very graceful response, basically telling them he would not renounce the woman he loved for Cameron's throne or any other damn thing. Tell Norma to check the mail. You'll like it."

"Do you think Chubb joined forces with the head of the board?" I asked. "That woman whose husband left her."

"Right on, Watson," Grant said. "Jesus, if you could see what you're doing to your bed. You look like a gunshot victim."

"How will the school manage without him, Grant?"

"They've got an interim guy, a retired headmaster from Dalton. Life will go on."

"Maybe, but it won't be the same. Not to mention that I'll probably lose my job."

"Look, don't get all in a twit. Can I find you something to calm you down? I think I've got a joint in a pocket someplace."

I read in his voice that he was concealing news, but I simply wasn't up to hearing it.

"How's the boyfriend?" he asked. Leave it to Grant to raise the germane issues.

"Oh, well."

"The fucker's deserted you in your hour of need!"

"First of all, keep your voice down. Furthermore, *I'm* breaking it off, not Joe. He's been perfect."

He fell silent for a moment. "Okay," he said finally. "I'm working on that."

"I feel obliged to explain it to Joe before I explain it to you. But tell me about my kids."

"They want to come see you. There's a plot afoot."

Total panic. "They can't."

"Why not?"

"They can't see me like this."

"Don't be an asshole!" he boomed. "It'll be good for them! A life lesson!"

"Shh, Grant. I don't want to be a life lesson. I just want to be their teacher."

"You look fine."

"It's unprofessional."

"So I'll go back and tell them they're not welcome."

"Do you know how hard it would be for me to see them without being able to see them?"

Another silence, not easy for Grant.

"But you can tell me about them," I said. "How's Rudy?"

"Nope."

"Come on, Grant."

"Not one word."

"That's blackmail."

"So it is. You have taco shell in your hair, darling." He reached to tidy me up. "Guess I'll be shoving off now."

"But what about Michelle, has she gained any weight? Did they hire a decent substitute for me this time?"

"Glad to note such a healthy interest," Grant said. I could hear fabric on fabric as he slipped on his coat. I was getting pretty good at this.

"Don't you dare leave me," I said.

But he bent down and gave me a kiss. "Mm, you smell like a south of the border cocktail dip. See you, darling."

"You rat. You king size rat. Thanks for stopping by."

As usual, I couldn't hear him grin. As he went out the door I called after him.

"Are you smiling? Grant Hurst, are you smiling?"

They stood whispering outside my door. Sukey was hectoring Eddie "Big Tits" Zimmer.

"Don't you dare say anything about, you know."

"I'm *not*, Sukey. Jeez, give me a little credit, will you?"

Then Rudy's voice. "Are we going in or what?"

I had asked Ma to bring me some street clothes, and had my hair washed and blown dry. The nurses helped me get to the window chair. I was still attached to my IV, but I figured I didn't look too frightening.

"Come in, people!" I called. Might as well get this over with. I was sweating with anxiety and supposed they all were, too. I cursed Grant for insisting on this extremely dumb idea.

They trailed in and I got an instant noseful of adolescents — acne medication, hair gel, and dirty feet. Somebody stumbled against the stool I used to climb into bed.

"Fuck!" Eddie said.

"Eddie, what's your *function!*" Sukey said, and I heard a whack.

I wanted to cry with joy.

"Hi, guys," I said. "So what's going on?"

"It's pretty lame without you, Ms. Bolles," said the divine Will Simmons, alias Johnny Depp. Straight D average and destined for expulsion. We'd probably both be chucked out of Cameron at the same time.

"Who all's here?"

Sukey piped up, "Rudy, Mark, Jennifer, me, and . . ." uttered scornfully, ". . . Eddie. Michelle's sorry she couldn't come. She's doing a dance recital."

"That's terrific."

Jennifer, Cameron's most accomplished dancer, spoke up. "She's gotten so good, Ms. Bolles. You should see — Oh. Sorry."

"It's okay, Jen. I'd like to see her perform. I hope that'll happen someday soon."

"When are you getting your sight back?" Mark asked.

I imagined Sukey's eyes rolling. *Mark, you're so inappropriate.*

"With MS, you never know what's going to happen," I replied. "Probably it'll gradually improve but I'll have some impairment. Then I'll get to wear some truly ugly glasses. I'm just warning you."

"We want you to come back, Ms. Bolles," Eddie said. "They gave us another horrendous substitute —"

"You always hand our papers back with a page full of comments," Rudy said. "She gives us one sentence."

"Yeah," Mark said. "Like 'This sucks. D-minus.' Real constructive."

Sukey jumped in. "She's stupid? I mean, all she does is make us read two hundred pages a week like we don't have any other subjects? And we've got semester finals coming up and she gets *us* to make presentations so she doesn't have to, like, review the material. She even filed her nails last week, like it's . . . So. Gross? My parents want to fire her."

They also wanted to fire me once, I remembered, but kept it to myself. I was getting aggravated over Sukey's portrait of my botched course. I decided to change the subject. "What's going on otherwise?" I asked.

I wanted to see if they'd raise the issue of Duncan Reese's departure. It was Rudy who cut to the chase.

"Dr. Reese left. There's someone new in his office."

"I'm glad he's gone," Sukey said. "Ee-yew, what a sleazoid."

"A person can't help it if he falls in love," Rudy said.

"Ms. Lassiter was *supposed* to be in love with her husband." Astonishingly, that came from Eddie.

"You don't have control over your heart," Rudy said in a voice of one who knew. That answered one question — he was still carrying a torch for Michelle.

"Who's going out with whom?" I asked.

"This school is so not into the social thing," Sukey complained. "Nobody does anything except watch stupid videos."

"I keep asking her out, Ms. Bolles," Eddie protested, "but she always turns me down."

I heard another whack followed by Mark's caustic, "I wonder why, Eddie."

"Michelle's with Wilson," Eddie said, undaunted. Wilson Parker was Cameron's sole football hero in a school that prided itself on never winning any sporting events other than chess tournaments.

"Yeah, they're going to the winter formal." Rudy tried, and failed, to sound upbeat.

"Don't give up, Cootie," Eddie said. "You never know."

"We brought you some candy, Ms. Bolles," Sukey said. "It's on the table."

"Skittles," Mark said. They knew my weakness.

Feet were beginning to shift. I sensed it was time to wind things up. "Thanks. You know I'll enjoy those. And thanks also for coming," I said. "It's wonderful to see you all."

I could imagine them glancing at one another over this. They started trailing toward the doorway.

"It's not the same at school," Jennifer said. "Dr. Reese's gone and now you're stuck in here."

"You have to come back soon." Rudy's voice. I wished that I could see his face, those brown eyes.

There was a chorus of " 'Byes" and they were gone. But I heard Sukey's stage whisper outside. "Oh. My. God? I think I'm going to *cry.*"

Which is exactly what I did. But not for long, not with a bag of Skittles lying in wait at my bedside. I ate them all.

Once I began to get my eyesight back, other symptoms cropped up in a trade-off. Two weeks into my hospitalization, I woke to find that I could make out a faint circle of light. If I passed my hand across it, there was a shadow. As the hours went by, shapes emerged from the murk. Dr. Klewanis was pleased, and launched into one of his sports analogies — the rewards of tenacity in long distance marathons or something. I didn't quite get the connection, but nevertheless his cheer was a comfort. Later that same morning, I began to have severe cramping in my calves and then the familiar weakness that put me back into the wheelchair.

On top of all this, Joe phoned to say he was coming into the city and would stop by to see me. This would be the first time since the upstate debacle, and I'd had a lot of time to ruminate about what I was going to say when this moment finally came. I had imagined that I was prepared. But of course I wasn't, not when I actually saw his face. Joe looked beautiful even through the distorting lenses of my science-fiction MS glasses. He leaned over the bed and gave me a long, lingering kiss. When I didn't respond in my ordinary breathless fashion, he stood back.

"I knew there was something," he said.

"Close the door, will you please, Joe?"

He did. Then he pulled a chair up next to the bed, where I could see him better.

"I said I'd give it a try," I began, "when I agreed to go upstate with you."

"You told me we were all right."

"I know I did. But I realize now that I was

only postponing the inevitable." I hated the way I sounded. That's what happens, I guess, when you rehearse something too much. Joe got up and started walking around, something he does when he's agitated.

"Okay, Anna," he said. "We might as well have this out once and for all. The way I see it, you're making a decision for me that you have no right to make. You're such a pathetic specimen that I can't possibly be in love with you. Not for the long haul. That's it, isn't it?"

"I'm not presuming to tell you what you should feel. I can only speak for myself. I don't know how I can make you —"

"Please don't tell me I can never understand what it's like to be disabled. You'll never get what it's like to be male. I'll never get what it's like to be a teacher. Nobody can ever understand what it is to live in anybody else's shoes. It's hard enough to figure out how to survive in your *own* shoes, for Christ's sake. People have a lot of differences. That's good. That's what makes it real and interesting. We don't have to be the same to be together."

"But there's such a thing as too much difference," I said.

Somebody knocked. Joe shouted, "Go

away!" and the steps retreated down the hallway. He went to lock the door and came back, twisting the chair around so he was facing me over the back of it. The slats made a barrier between us.

"You think I haven't thought about this," Joe said, "that I'm just brainlessly walking into it?" I didn't answer. "After I met you in the gallery," he went on, "I spent weeks mulling it over. I told myself I wasn't involved yet and I could still choose not to pursue it. I read everything I could get my hands on about MS, and we all know it's not a happy story. But I also realized that what happened between us was rare and amazing. What you could mean in my life, and I wasn't wrong. Goddamn it, Anna."

He stuck his finger out at me and went on. "I want you to explain to me why two people who are so completely connected to one another can possibly live apart."

For somebody who didn't talk much about his feelings, he was on quite a roll.

"Because one of them needs it so badly," I answered.

There was a long silence and then I continued, haltingly, but at least now I was speaking from the depths of myself and not just rehashing some glib speech I'd been reciting for days. "I've had almost six years to

329

figure out a way to live with MS," I said. "Plenty of times it seemed easier to just throw myself off a bridge. Pardon the image." Full circle, back to his photograph in the gallery that first summer day. I could tell by his ironic grimace that he'd thought of it, too.

"I'm sorry if I sound maudlin or self-pitying," I went on. "But the fact is, when I met you that day, I had finally come to terms with my life and my future. I was even pretty happy."

"I screwed that up, did I?" Joe asked. His voice was an even mix of sadness and sarcasm.

"Yes."

"By dragging you back into the world?"

"Being with you makes me feel like a walking sack of symptoms!" That was cruel, but I couldn't seem to get it across to him. "I didn't dwell on my illness, not even when I had a relapse. I just got on with my job and the life I'd carved out for myself. But once you showed up, I started having major regrets again. I kept thinking about all the things we couldn't have together — like a normal sex life and a normal marriage, and kids. What I regret the most is that I hauled you into my denial. But I can't do it, Joe. It's just too painful."

"I want to be with you the way you are and the way you'll become," Joe said. "If I can do it, why can't you?"

"Because you're not the one who's sick. I hate having to worry about leaking all over the bed when we make love. It can get a lot worse, too. My intestines will be next. You want to be changing my diapers in the middle of sex?"

"Look, Anna, when my grandmother was dying of colon cancer, I shoved suppositories up her rectum twice a day. It didn't change the way I felt about her. Your shit is just another part of your body."

"Did you ever think that maybe I'm a replacement for her?" I asked.

"And maybe you believe every male is a jerk just like your father," he shot back.

We sat in silence for several seconds.

"If I'm the kind of person who needs to take care of someone," he said quietly, "is that so terrible?"

"I can't help it, Joe," I said.

He was staring into my face. Even through my strange lenses, I knew I'd never seen his eyes so dark. He got up and carefully replaced the chair in its niche against the wall. My heart started crashing in my ears. Watch him, look at him, it's the last time, I told myself. Burn it into your brain so you never forget the beauty of him. The grace of him. The goodness and miracle of him.

" 'Bye, Anna Marie," he said. And he walked out the door. I strained to hear his footsteps all the way to the elevator. I told myself he wasn't really gone until the elevator bell dinged. I could still call him. I could still begin screaming from the bottom of my soul, "Stop him! Stop that man!"

But I didn't. I took off my glasses and laid them on the table and waited until at last I heard the little bell sound. It tolls for thee, Anna, I thought. It's over.

18

When the newspaper arrived with breakfast the next morning, I noticed the date: January 16. The anniversary of my father's departure. It was a day I had always remembered to mark in some fashion. One year I wore one of his old neckties to school. Once I made a little shrine of photos and artifacts — a cigarette lighter, a *Playbill* from a musical he'd once taken me to, a Tootsie Roll — a miniature one like the kind he always carried around in his pockets. I lit candles and prayed on my knees that he'd come home again. Then when I was fifteen, Patsy and I collected the videos he'd produced and systematically yanked out the tape from every one. It made a mighty impressive pile of mediocre acting and predictable dialogue. Then we wrapped a Ken doll in that same old necktie and skewered it with half a million needles. All of it went into a pillowcase and down the chute into the garbage compactor.

I stared at the IV in my arm, which was

the color of a ripe plum from so many punctures. It seemed very clear to me now. With that private ritual so long ago, I had sealed my own fate. My father frolicked in the playing fields of California while I lay impaled here in punishment for my own vicious brutality. I was bad. Always had been.

I looked up toward the foot of my bed where a row of nurses had suddenly appeared. I didn't recognize them, and it was strange that they had arrived so silently.

"You're not the regulars," I said, squinting at them through my special glasses. Their uniforms were white leather, an extravagance, I thought, given this era of HMOs.

They raised their forefingers simultaneously. "Evil girl," they said. "Disgusting girl." I watched as their hair, even their eyelashes and brows, sprouted like barbs on a cactus. Suddenly I realized that these weren't nurses at all but prosecutors come to exact vengeance on behalf of all those people I had wished ill over my lifetime.

"How did you get in here?" I cried. "It's not visiting hours!" In lock-step, they swayed toward me with thorns rattling. They smelled foul with the rotten-egg stink of sulfur.

I tore at my IV, sending a spectacular

fountain of blood spurting over the sheets. I tumbled onto the floor and tried to run but my legs were too weak. The nurses reached for me, laughing at my pitiful attempt to escape. I sliced my head on the edge of the door as I fell and then everything went dark again as they caught me and buried me alive in a suffocating hole. There wasn't even a coffin, just heavy clods of dirt that clogged my mouth when I opened it to scream. I could barely breathe and all I could hear was the high-pitched howl of my own blood coursing through my veins. I willed myself to die — anything to release myself from this hell. Bad. Bad. Bad Anna.

"Anna. Anna." It was too bright. After the darkness of my grave it was painful to open my eyes. But at least I was out of the hole.

"Did I die?" I asked. Perhaps this drifting sensation meant I had at last been purified and sent on to another easier life, a life with no MS, no loss, just peace.

"You want me to close the blinds?"

"Yes, please."

I risked opening my eyes a crack and saw Dr. Klewanis sitting beside my bed. I made a quick survey to make sure there weren't any evil harpies hanging around.

"You've had a reaction to the drugs," he said. I tried to grasp the words but they seemed like a puzzle. "Do you understand me, Anna?"

"No," I said.

"Do you remember coming to the hospital? You couldn't see."

"Yes." And then I remembered a worse thing. "No more Joe," I said. A cry seeped out of my mouth.

"Would you like me to call him?"

"No," I said. "Where's Ma?"

"In the hall outside. I just need to take a look at you first. All right?"

He had never spoken to me this way, as if I were breakable. But I felt myself gradually coming back into focus, like a photograph floating in its chemical bath. "Who won the game?" I asked him.

"What game?" He was looking into my eyes with that dreaded mega-wattage flashlight.

"Any game."

"Philadelphia," he said bitterly. "Bad calls."

He leaned away and I took a look at my aching arm. It appeared I'd had a run-in with somebody's Cuisinart.

"You got rid of your IV," Dr. Klewanis said.

"What am I on now?"

"Lower dose of steroids and a little something for the mood. Sorry about the bad trip."

"I got my sight back."

He stood. "Okay, sport. I'm sending your mother in. She's been what you might call a trifle anxious."

I closed my eyes for maybe longer than I thought, and when I opened them again, Ma was there. She looked haggard but gave me a smile. She'd shoved the table across the bed and put a plate with some kind of cake on it.

"What's that?" I asked.

"Tropical fruit cake. It's got mangoes and papayas. The nurses say it reminds them that warm weather still exists somewhere."

I realized that I hadn't spoken with Ma since Joe's visit. This wasn't going to be easy but at least I was under the influence of some drug that gave me a pleasant what-the-hell feeling. It made me understand addiction.

"Nice to have you back," Ma said. "You feel okay?"

"Dandy," I said. For someone's who's been buried alive. I pinched off a snippet of cake and chewed. We both knew I was doing it for show.

"Joe called the bakery to see how you're doing," she said. "He sounded like shit."

I didn't say anything.

"You're not paying attention. You stoned?"

"Broke up," I said.

"What." It wasn't a question exactly, just another of Ma's symphonies of meaning in one syllable.

"We broke up."

"You or him."

"It was mutual."

"Like hell it was."

"I gave it the old college try."

"If you can't make it with Joe, you can't make it with anybody."

"That's correct."

"Single forever."

She was silent for a long while. This was unexpected. I had imagined outrage and what I got was a face that had suddenly acquired a few more creases. She went to the window.

"Would you do something for me?" she asked, turned away from me.

"If I can."

"See a psychiatrist."

"I don't think so, no," I said. "It just isn't for me. Everything's so much harder to bear."

I watched her absorb the blow as she had so many others. After a moment she squared her shoulders and swung around. "Well, I'll miss him. He was a goddamn saint, only a lot more fun."

"You want to take the rest of the cake to that kid next door? I'm not all that hungry."

I left the hospital in my wheelchair a week later. Alone in the apartment, thoughts of Joe propelled me into a kind of panic. So despite the fact that there were icy patches and that New York taxicabs were notoriously casual about crushing disabled people, I took daily forays into the urban winter. I wheeled myself up and down Third Avenue, stopping to look in the windows and to chat compulsively with the dry cleaner and the deli owner.

My neighborhood felt unfamiliar, as did everyone in it. The druggist appeared surly, almost menacing. I asked him if he'd grown that moustache recently, and with a startled look, he told me he'd worn one for fifteen years. I told Ma I didn't like the ugly color of the new paint on the bakery window trim, but there'd been no paint job. With all this pointless babbling at people and zooming around, I quickly wore myself out and was forced to retreat to my room where I stared at my wallpaper and curtains and bookcases and realized that they weren't the same either. When I said good-bye to Joe, colors dulled, events lacked interest, nothing much mattered. I told myself that I'd get over it. After all, I'd adjusted to MS, hadn't I? It was simply a matter of patience.

"Did you feel depressed and strange when Dad left?" I asked Ma. We were watching a video of *Barton Fink*. I had discovered that movies by the Coen brothers coincided perfectly with my bleak state of mind.

"No. Relieved. Why?"

"Just curious." My left leg did a little hop by way of punctuation.

"You sure you're ready for work?"

"Oh yeah." I was depending on my job to save me. From the anxiety, the loneliness, the conviction that without Joe nothing meaningful would ever happen to me again.

I had arranged to start the next week. With a new semester beginning, perhaps I could repair some of the damage inflicted by my substitute. By prearrangement, Grant picked me up in my lobby.

"Whoa, you look wiped out," he said. "You sure you're ready for this?"

"Why, thank you so very much," I said. I didn't tell him I'd woken up at five and lay there for two hours trying not to wonder what city Joe was in.

"I forgot how long it takes to get ready

when your feet don't work," I told him. "Can we pick up some coffee on Lex?"

"Sure, honeybaby. My, but aren't those perky little Lana Turner glasses?"

"Lana Turner didn't wear glasses," I said, giving my chair a mighty shove to get up the curb at Eighty-fifth Street.

"You're not going to quibble, are you?" he asked. "I hate it when you're quibbly."

"I'm nervous about work, that's all." People glared at us for taking up too much space on the sidewalk, but Grant knew I liked him to walk beside me so we could talk. He held the door while I zipped into the *Refill*, a coffee dispensary whose only asset was its wide doorway. Despite the fact that I was directly in the counterman's line of vision, he looked up at Grant.

"I'll have the Colombian, black," I said.

"To go or to stay?" the clerk asked Grant.

Why is it that if you're sitting in a wheel-chair, people assume you require a spokes-person? This guy was no more than thirty inches away from my face. It was far more trouble for him to crane his neck up at Grant.

"To go," I replied.

Again, the next question went straight over the top of my head. "She want sugar?"

"The asshole wants to know if you'd like sugar," Grant said to me.

"Hey," the clerk objected.

"Please tell the man no sugar, won't you please?" I said to Grant, handing him two dollars. "And would you be so kind as to pass this along? I'm simply too invisible today." I was instantly sorry. The guy didn't have a clue so what was the point in torturing him? Grant opened his mouth. "Close that thing, Grant," I said in my sternest teacher voice. "We're out of here."

"Don't you *dare* tip," Grant bellowed, and we sailed out.

"He can't help it," I said.

"I hope he gets his dick caught in the cappuccino machine."

"You must have a grotesque fantasy life. When's the next faculty meeting?"

"Yesterday," Grant said.

"When were you planning to tell me about it?"

"When you asked."

"Uh-oh," I said.

"Chubb's on the selection committee for the new headmaster."

I was dumbfounded. Who would trust that slug with such a crucial task?

"He's also put in his bid to run the English department when Mary Feeny retires."

"But she's not going for another couple of years."

"Well, her daughter just lost her husband. Cancer, and she's got little kids in the wilds of Massachusetts. Mary wants to help out."

"You couldn't have broken this to me before?"

"Oh, hell, Anna, you know I'm a coward when it comes to this stuff."

"You mean when it comes to giving me bad news."

"All right, yes. I don't like it. I don't like it." He was getting excited. Steam poured out of his mouth like Puff the Magic Dragon on bad drugs.

"Think they'd hire a crippled teacher at Dalton?" I asked.

We paused at the end of the block. The younger kids were hurrying inside while the older ones hung out on the sidewalk, many of them concealing cigarettes.

"Okay, Grant. I can take it from here. Call me tonight, will you?"

"Sorry to be so clumsy," he said. He kissed his finger and pressed it to the top of my head. Then he disappeared through the front door. I averted my eyes from the gate where Joe had stood when he picked me up on the motorcycle. *Swallow it down, Anna,* I told myself. That lump will just have to go.

I wheeled up to Michelle. She saw me too late, and while trying to ditch her cigarette brushed Sukey with the hot end.

"*Ow*-wah!" Sukey yelped.

But I was too pleased at the sight of them to complain. Michelle had obviously put on weight over the past month, maybe even ten pounds. She looked great.

"Ms. Bolles!" Her face was a confused jigsaw of guilt over the cigarette, delight in seeing me, and dismay at the wheelchair and strange glasses. I held out my hand and she took it. No gloves on this frozen day and I could see she was still biting her nails. "Are you okay? I mean, oh. My. God. We had the *worst* teacher. We so didn't learn one thing."

"I heard you were in the dance recital," I said.

Sukey, rubbing her cigarette burn, piped up. "She was amazing, Ms. Bolles. Everybody said so. There was somebody from a dance company there who wants her. They didn't even ask Jennifer."

"I felt weird about that," Michelle said.

"Well, congratulations," I said. "We'd better get inside." There were only a few stragglers left on the street, and my inner clock told me the bell was going to ring before we made it upstairs to homeroom. "You girls go ahead. I'll be there in a minute."

I waited inside the lobby for a moment, soaking in the atmosphere, listening to the sounds of shouts and running feet, and smelling the mix of steam heat, wet wool, and sweat. It saddened me to think of Duncan Reese's office occupied by someone else. How could Duncan be feeling, with a stranger usurping that battered leather chair he had occupied for two decades? I hadn't realized until this moment how much I had depended on his support. I felt vulnerable and ridiculous in my wheelchair.

On my way past, I glanced at the notice board just to check out the current climate — a batch of flyers decrying cruelty to animals with photos of mutilated creatures in traps. An index card tacked to the bottom caught my eye. Scrawled on it in red pen was the observation: *BULLETIN: Martine reached her goal! She's a C-cup!* Ah, it was good to be back. I ripped it off and stuffed it in my pocket for filing with other such treasures.

It turned out that my teaching reentry wasn't so easy. The relapse had tampered with my cognitive function. That first morning, I tried to sign a trip-permission form for Sukey. I gripped the pen and stared down at the black line but my fingers simply refused to move.

"But you *said* I could *go*-wah," Sukey

complained, misinterpreting my paralysis.

"Bring it to me later," I said. "I'll sign it then." She backed off as if I had the plague, but there was no use trying to explain.

I could feel myself struggling to pin down vocabulary and, once I retrieved the word, to express it without slurring. I said "Whit Waltman" the first time, then "Joe Whitman" — which perhaps I couldn't blame totally on MS — and "poetry" came out "moesry." I could see confusion on certain faces. Most were tactfully silent, except for Eddie, of course, who called out, "What, Ms. Bolles? I can't figure out what you're saying!" Rudy shot him a look of disgust, but why shouldn't Eddie protest? If I couldn't make myself understood, I shouldn't be teaching.

It didn't take long for the word to get around. There were sympathetic looks from other faculty members, as if they were trying not to notice the ax hanging over my head. The scariest thing was that every time I caught a glimpse of Leonard Chubb, he'd disappear around a corner or slink into a classroom so he didn't have to speak to me. I took that as an ominous sign, guessing that I no longer even appealed to him as a political partner. Anyhow, he was doing just fine without me. The few times I actually spotted Peevik, the interim headmaster, Leonard was with him and they seemed very chummy. In fact, Peevik never bothered to introduce himself. I supposed that I was as invisible to him as I was to that clerk at *Refill*. All this spurred me to write an overdue thank-you letter to Duncan Reese telling him how much I admired what he had done for Cameron, how much I had appreciated his support, and that I missed him.

In school, I concentrated all of my energies into preparing my classwork, making reminder lists, and speaking up in departmental meetings in an alert sort of way — though this could be dangerous. I lapsed into some mirthless giggles one day after an inability to get my tongue around the word "curriculum." It kept coming out "curried cumin," as if I'd got my wires crossed with the menu from an Indian restaurant.

At the end of each day I would roll out the school entrance with a cheery wave to anyone standing in the lobby. But it was all show. Oftentimes I'd see the garbage truck on Eighty-fifth and wish that they'd just pick me up, chair and all, and compact me with the rest of the useless trash.

19

Joe disappeared off the planet. Last summer there had been the incessant media deluge from ads and articles. During those weeks, I had pictured myself standing under a cartoon umbrella showered with the words *Joe* and *Malone*. But this time the winter dragged on and there was total drought. He could no longer be part of my life, but I grew desperate for some indication that he still existed. Once, in the elevator of my building, a toddler peered up at me with Joe's eyes. Its mother, no doubt accustomed to comments about the unusual color, was nonetheless caught off guard by my over-the-top rhapsodizing.

There was no mention of AirMalone in the business section of the paper, nothing about Joe in another of those breathless eligible-bachelor articles. Lola Falcon's latest publication emerged but I only knew because I ferreted it out in the bookstore. I flipped it over to check out the author's photo, but this time there was a slick air-brushed picture credited to somebody else. I had wanted so much to see Joe's name, imagining myself running a finger across it as if the typed words could transport the comfort of him. I sat in my wheelchair in the back of Barnes & Noble clutching the book to my chest and weeping. It was the first time I had cried. Wouldn't you know I'd choose a place crawling with self-possessed people browsing for books on how to maximize their sexual potential.

After another couple of weeks, Dr. Klewanis told me I could fold up my wheelchair and ditch the Lana Turner glasses. I'd embarked on a regimen of injections, and as before, they left me feeling as if I had the flu. But rubbing aloe on the injection site kept the swelling down and I did feel stronger. My tongue was definitely more supple. The acid test was pronouncing unfamiliar names. At first, I practiced on the Sunday *Times* newlyweds, muttering the more difficult names out loud: *Gwyn MacIlvennie, Huson Klenawicus, Ryan Van Buskreek*. But in short order, all those smiling brides depressed me and I moved on to the obituaries.

No one close to me had ever died, but I

began to understand what it meant to mourn and how Joe must have grieved over his grandmother. It's the specificity of a person — the habitual gesture, the curve of the mouth, the chipped tooth, the idiosyncratic catch in the throat to signal a laugh — the loss of these things are what cut so deep. I suppose when they begin to recede from memory, that's when you begin to mend. But I didn't want them to fade. I clung to them, willing myself to remember that Joe said "roof" to rhyme with "woof," that he was ticklish at the back of his left knee but not the right, that I didn't need to see any part of him except his eyes to know that he was smiling. I hung on to those memories because they kept me company in a bleak sort of way. I could understand people who built shrines.

During my recovery, Ma had been uncharacteristically quiet. I suppose I expected a battle over the breakup, or at least a lot of questions, but she never mentioned Joe's name. Her silence only contributed to the strange vacuum that intensified my yearning for him. One Saturday night in late March, I raised the subject. We were watching a rerun of *Chariots of Fire* while a tease of spring slipped through the window, making my heart ache. On the TV screen, the aristocratic hurdler had set champagne glasses on a series of barriers and was leaping over them.

"That actor reminds me of Joe," I said. Wonderful angular features and that silky blond hair. Not to mention the athletic grace. It gave me a sick feeling, as if I hadn't eaten in too long, and yet I couldn't look away.

"Mm," she said.

"Don't you think so?" I pressed her.

"Not really." She got up. "You want mocha chip or butter pecan?"

When she came back with the ice cream, I said, "Ma, how come you don't ever talk about Joe?"

"I don't?" she said.

"You never mention him."

"Oh."

"You liked him, didn't you?"

"Yes."

"Are you pissed at me for breaking it off?"

"Of course not," she said in that subdued tone I kept hearing out of her lately. "I guess it just seems pointless to dwell on a closed chapter. Don't let that ice cream melt."

Her reticence didn't encourage discussion and it made me feel even more isolated. A week after this conversation, Ma announced that she was going on a vacation.

"A vacation," I repeated uncomprehendingly. She'd never taken one as far as I could remember.

"Yeah. I need a break."

"A break." I knew I sounded like a dim-witted child but I was having a lot of trouble grasping the concept. Ma got up from the dinner table and started making noise in the kitchen.

"Where will you go?" I asked.

"Key West," she said over her shoulder. "I hate this fucking weather."

"It's almost spring," I said.

"Almost doesn't count."

"All by yourself?"

"Sure." In the sink, silverware ricocheted, pots crashed. "It'll be nice to just lie around and read a good book."

Nice without me to look after. Maybe that was what it was all about. She was tired, and why not? My latest relapse had carved a new wrinkle in her face, a deep slice between her brows. But I felt bereft and angry, abandoned. I knew I was going to cry again. Ashamed, I crept into my room and shut the door. I curled up on my bed and thought I might as well just complete the picture by sticking my thumb in my mouth.

"So when are you planning to leave?" I asked casually at breakfast in the morning.

"Next week."

352

"Next week!" I couldn't stifle the panic.

"Mrs. Wellaway says she'll run errands if you need her."

I was thinking that Mrs. Wellaway couldn't help me with my exercises and I would certainly never want to plunk myself down on that bony lap.

"Why are you doing this, Ma?" I asked.

"I told you. I need a break."

"But I just got rid of my wheelchair."

"You'll be fine. I checked it out with Klewanis."

There was no responding to that so I tried another tack. "How will Carmen ever manage the bakery all by herself?" Dirty pool, but Ma didn't rise to the bait.

"If she has a problem, I'm only a phone call away."

"I feel like there's something else. Are you sure you're not angry with me?"

"Of course not. Since when wouldn't I tell you if I'm pissed?"

"Okay," I said. But I was thinking, *Since the alien came and took over your body.*

A barrage of blue language emerged from Ma's room as she packed for Florida. Her suitcase was too fucking small, the goddamn handle was for shit, her lone bathing suit was a cocksucker that made her look like a fucking manatee, etcetera, etcetera. I took secret satisfaction in this display, attributing it to separation anxiety. God knows I was flooded with it. But rather than curse, I withdrew into that place I was finding ever more hospitable, a walled room inside my lesioned brain where silence was the language of choice.

We ate breakfast together the day of Ma's departure. I was swollen with feelings but there was a new carefulness between us now. I couldn't tell her how much I loved her and depended on her, and how fearful I was that I'd never see her again. I couldn't tell her how much I didn't want her to leave me. Ever.

"Save the Style section from the Sunday paper," she said. We liked to giggle over the more outlandish fashions.

"Okay. Well, I'd better get to school." I got up from the table, grabbed my cane and my coat and bent to give Ma a kiss on the cheek. "See you in a couple of weeks."

"Take care of yourself, Annabelle." I was kind of counting on a tear or two but she kept her face averted.

That was it. Ma's flight took off midday, so when I came home that evening, the place was dark and quiet with no comforting smell of dinner cooking. I stuck my face into the apron hanging on a hook in the kitchen and breathed in the scent of bath soap and flour.

"Grow up, Anna," I told myself, and grabbed a fork for my Chinese takeout.

I look back on that time as a kind of purgatory. First, the very next day, I got fired.

I should have known something was up when I ran into Leonard Chubb in the teachers' lounge. Rather than curling up in his corner of the couch, he was standing in the middle of the room with legs apart, arms folded, every inch the squire surveying his estate. He'd parted his hair on the opposite side and stuffed a silk handkerchief in his pocket.

"Glad to see you on your feet again," he told me, managing to convey that he wasn't. But clearly he was cheered about *some*thing. He started fiddling with one of those palm-size computers. "Just want you to know," he said, peering at the screen, "I didn't have anything to do with it."

Ah. I stood in silence for a moment, then wheeled around — or tried to wheel, which is not easy with a cane — and headed straight to my homeroom.

My e-mail asked me to stop in at the high school dean's office. I took a deep breath.

Perhaps because of my close connection to Duncan Reese, I'd had a distant relationship with Conley Mellen. In fact, the only other time I'd been summoned to his office was as a student when I'd organized a snowball fight during a fire drill. Mellen and I smiled at one another a lot but didn't have much to say. When he saw me standing in the doorway, he quickly dropped his eyes. I knew right then that it was over.

"Should I bother to sit down?" I asked.

"Of course." He moved some files from one stack to another but I knew he was just looking for something to do. I'm pretty adept at the file-pile maneuver myself when trapped in an awkward parent conference. "Anna . . ." he started, letting his eyes flicker to my face for a moment. He faltered, but I was damned if I was going to help him out. I noticed for the first time that he had the veined face of a heavy drinker. My mind wandered back to past faculty events. I pictured the glass in Conley's hand. It was always filled with Diet Coke. A recovered alcoholic. I fought sympathy. After all, this person was about to fire me.

"I'm afraid we just can't continue keeping you on in your present capacity," he said.

"In my present capacity," I echoed. What exactly did that mean? Precise language, please. In my present capacity for bringing dusty old literature to life? For empathy with my students? For tripping over the furniture? What?

"We wanted to give you plenty of time. To finish out the year. Under the circumstances. To examine your options."

"I'd appreciate your telling me why."

He got up and went to the window. I figured he was thinking he could use a stiff drink right about now, and I have to say I wouldn't have minded one myself. He addressed his remarks to the brick wall on the far side of the courtyard. "There have been complaints," he said, "particularly since your recent hospitalization. As you're aware, it's always difficult to find a satisfactory substitute. It's disruptive for the students and, unfortunately, we can only expect to be placed in the same situation more frequently in the future."

I didn't know what to say. I blurted out finally, "I could go for years without a relapse. I love teaching. I think I'm a good teacher."

He turned to look at me at last. "You're an exceptional teacher, Anna. But we have demanding families and an active board of trustees."

"Can you tell me something specific? It would help."

He sat down and retrieved a file from the heap. "Since your return, you've misgraded two papers. You lost one student's quiz before reading it. Your speech has sometimes been unintelligible to the students and to other members of the faculty." He flipped a page. Somebody had been keeping close tabs. Wonder who.

"That's enough, Conley. You don't have to go on." I'd fire me myself.

"As far as I'm concerned," he said, "these problems, while serious, don't counterbalance what you give to your students, and from what I understand, you could be in remission for some time. No one prepares their students better than you do, and you always find imaginative ways to keep them excited about literature." He sighed, a big one. "Off the record, I want you to know that this is happening over my protest."

"Thank you," I said. "That's a comfort." I stood up and took the hand he offered across his desk.

"You should be very proud of what you've accomplished here, Anna," he said. "You just got a bad break."

I stood in the hallway outside, leaning on my cane and watching the students. There were no classrooms here on the ground floor but there was a view of the lobby and the entrance to the auditorium. I knew that a rehearsal for the spring musical was going on in there. I'd been influential in the selection of Stephen Sondheim's *Company* and had encouraged Michelle to audition for the part of Kathy. She must have nailed it because she was standing just outside the auditorium door listening raptly to Don Stein, the head of the theater department. I noticed that the haunted look had disappeared from her face. Rudy passed by with a sixth-grader whom he was tutoring in math. I watched his eyes linger on Michelle, saw the pain in that flickering glance, even now after all these months — a lesson to those of us who underestimate the constancy of an adolescent passion. Puppy love, indeed.

I must have stood there for ten minutes watching the ebb and flow of students, the younger kids straining with backpacks almost half their size, the high-schoolers who typically managed to crash into somebody or something on their way through. A few of those enormous seniors had been pint-sized themselves when I first began teaching. I wondered how I was supposed to go about disengaging myself from a place whose rhythm was so familiar that I felt the bell ring on Saturdays.

I walked out of the building and headed

for the park. I didn't have my coat, but physical discomfort was almost a relief. I took the Ninetieth Street entrance to the reservoir and stood watching the gulls wheel over the wide expanse of water. Ducks walked with webbed feet on a transparent skin of ice. The sky was dull gray, and over on the West Side somebody had released dozens of balloons, tiny pinpricks of color rising like wishes. I followed their ascent until my eyes caught sight of a small plane, a toy against the clouds. I imagined that Joe was in that plane. Another wish, another dream, so far out of reach, like everything else that mattered.

I ricocheted between the silent apartment and the corridors of Cameron where I already felt like an intruder. I could tell by the way my fellow faculty members behaved toward me that the word had gone out. My old friend Dee Sunderland asked if she could take me to lunch. Grant haunted my homeroom and left me e-mail messages about the evils of repression. But I avoided everyone. I suppose I was in shock, which seemed a bit ludicrous after all my prior twittering about the imminent possibility of getting fired. Maybe I'd labored under a superstition that worrying about it would prevent its actual happening.

Ironically, what kept me sane was work. I knew I had papers to grade, exams to prepare, problems to solve. Beautiful Will came to say he'd gotten the word that he wouldn't be coming back next fall. As we discussed life after Cameron, I felt a silent kinship with him. Jennifer had had surgery on an ankle broken in the dance studio and needed extra help with missed classes. So between eight and four every day, I was anchored to something real. It was in the empty hours afterward that I sat around like a leftover on an hors d'oeuvres platter, gradually turning brown at the edges and waiting for the slide into the garbage pail.

I ate my dinner in front of the TV at night, often keeping the audio off on account of the jarring voices. One night, I caught a glimpse of myself reflected in the window, sitting on the couch with my take-out carton. I was so transparent that the painting on the wall behind me was clearly visible. Anxiety rose in my chest like indigestion. I got up and retrieved pen and paper from Ma's desk. I could feel my pulse beating in my fingers where they held the pen. I was sweating, the cold drizzle sweat of fear.

ANNA MARIE BOLLES, I scribbled, and underlined my name several times, as if to ensure that I did in fact exist. Then I started compiling a list:

Joe's girl
Ma's daughter
Teacher
Athlete
MS victim

I couldn't think of another thing. I stared at the words, slowly coming to the realization that the only accurate descriptions at this moment were daughter and victim. Everything else warranted an *ex-* in front of it. The anxiety thickened into something darker. I hastily added *Friend* to the list with *Grant* after it in parentheses.

It seemed unthinkable that something as important as losing my job could occur without Joe's knowing. My need for him felt physical, as basic as hunger, thirst, the craving for sleep, the avoidance of pain. I stared at the phone and half expected it to ring, as if a psychic connection between us would inform him. I put my hand on the receiver, leaving a clammy palm print. I was so cold, cold as a corpse.

That weekend, I walked alone with my cane across Seventy-ninth Street. There was a motorcycle chained in front of the New

York Society Library. I stared at it, remembering the rumble of the engine, the leather under my legs, and the warmth of Joe's back. What a euphoric ride, both of us leaning into the curves in unison as if we were one creature. I knew I was hanging onto my memories with the same tenacity that I had clung to Joe that afternoon. It might not be healthy, but I simply couldn't help it.

Then outside the Guggenheim Museum on Fifth Avenue, I saw a woman pushing a man in a wheelchair. The woman's face was weary and sad. At the curb the man looked up at her to speak. Instantly, she masked the exhaustion and replaced it with alert interest. As if performed for my benefit, here was the portrait of our future had we stayed together.

When I got home, the phone was ringing. My heart started beating fast. It was a difficult habit to break, imagining Joe calling in from some anonymous hotel room in Burlington or Montreal. But it was Dr. Klewanis.

"Hiya, sport," he said. "What's up?"

"Just took a walk," I said. "You checking up on me?"

"Yup. How's the vision?"

"Pretty good." I didn't feel like telling him I'd just been fired.

"How's your ma?" he asked. "I'm more worried about her anyhow."

"What?" A surge of panic. Did he know something I didn't?

"I practically had to get a court order to make her leave town. She's still away?"

"Yes."

"Excellent. Okay, kid, I'm outta here. Keep me posted."

He hung up. *Thanks for removing my life support, Doc,* I wanted to tell him.

I sat by the phone for a moment and tried to get my bearings. Joe was gone, Ma was gone, and I could no longer turn to my work for respite. I walked to the TV and snapped it on. There on the screen was an old movie with Robert Redford shushing expertly down a ski slope. It almost made me laugh.

20

The weekend inched along as did I, since a severe case of mock sunburn made every movement torture. Since this particular symptom hadn't cropped up in a while, I thought perhaps it had surfaced in honor of Ma's Florida vacation. Not that my skin showed any tinge of pink. It was just confused pain receptors.

"I hope you're using plenty of sunscreen," I told her when she called Sunday evening. Her voice made me ache to see her. Only four more days and she'd be home to cheer me with her prickly comfort.

"Yep. Not a freckle on me. How're you doing? Work?"

The words were on my lips. *They fired me, Ma. There's nothing left for me now.* But it was only the slightest hesitation. "The usual," I lied.

"You sure? How's your speech? You sound funny."

"Fine. I'm eating a bagel." She'd be angry

when she'd find out, but I knew the truth would bring her home on the first plane. "How about you? Dr. Klewanis wants to know if you're getting a good rest."

"Uh, I'm having a great time," she said. "I think I'll hang around awhile longer. That is, if you're feeling all right."

"I'm perfectly okay, Ma," I said. "How much longer?" I think I succeeded in keeping my voice neutral.

"Couple of weeks, I guess," Ma answered.

Two more weeks! I had thought I was managing very well under the circumstances; i.e., I had not yet flung myself out the window. But two more weeks! "What'd you do, meet a guy?" I asked.

"Shit, no. Unless you count the hotel gardener. He may be ninety but he pinched me on my way past the begonias."

"Do you have another cold?" I asked.

"Maybe." I heard her blowing her nose. She never got colds.

"Ma, are you thinking of giving up the bakery?" Maybe that's what this was all about, a career crisis.

"No."

I wasn't going to ask her if she was going to give *me* up. "I haven't checked on Carmen today," I said. Hard to do that when it feels as if your skin is peeling off down to the bone.

"I phoned. She's fine except for Father Dewbright. He shows up every day looking for me no matter what Carmen tells him."

"So when exactly should I expect you?" I asked. I wanted her home, to make me believe that somehow things would turn out all right.

"I'll let you know. I've got an open-ended ticket." She blew her nose again and I heard her mutter, "Goddamnfuck."

When I was on my own, straight out of college, I'd lived on ice cream, pizza, and Ritz crackers. But now it was time to take a crack at cooking. How tough could it be to make spaghetti sauce from scratch? I figured. What I learned was, the can opener remains a blessing.

The sunburn gradually eased, and I only needed my cane for street security and for brandishing in the face of certain unruly students like Eddie, whom I caught building a snowman in Sukey's locker. It was a good trick requiring a fair amount of resourcefulness, given the fact that it hadn't snowed in almost two months. He claimed he was making a creative statement about the cycle of the seasons, but nevertheless.

The week passed, and the next. I began to

take some pride in my newfound self-sufficiency. When my hands were uncooperative at the end of the day, I used kitchen utensils especially made for the disabled. Most of them were still in their bubble wrap in the drawer. Who needed them when I had Ma? The same applied to managing my clothes. It took a little maneuvering to learn some of the techniques, but pretty soon I was quick with the buttons, even little ones. I found that Mozart could be depended upon for moral support when hooks and zippers were recalcitrant.

For the first time since I got sick, I began to imagine moving back into a place of my own. Surely I could fend for myself, and in the event of a serious relapse, Ma would take me back in temporarily. I resolved to discuss it with her when she got home. I lay on my bed listening to *Don Giovanni* and decorating my little studio apartment. I imagined the wallpaper — Joe's face reproduced hundreds, thousands of times — so that no matter which way I turned, he'd be there.

The morning Ma was due home, the dean called me back into his office. I figured they'd found someone to fill my position and weren't even going to let me finish out the semester. I rehearsed my defense all the way to Conley's office, how I had regained nearly all my speech proficiency and hadn't misplaced anything more valuable than a paper clip. Conley was standing against the window, backlit so that I couldn't see his features, merely the glowing outline of his body.

"Sit down, Anna."

I could tell by his voice that I'd better damn well do it. So I sat.

"You'll have your job here next fall if you want it."

The Ma lurking in my lower layers burbled up as I thought, *Look, don't fuck with me, man.* It must have showed. Conley took his seat and emerged into focus. He was smiling.

"I mean it," he said. "You're unfired."

"How can that be?"

"The department's had a change of heart."

"Wait. I'm trying to . . . you wouldn't kid a person?"

"A number of us felt you got a raw deal and that the students would lose out if you were to leave."

"But what if I get sick again? I mean, I could go for years without another relapse, but there's always the chance." I wanted it sorted out once and for all. A roller coaster is no place for somebody with compromised balance.

"We'll deal with it if the need arises."

I sat there in numb silence. I felt as if I'd been clubbed over the head, but with affection. "The bell's going to ring," I murmured, and it did. "I have a class to teach." I got to my feet and shook the hand that Conley extended. "Thanks. Thanks." It was all I could think of to say.

I tried to concentrate in class but I suspect that I gave Thomas Hardy short shrift. As soon as I had the chance, I e-mailed Grant. He showed up in my doorway at the end of the day. "Tea, darling?" I could see he knew all about it.

"Oh, yeah," I said.

Spring was far enough along now so that the four o'clock daylight was not too dreary. Grant took my arm and hurried me in the direction of the park. I started to say something.

"Hush," he said, cutting me off. "Not till we're in neutral territory."

"Where?"

"Where no teacher on a private school salary ever goes," he said. "The Stanhope."

It was bliss in the old hotel's tea room — overstuffed furniture and brass lamps with Victorian shades. Grant commandeered a corner table and sat, ludicrous with his lanky frame sprawled across a chintz settee. There were other muted conversations going on, but none in English.

He raised his teacup. *"Salut,"* he said. "This has to be a first."

"Did you do it?" I asked.

He sniffed. "Not hardly. Nobody on the staff has that kind of clout."

"Does everybody know?"

"Just those of us on the inside track. But of course it'll get around."

"Poor Leonard's nose must be out of joint."

"A solid punch'll put it back." Grant helped himself to a scone.

"Were they worried I'd go to the A.D.A.?" Grant had urged me to make a formal protest with the association. As a disabled person, I qualified for their assistance. But the problem was, I half agreed that I was no longer fit to teach.

"No." He checked out the patrons for possible undercover agents and leaned across the table. "It was Deke Cross, but don't ever say I told you."

"Michelle's father?" I wasn't sure I'd heard him right.

Grant nodded and stuffed a tea sandwich into his mouth.

"I have no idea what you're driving at."

"I know," Grant said. "I'm having so much fun."

"Come on, come on, you're killing me."

"Well, you know how Cross is financing the new science lab with his millions?"

I nodded.

"Michelle found out you were fired and she went straight to her daddy. He called an emergency meeting of the board and informed them that unless you were reinstated he was withdrawing the funds."

I dropped my teacup. It smashed to smithereens on the table. I knew it was the kind of thing you see in bad movies, but the combination of shock and MS fingers just did me in.

"Well, Christ, if I'd known you were going to start breaking things, I would have taken you to the diner," Grant grumbled, mopping at the spill. A waitress with a ruddy Irish face came over with a new teacup and efficiently removed the shards of china.

"What should I do?" I asked.

"Oh, don't be an ass," Grant said.

"I love teaching," I said.

"Yes, Anniekins, we know. Don't you recognize the footprints of fate here?"

"Deke Cross's size ten Guccis?"

"Look, if Cross thinks you're worth two

372

million bucks, maybe we'd better respect his judgment."

"Shouldn't I write him a thank-you note or send him a box of chocolates or something?"

"I think you've got it backward. The way Cross sees it, you saved his daughter's ass and this is *his* thank-you note."

I waved at the waitress. "Could we have two glasses of champagne, please?"

The waitress looked a little confused, but Grant grabbed my hand. "We just got engaged," he explained.

I went home and slept off the crushing fatigue that hit me with the second glass of champagne. I hadn't been near a glass of wine for weeks and my tolerance was low. But Ma's plane was due in at eight, and by the time she got home, I had heated up a vegetarian lasagne from my weekend cooking experiment and thrown together a green salad. When she walked in, the table was set and there was the pleasant smell of food wafting through the apartment. She looked tan and dramatically thinner. I gave her a hug and inspected her at close range.

"You've lost a ton of weight."

"They put all kinds of sickening crap in the food." Her typical lament. Never eat out for fear of toxins. She removed her coat and sniffed the air. "What'd you do, hire a caterer?"

"Simply moi," I said. "I'll put dinner on while you wash up." I watched her head off to the bathroom. She'd bought a new pair of slacks that looked like they were maybe a size ten. This new sleek Ma was disconcerting. It would take me some time to adjust.

At the table, Ma stared back at me with the slightly baffled expression I suspected I was wearing myself. "You're pretty skinny yourself," she said. "A tad on the wan side. Everything all right?"

"Actually, Cameron fired me, but don't freak out. I just got rehired today."

"Holy God," she said. "You'd better start from the beginning."

We sat at the table for a couple of hours, then moved to the couch with our peppermint tea. A month is a long time when you're accustomed to sharing most of the details of your life. Furthermore, we were both conscious of a shift and were struggling to reconnect.

"Ma," I said after my third cup. "I've been thinking."

"Always a frightening prospect," she said.

"Do you suppose I could manage on my own?"

She had switched to Diet Coke. "What do *you* think?" she asked me, setting the can down.

"That's a shrink response," I said.

"What's the difference what I think? You're the one who's got to feel confident enough to do it."

"I have to say it surprised me how well I did once I got used to being alone. You've spoiled me rotten." I could see I'd blasted her with too much at once, the job and now this. "Anyhow, it's just something to think about. For sometime in the future, maybe."

"Anna, you've lived on your own before and I've already gone through the empty-nest thing," she said, sliding her soda away. "Don't be worrying about my tender sensibilities, because I don't have any."

"Yeah, and the Pope wears high-heeled sneakers," I said.

We smiled at one another. Things were beginning to feel more familiar again, but still, something had changed, that was certain.

The sense of disorientation, palpable since my hospitalization, persisted. I still felt that I was picking my way across territory that had been ravaged by an earthquake. I stepped gingerly over jagged crevasses and struggled over chunks of rock. First and foremost, there was the absence of Joe. A dozen times a day I felt the impulse to tell him something. An anecdote about one of the kids that I knew would reward me with his laugh. Or the glimpse of a head of streaked hair disappearing into the subway entrance made my throat constrict. The hurt from missing him became as familiar as the feeling of air against my skin. It was always there.

Then, there was the peculiar alliance between me and my job. I was out, now I was in, but my confidence was damaged. I found myself giving thought to the issue of my competence. If I couldn't be a great teacher, I didn't want to hang around. And if I wasn't teaching, what would I do with myself?

And lastly, there was my relationship with Ma. Not that we didn't share stories about our day, and laugh as always, and confide our frustrations. Not that Ma wasn't as tuned in as always to every nuance of my gestures and speech patterns. Yet there was an almost imperceptible stepping back from one another. Only a crack, perhaps, but cool air penetrates even such a tiny fissure. And now that Ma had lost weight, I suspected that her lap wouldn't feel the same. Anyhow, I didn't find myself so inclined to sit there anymore.

One Friday afternoon when I was packing up exams to grade over the weekend, Dee Sunderland poked her head into my homeroom and asked me if I felt like joining her for a cup of coffee. She'd done this every few weeks over the years, faithfully demonstrating that her friendship was still available. This time, I zipped up my bag and told her I'd love to. I'd forgotten her ear-to-ear grin. It made her look like she'd just hatched a plot to abduct her favorite Renoir from the Metropolitan Museum. We headed straight off to Starbucks and started dishing the dirt as if there'd been two weeks instead of three years since we'd last gossiped together. I noticed a couple of gray threads mixed with the tangle of auburn curls, but her hands were the same as ever — in perpetual motion and stained with every conceivable color.

"Do you have any recent pictures of the kids?" I asked.

She gave me a look. "Are you sure?"

"I'm sorry that I've been a jerk," I said. "Let me see."

She dug in her bag and produced some tattered photos of the five children, all with smiles just like hers, and her husband, Van. That was the shocker.

"I know, bald as a beach ball," Dee said with a laugh. "It all fell out two years ago when I thought I was pregnant again."

We sat for more than an hour while I gobbled up details about her life. Then she asked me if I ever heard from Bobby Zaklow. Bobby and I had gone out to dinner with Dee and Van a few times before the final break.

"No," I said. "Not a word. Oh, God!" I wailed as the tears pumped out of my eyes in rivers. Thankfully, Jennifer and a few of her friends had left moments before. Dee just waited.

"Why don't you call him?" she asked finally.

"Who, Joe?"

"Who's Joe?"

We were beginning to sound like an old Abbott and Costello routine. "Oh, you mean call *Bobby*. Oh, God!" Again. My nose was running on top of everything. I tried to blow it, but my stomach muscles weren't cooperating. Until you've got MS, you don't appreciate what it means to be able to blow your nose efficiently. "I *hate* Bobby," I said. "He's pond scum."

"You won't get any argument from me,"

Dee said. "Who's Joe?"

I explained as best I could, winding up with the sad finale. "Please tell me you get it," I said.

She thought for a moment. "I think so," she said finally. "Being with him throws your MS into high relief."

"Thank you. Spoken like an artist."

I walked Dee to her car. She unlocked it and turned to me. "I was pissed at you," she said. "You just disappeared out of my life."

"I know. I'm sorry."

"Are you back now?"

"Yes."

"Not going to head for the hills?"

"No."

"Promise?"

"Promise."

She hugged me gently, sensitive to the fact that I might be hurting, and hopped into her car. "Want a lift home?"

"That's okay. I feel like walking. Dee, thanks for not giving up on me. Thousands would."

She drove off, fluttering her multi-colored fingers at me out the window.

When I got home there was an innocuous-looking letter stuffed in our box in the lobby with the junk mail. I have since replayed this scene over and over in my head, along with everything else that followed. It was a plain white envelope with the address typed on an old typewriter that smeared the letters. The return address said: *Hartwicker, 220 Mill Road, North Lockville, New York.* That's when I started to hear the pulsing crashes in my ears as if the Upper East Side were being rhythmically pounded by artillery. I tore the envelope open. A newspaper clipping fell out onto the floor but I let it lie there for a moment. I glanced at the bottom of the brief letter and saw the signature: *Steve.* Then I read it, not an easy task with that cacophonous thundering going on. By now I had realized that it was my heart making all that racket, but there was nothing I could do about it except hope I wasn't having a coronary.

Dear Anna, the letter began. *I know that Joe has been conflicted over whether to tell you about the enclosed. After giving the matter a lot of thought, I decided to relieve him of the responsibility. I'll tell him I've written after I've sent this. He's as okay as he can be under the circumstances. Hope you're well. Best, Steve.*

I bent down and picked up the clipping. It was from the *Lockville Dispatch*. Gus, a much younger Gus, was smiling at me. He had a neat part in his hair and was wearing a jacket and tie. I knew then that I'd better sit down. I crouched on the floor in the corner and read the obituary:

On March 12, Augustus Malone died when his hand-crafted single-engine airplane crashed in the Adirondacks near Old Forge. Better known as "Gus," Malone was born in Westmoreland, educated at the Rochester Institute of Technology, and served with distinction in the Vietnam War. In 1964, he married Celeste DeLand from Saratoga Springs. The couple had two sons, Frank and Joseph, both of whom work in the family business, AirMalone, the charter airline founded by Malone in 1975. A detailed obituary will appear in the Sunday Dispatch. *Services are private. The family asks that in lieu of flowers, contributions be made to the Nature Conservancy or the National Multiple Sclerosis Society.*

I don't know how long I sat there among the dust balls, the discarded catalogs and junk mail. Finally Big Bob appeared. I remember the effort it took to lift my eyes from his feet, big black shoes with a crust of mud dried around the soles.

"You all right?" he asked.

"I'm sad." That's all I could say. My heart

had stopped pounding. Instead, it had begun to rain. It was raining everywhere, right here in the lobby of my building and in Palm Springs and Juneau and in Rio and Tokyo. It was raining on Mars and on Pluto. It was raining on the sun, and soon it would be extinguished with a big hiss and that's the last we would see of the light. I just kept hearing the name. *Gus. Gus.*

Big Bob reached down with his huge paw and lifted me up. "You just come with me, miss." He took me with him to the front door and used the lobby phone to call my mother at the bakery. I don't know how long it was before she came. I just knew it was raining hard. It was raining down on the broken plane, on the dark trees and the rocks and the melting snow.

Big Bob and Ma got me upstairs. "I want to go to bed," I told Ma, and curled up in a tight ball. It was raining on my bed. All I could do was clutch my knees and let it pelt down. *Gus. Gus. Oh, Gus.*

21

Ma just came in every now and then to check on me and leave a cup of tea beside the bed. The next morning, I picked up the cold brew and carried it to the kitchen. Ma was in there rolling out dough for biscuits, the plain ones I love to eat hot with a little raspberry jam. She held out her arms and I went into them. The terrain of her body may have changed but not that comforting scent. One batch was already out of the oven. We sat down at the table and ate and talked. She let me tell her again about the skis, listened to me describe the barn, though she'd heard it all before.

"I noticed in the obituary about the MS Society," she said.

"Maybe it was Joe's idea. Poor Joe."

"Yeah," Ma said, and again that thick silence. The vibrations hummed off her like a radio with the sound turned too low.

I crept around inside the apartment that weekend, feeling bruised all over. Ma left little plates of things around, hoping I'd nibble — grapes, cheese, chunks of currant bread. I stood at my window, facing east and watching the airplanes rise over Queens. The sky was a pale watery blue, the kind you see in April after it's been raining for a long, long time. By Monday morning, Steve's letter looked as if it had been through the laundry a dozen times. I kept staring at the word *Joe* — three letters that seemed impossible to grasp. A black cyclone had ripped through my brain. Nothing made sense anymore.

On Monday, I tiptoed back to school on feet that didn't feel up to the job. Grant ran into me as I was walking to the library, keeping close to the wall for security.

"You're looking furtive this morning," he commented.

"Not up to snuff, actually," I said. "Talk to you later." It was easier to let him think I was ill than talk about Gus. I just wasn't ready. The students also sensed my frailty and were hushed and respectful in class, even Eddie, who asked if he could fetch me a cup of coffee during break. Michelle was giving me penetrating looks. She and I had not yet discussed the issue of my employment. I wasn't certain how to address it, and now I was having trouble thinking about anything but the woods, the plane, and the people left behind. I stayed late to grade papers, not that I was particularly reluctant to go home, merely that I was afflicted with inertia. It was such an effort to make any move at all.

I fastened my attention on the essays, taking comfort in the familiar exercise of removing and inserting apostrophes, hunting for structure in what seemed a morass of adolescent free association. But after an hour, the words began to blur into gray streaks and I realized that it was pointless to continue. The last bell had rung, the halls had emptied out, and I could hear the sound of the janitor's mop clicking across the floor outside. I stuffed the remaining papers into my bag and shrugged on my jacket. Then I noticed the half-empty container of coffee, courtesy of Eddie, that had grown cold on my desk. There was a sink in the art studio. I would just empty the coffee on my way out.

The studio was dark. I snapped on the light and caught a flicker of movement out of the corner of my eye. The art-supply door closed with a tiny click. I stared at it a moment, then approached and asked, "Who's there?" No answer. I wondered if I was hallucinating, a symptom stimulated by grief, perhaps. I reached out and opened the door. Crushed inside amid the jars of paint and rolls of paper were Rudy and Michelle with their arms clutched around one another.

Rudy was the first to speak. "Hi, Ms. Bolles." There on his face was that beatific smile, and on his neck a strawberry love bite.

"Are we in trouble?" Michelle asked.

I studied them, feeling the way I suspect Newton did, sitting under the tree and minding his own business when suddenly he got clonked on the head by an apple. Teachers are always mouthing platitudes about learning more from their students than they can possibly impart to them. I hoped that from now on, whenever I was tempted to think *impossible*, I'd remember the sight of Rudy and Michelle grafted together in that closet.

"I guess we should come out?" Rudy said. They were looking increasingly alarmed by my silence. But I was simply too stunned to respond.

"Okay," I said. "I get it now." Then I went home to call Joe.

The electronic voice on his answer machine in North Lockville said he'd be back tomorrow, Tuesday. I decided to take a chance and hopped in a taxi for the West Side. The doorman waved me in without announcing me, a first. I stood outside the door to Joe's apartment and knew he was in there. I felt him breathing, felt his heart beating, felt him hurting. I rang the bell. He must have been just inside because he flung it open. He had a bag in one hand and another beside him on the floor. His eyes were red-rimmed, his hair shaggy, his face pale under two days of whiskers. He looked awful and wonderful.

"I'm so sorry, Joe," I said.

He dropped the bag and wrapped his arms around me. Gradually they tightened until the muscles were like steel against my back. When he laid his cheek against mine, the stubble was damp with tears. "Oh, God, Anna," he said.

"I'm sorry. I'm sorry. I love you, Joe." I didn't care if he had moved on, if he was with Lola, even if he was married. Nothing mattered except that I could say these true things. The earth circled the sun, I was sorry Gus was dead, and I loved Joe. That was all.

After a while I led him to the couch. So far, he hadn't spoken a word. We both sat down. I could see he was trying to talk, but he was so full of emotion that he couldn't push any words out. I took his hand and held it to my heart.

"You gave him back to me, Anna," he said

finally. His voice was hoarse.

"I should have been with you," I said.

"Yes, you should have."

We clung together until we actually fell asleep all tangled up on the couch, both of us in our jackets and me with my handbag strapped around my shoulder. It was as if after all the months of fitful nights, we could finally rest. The numbness in my left side woke me. When I tried to sit up, Joe tightened his grip on me in his sleep so I shifted against him to relieve the prickly discomfort. Through sleep-blurred eyes I noticed that the apartment was barely recognizable. There were plants on the windowsill and the coffee table. A plaid Adirondack blanket was flung over the chair and there was a guitar leaning against the wall. I wondered fleetingly if he had a musical girlfriend. The most striking change was the photographs. A few of the old ones remained, but mostly they'd been replaced by portraits — color photos of locals from upstate, some of whom I recognized from the New Year's party, all of them elderly. There was a luminous quality about them that reminded me of the Dutch portraits Joe and I had seen at the museum on our first date.

Joe stirred beside me. I helped him sit up and he almost smiled at me. "Then I wasn't dreaming," he said.

"Do you have to be somewhere, Joe?"

"It's all right. I flew down to LaGuardia so I could pick up a few things. I have to stick around upstate for a while."

"How's your mother? Frank?"

"Frank's okay. Eva's been a brick. But my mother's a mess. How am I supposed to leave now?"

"I'll be here when you get back."

There was a long silence.

"I will," I said.

"I need it in writing."

"You can have it in blood," I said.

The haggard anguish lifted into a more convincing version of a smile. "Let's drink something," he said, and rose stiffly. He put the teakettle on and came back to sit on the arm of the couch.

"What brought you back?" he asked. "Was it Gus?"

"Gus and some kids in a closet. I'll try to explain." But the cursed fatigue was crushing me. I leaned back against the corner of the couch. He would be leaving me soon and there was so much to say, but my eyelids weighed fifty pounds apiece and my mouth was too weary for speech. In the distance I heard the teakettle whistle and I felt Joe breathing into my hair.

"I'm not like sports, Anna," he said. "You don't have to give me up."

I fell asleep again and dreamed of Gus. It wasn't a sad one, more like he was paying me a visit from someplace where the sun was shining. He took my hand and I could feel the calluses. I said to him, "I thought dead people were cold. How come you're so warm?"

"Been sitting by the stove," he said.

"But you're in heaven. You're an angel now," I protested.

"Don't go getting mystical on me," he said. Then he gave me that little wave and walked off.

Joe brought the car around to the front of his building and tossed his luggage in the trunk. There was bumper-to-bumper traffic on Central Park West so we sat and talked, mostly about Gus.

"We started flying together whenever I was home," Joe said. "And we were working on a hinged door in the wing of the Stearman. He saw it was hard for you to get in and out of the passenger seat and it gave him the idea."

"What went wrong, Joe?"

"Nobody knows. He lost power and stalled."

For the first time, it occurred to me that Joe could easily have been in that plane. The nerves in the surface of my skin sent prickles from the back of my head down into my fingers.

"I don't want you to fly anymore," I said.

"I wasn't in a hurry to get back in a plane," he admitted. "It's getting easier."

"You could do something else for a living."

"It's too late," he said. "You taught me that I like what I do."

"I did?" I said. Joe had turned into the park to cross to the East Side. The trees were furred with green, and forsythia dripped from the stone walls along the road.

"I didn't hate my job," Joe said. "There was just something missing from the equation."

"I'm not following," I said.

"Appreciation," he said.

"That's pretty zen. I don't get it."

"You will. I'm just not explaining it very well." We were only blocks away now. I was awake enough to suffer over his leaving. "How's Norma?" he asked.

"Too chic for words." I told him about her new figure. "Joe, when are you coming back?"

"There are a lot of things to settle, and

391

my mother is still on medication. She collapsed completely."

"I guess I'm surprised at that."

We drove up in front of the building. When Big Bob saw Joe's car, he broke into a grin and saluted. Joe leaned over and gave me a kiss. I was trying to hide my panic. All I could think of was that I might never see Joe again. He would crash or there would be some terrible catastrophe. My eyes must have been the size of hubcaps. Joe gave me a sad smile. "We've had enough tragedy, Anna. I'll phone you as soon as I get home."

Ma was working late. When she came in I was watching a game show with my feet stretched out on the coffee table and a glass of wine in my hand. Ma stood in the doorway, her face swiveling from the TV screen to the wineglass. I could see the muscles in her jaw bulge with the effort not to ask.

"I saw Joe," I said.

"And?"

"I don't know what's next."

"What do you want to be next?"

"He said he'd call the minute he landed. That's all I can think of." I looked at my watch, then took another slug of wine.

"Did you eat?"

"No. Can't. Later." I glared at the phone.

That bastard. Ring already.

After a while Ma sat down beside me with a plate of melon and prosciutto. The phone rang. Vanna White clapped her hands with glee.

"I'm here," he said.

"In the airport or at your apartment?"

"Airport. There were delays at LaGuardia. The worst runways on the eastern seaboard."

"Joe, will you marry me?"

There was a long silence. "I don't know," he said. "Maybe."

"At least it's not a no."

"It's not a no."

"So you're going to think about it."

"Yes."

"You're the love of my life," I said.

"I knew that," he said.

We hung up and I looked at Ma. Her eyes were full of tears.

22

Joe e-mailed me later that night:

April 22

Dear Anna,

If you had asked me a couple of months ago, I would have dragged you to the nearest judge. But I have to wonder if it's going to stick this time. I think you owe it to both of us to find out.

Gus and I talked about you. He wasn't exactly wordy, as you know. "She'll come around," he told me. More than once, he mentioned that you've "got guts," the supreme compliment. We fixed a busted altimeter together and argued over his conviction that if I had guts of my own, I'd pursue you until you gave in.

Your withdrawal was tough on me, as was losing my father so soon after finding him again. I'm pretty beat up. For the time being, I think we should spend some time together and see how things go.

Love,
Joe

The first thing I noticed was that he signed off with *Love* instead of *Your*. I wasn't certain it was a good sign. I sat in my room listening to Vivaldi until long after I heard Ma close her bedroom door. Of course Joe would feel this way. Was I imagining that he'd fly down here tomorrow with a wedding band, all gratitude and joy? It was tempting to compose an e-mail assuring him of my constancy and listing all the reasons why we shouldn't delay. But Vivaldi was reminding me that the seasons came around again and again regardless of how frantically we humans behave, and that possibly Joe was right about being patient. Maybe I was in the grip of a symptom. Perhaps grief for Gus had impelled me to reach for a union I couldn't really sustain. So I sent him a note that said: *Fair enough. When do we start?*

He didn't show up in New York right away. I talked to myself a lot during that period. Grant actually caught me at it on the street a couple of blocks from school. He must have been shadowing me for a while.

"Talking to our little imaginary friend, are we?" he asked at my elbow.

I think I leapt a foot off the ground. "Don't *do* that to me."

He took my arm. "Just out of curiosity, Anniekins, what does Betaseron have to do with commitment, or did I hear you wrong?"

It took me a moment to retrieve my internal conversation with myself. "There's a connection. I haven't figured it out yet but I'm working on it. Care for a cappuccino?"

We sat outside in the spring sunshine gossiping and laughing, while all the time I was carrying on that inner dialogue, convinced that I was on the verge of some crucial revelation.

Finally, in early May as I prepared for finals, Joe called to say he'd be flying in on Friday night. "Meet me at the sushi bar?"

I agreed, and we hung up. Joe and I had never established a habit of prolonged telephone conversations. I glanced over at Ma, who was pretending to be seriously enraptured with a beer commercial. "He's coming in," I told her.

"Fine," she said. Four paragraphs inside four letters. I went back to inventing an essay question that would prove provocative yet not terrifying.

Joe got to the restaurant first. It pleased me to see him sitting at the sushi counter checking out the array in the glass case. Initially, the notion of eating raw fish had disgusted him. "If it swims, cook it," he told me.

"Oh, come down out of the mountains, country boy," I'd complained. "You're a New Yorker now." He gave it a try, and soon became an enthusiast. It pleased me that I had opened his world just a little, considering how much he'd expanded mine.

I slid next to him and we exchanged a light kiss. We were both feeling the constraint of absence and of unresolved questions. Furthermore, it seemed uncouth to lock lips within the hushed walls of Japanese propriety. In fact, we barely spoke, other than to order our food. Joe was wearing jeans, a white T-shirt, and a blazer. Even when the fabric brushed my arm, I felt a thrill. I ignored it because of the conversation in my head, which was proceeding full throttle. No sake for me either. I felt so close, so close to something. Not that I could have articulated what it was, but inside my head there was music building to an almost unbearable pitch, along the lines of Ravel's *Bolero* where the suspense is enough to make you stop breathing.

It happened over the *tamago*. As soon as the yellow rectangles arrived on my palm-leaf platter, I turned to Joe and interrupted him in midsentence.

"Okay, Joe, this is what it is." I kept the elation out of my voice for fear he'd think I was being hysterical or symptomatic. "I wasn't ready to believe that I had MS. I know it sounds crazy, but I just couldn't accept it, even after five years."

He was gawking at me with one hand in the air, balancing a shimmering sliver of yellowtail.

"You presented a problem for me," I said, "because around you there was no way to duck being sick." He just kept staring. I reached out, captured the fish from his fingers and popped it into his mouth. I could sense that the businessman sitting next to me was leaning in, trying to catch every word. I always hope that I'll get to sit next to a conversation like this, but all I get are discussions about interest rates and municipal bonds.

"Are you with me here?" I asked Joe.

"I'm trying," he said.

"It seems so obvious to me now," I said.

"But what's changed?"

"The injections symbolized something. I used my initial reaction to Betaseron as an excuse to avoid them. Dr. Klewanis tried to tell me. Ma tried. I didn't want to hear about it. But after this last episode, I was finally able to commit to them. It took a while, but whatever had me by the throat — I suppose it was denial — loosened and let me go." I ran out of steam for a minute. I was feeling wildly stimulated and exhausted simultaneously, a bewildering mix.

"What you're telling me," Joe said, "is that you couldn't accept me until you accepted your illness."

I laughed at the brevity of his totally accurate summation and gave him another kiss, with a little voltage this time. I figured the restaurant would forgive us. Clearly, we were in the midst of something important. When a waitress came to ask if we wanted anything else, I saw the sushi chef's minimal gesture, waving her off.

"I don't know, Anna. It sounds so simple."

"That's what they said when Elvira Hopsaddle invented the umbrella."

"Elvira who?"

"Well, I don't know who invented it, but you know what I mean. It's only simple in retrospect."

"You got me mixed in with your MS," he said.

"You were kind of a symbol, too. I can't help being seduced by symbols. I'm an English teacher."

"I'd prefer to be a person."

"Well, you are now, Joe. You always were. I just didn't know it enough."

The businessman was almost in my lap. I wanted to ask him if perhaps I should repeat myself in case he hadn't heard me clearly. Joe still looked dubious. There was a kind of expectant hush at the sushi bar. I got the feeling everyone was waiting for the denouement. I know I was.

"Look, Joe, in my experience, epiphanies aren't a dime a dozen," I said. "I've been working on this one for weeks."

He gazed off into space as if there were nothing on his mind more weighty than the dessert menu. Then he turned to me and said, "Then I think we'd better get married."

"What a great idea," I said. It had been a long time since I'd seen his eyes lit up like that. They were Fourth of July sparklers.

Moments later and without comment, our waitress set a fruit platter down in front of us. It looked like an abstract painting, something Christie's would auction off for a few million dollars. The businessman shoved his card across to me. It said: *Bob Weinstein and Sons, Caterers. Weddings and Bar Mitzvahs Our Specialty.*

Joe and I decided not to worry about such minor incidentals as: (a) Where were we going to live? and (b) What about my job? We just wanted to get married, the sooner the better, and preferably while I was still in remission. It turned out that Bob Weinstein worked out of Orlando, Florida, but we figured we already had a pretty good source for food.

Ma commandeered Father Dewbright, who initially misunderstood and thought she was at last agreeing to marry *him*. Once he recovered from his disappointment, he was delighted to preside. Before his retirement, he had been the pastor of a gingerbread-style church off Madison Avenue, and so was able to arrange for an evening ceremony on a Saturday in early June.

That Friday night, all of our guests and members of the wedding party arrived at Ma's apartment for a rehearsal dinner. Not that there was anything much to rehearse. But since Joe and I were planning to head off immediately after the ceremony, we figured we'd have the party the night before. Ma closed the bakery and she and Carmen cooked up a spectacular spread. There was lobster bisque and baked salmon en croute and roasted vegetables and a leg of lamb and rosemary focaccia and watercress salad and a fabulously ornate wedding cake, chocolate in honor of the groom, that was topped with an odd pair: a pilot sporting a Red Baron hat and a sadistic-looking teacher whose ruler looked like a bayonet.

My father had sent a large check and regrets due to a commitment in Toronto to tape a video called *Warm Guns and Hot Beds*. I felt he would have added a jarring note and was just as glad. I had imposed on Duncan Reese to give me away. To my surprise and gratification, he seemed deeply moved at the invitation and agreed. Steve, Celeste, Frank, and Eva flew down, and I invited Grant and Dee and Van Sunderland to hold up my end. It's always risky to stir ingredients from the various canisters of one's life into a single stew, but I hoped that if we spiked it with enough champagne, all would be well. As far as Joe and I were concerned, the crucial issue was the confrontation of the mothers. I was dreading a clash-of-the-Titans type of situation and had warned Ma that I expected tractability if not submissiveness on her part. I knew it was futile to request clean language. Suddenly it seemed like a better idea to just head down to City Hall, Joe and me, and forget the rest of it.

I sat on the edge of my bed and stared at the absurdly impractical wedding dress Dee and I had bought, which was now hanging on my closet door. What the hell, Joe and I had weathered worse things than Norma and Celeste under the same roof. Maybe.

The intercom buzzed and Ma shouted at me to move my ass, she was tangled up in panty hose. I got up and opened the front door to Duncan Reese, Dee, and Van. Duncan wrapped me in a bear hug and told the Sunderlands that I was his "honorary daughter." I hadn't seen Van in three years, but other than the bald head, he looked exactly the same, with a sweet ruddy face that suggested an outdoorsman rather than an accountant. I led them all straight to the punch bowl.

"We all have to get drunk," I said. Ma emerged to greet everyone. She barely acknowledged Duncan, an oversight considering his special kindness, so I handed him a drink and took him by the arm. We stood together by the window. The light was a mixture of pink and gold as the day began to wane. It cast every detail of the skyline into sharp focus.

"Thank you for doing this," I said to Duncan. "You're so good at showing up when I need you."

He beamed at me with the kind of pride I hoped a father might feel. "What are your plans, Anna? Will you leave Cameron?"

"I can't imagine not teaching, but I have

to take this step first. We don't even know where we're going to live." I turned to look at Ma who had extracted the family photos out of Dee. "It will seem very strange, not seeing her every day." This was a subject I had hardly dared to contemplate. I knew that an era in our relationship was ending. I also knew that it was time, but that realization didn't muffle the sound of Velcro tearing every time I looked at her.

The buzzer rang and Ma's head lifted. She looked pretty in a light blue dress that showed off her skin. There was that ache beginning under my ribs.

"You'll miss her very much," Duncan murmured. Something in the way he said it was arresting. I looked up at him, but then Joe burst through the door with the upstate entourage in tow and the sight of him gave me such a jolt of pleasure it was embarrassing.

Celeste was barely recognizable. Her designer suit hung on her and she'd cut her hair shorter so that the gaunt bones of her face were even more prominent. Her glance swept the room, hawklike, until it settled on me. The muscles at her jawline clenched into a ghastly smile. Joe led her over to me and she planted a cool kiss on my cheek.

"This is Duncan Reese, who I hope

you've noticed is wearing a Bill Blass sport jacket," I said. No, I didn't. But I made the introduction and watched Duncan begin to reel her in.

"I understand you're originally from the Saratoga area," he said. He'd done his research, presumably with Ma. "You aren't by any chance acquainted with the Forresters, Gwen and Ralph?"

"Why, I grew up with Ralph Forrester," Celeste gasped. "He's the foremost real estate developer in the county."

Hook, line, and sinker, I thought, blessing him silently before turning to the other guests. Grant was talking to Joe while munching on flatbread and shedding not a crumb. I watched for a few seconds, experiencing the strange sensation of worlds colliding, and quickly sank into maudlin territory: *My guys. My two guys. Aww.*

I wasn't permitted to wallow for long. Over by the grilled vegetables, Duncan was introducing Celeste to Ma. Of course, it should have been my responsibility to perform that particular ritual, or Joe's, but neither of us was thinking very clearly. I could tell that despite Duncan's formidable skill, there was a crisis brewing. Celeste's eyes were narrowed and Ma had a dangerous flush in her cheek. I went straight to Joe.

Grant swung around and nearly poked me in the eye with his punch glass.

"Boys," I muttered, "I think it's time to elope." I slid my eyes in the direction of the Mothers. By now, Ma was talking, and I could see it wasn't pretty. Duncan had hold of her arm and wore the smile of someone who was pretending to make a joke out of a diplomatic disaster. Nearby, Dee and Eva had interrupted their conversation to watch the women.

"What should we do?" I asked Joe.

"Oh, for Christ's sake," he said. "Come on."

"I knew I should have taped her mouth," I muttered. "I couldn't find the duct tape."

As we came within range, Celeste was sputtering something about "breeding," and Ma retorted, "Don't talk to me about breeding. I'm not one of your fucking race-horses."

"Ma," I said.

But she ignored me and reached out to grab Celeste by the arm. "We're gonna go duke this out. Come on." The two of them marched stiffly off to Ma's bedroom. Just before Ma kicked the door closed, I caught a glimpse of their faces.

"Scylla and Charybdis," I said. Duncan burst out laughing. I could see that he was

406

actually enjoying this. He caught me staring and tried to replace his amusement with an expression of concern.

"What happened?" Joe asked him. Grant had tagged along behind, and now Eva and Dee edged in closer.

"I think you'd better ask the ladies," Duncan said. "Gosh, that lamb is outstanding. I'm going to help myself to some more." He slid away, leaving us in the dark.

"Do you think there might be a murder?" I asked.

"Whatever makes them happy," Joe said. "Meanwhile, let's eat."

"I like your boyfriend," Grant said, and went off with Joe to fill his plate.

I spent the next twenty minutes chatting with Father Dewbright about the months he'd languished in jail during the sixties on account of his radical politics. But I had one eye on that bedroom door, wondering if there were bleeding bodies stretched out on the floor behind it. Eventually it opened and the mothers trooped out. Celeste's eyes were swollen and her nose was scarlet. Ma looked perfectly composed. A hush fell. All attention was riveted on them as they headed straight for the punch bowl. Ma poured two drinks and handed one to Celeste. They clicked glasses and downed half in one swallow. Then Celeste marched up to me and began a monologue about Gus — whom she referred to as "Augustus" — and his interest in multiple sclerosis, which she attributed in equal parts to me and to his lawyer friend who had worked with him on the planes. She said that since Gus's death, the Society had received over three thousand dollars in his name.

Joe came up to put his hand on my elbow. I could feel the energy in his fingers. "Frank is looking for you, Mother," he said. She backed off gratefully as Joe practically shoved me into my bedroom. He locked the door behind us and pulled me into his arms. "What do you say we get Father Dewbright in here right now and do this thing?" he murmured against my neck.

"I'm not sure he's up to it at the moment. He likes that punch. Do you have any idea what got the Mothers so riled?"

"Nobody heard the opening shot." He kissed me and I kissed him and then it got a little dicey in terms of decorum. My bed was looking awfully inviting.

"Maybe it's purely physical attraction," I said when I could catch my breath.

"Probably," Joe said. "Let's take advantage of it before it wears off." He reached around and pulled me against him, pelvis to pelvis.

There was a sudden pounding on the door. "We know you're making out in there!" Grant bellowed.

"We'll be out in a minute!" I shouted back.

But I put my arms around Joe and held on. "Promise me we'll never forget the way we feel right this second."

"Can't do that," he said.

"Do you have to be so honest all the time?" I murmured.

"Yeah," he said. Then we straightened our clothes and headed back out into the fray.

"What *happened?*" I asked Ma when Father Dewbright finally left, last to go and somewhat the worse for wear.

"Your mother-in-law's got a mouth on her, I'll give her that," Ma said. "Let's talk in your room so you can lie down."

Carmen had hired three of her cousins to help out and was having a grand time ordering them around in the kitchen.

I propped myself up on some pillows and waited. As usual, it was impossible for Ma to perform only one task at a time so while she talked, she massaged my feet.

"First thing she did," Ma said, "was give me the old-fashioned check, you know, the eyeball slide from head to toe to figure out where I got my frock. So I tried to save her the trouble by giving her an inventory right off the bat: dress from J. Crew summer sale catalog 1995, shoes on loan from Mrs. Jake Wellaway's closet, Apartment 9B —"

"You didn't."

"Lookit, Anna, I figure you and Joe are in this for the long haul. I don't plan on taking any crapola from this broad, and she might as well know it from the get-go."

"She got mad?"

"I could see she was a bit peeved, so then she started in on how it was so sweet to see the way her boy took such good care of you and how he's always been so charitable with the helpless, impaired, and pathetic."

"No, now she didn't —"

"She gave me this song and dance about Joe and his collection of abused fucking field mice or something. . . ."

"Not the strays. I've heard about the strays."

"Pissed me off, I have to say. But we got it straightened out."

She started working on my calves. Standing around had worn them out. I wondered fleetingly when I'd ever feel her fingers again, but that wasn't a constructive thought. "What'd you do, flog her with your bathrobe belt?"

"We had a little chat, that's all."

"Come on, Ma."

"I told her I thought you two had a shot at a lifetime deal here, especially if you didn't have to endure extra grief from outside influences. I allowed as to how my intuition told me she had the makings of a true pain in the butt in that department and we ought to squelch it right now. First she started in with some asshole rant about how I had some nerve and all that, but then she just ran out of steam. She's pretty broken up about losing her husband."

"She paid no attention to Gus whatsoever. I don't think they ever even talked to one another."

"Anna, don't make that mistake. You can never know about anybody's marriage. They're mysteries, even to the people living in them. She kept saying how he could fix everything, as if now it's all broken. It was pitiful. And let me ask you something. Did you know she had polio as a child?" My jaw dropped. "Oh yes," Ma said. "She was the last kid in her community to come down with it. Even wore braces on her legs until she was eight years old."

"Joe never told me."

"When that subject came up, she just lost it completely. Cried her heart out."

"Well, I suppose that explains a few things."

"Anyhow, she's not going to give me any lip." Ma got up and turned out the light. "I'd better do some damage control in the kitchen."

I grabbed her hand and pulled her back to me. "Ma. Wait. I've got to figure out how to tell you —"

"Oh, shut up," she said, extracting herself. "Nobody wants to hear that bullshit." But she bent down and gave me a kiss on the forehead.

As a little reminder, or maybe a tiny private jest, God decided to scare the hell out of me on the big day. When I first woke up in the morning, everything seemed normal except for the outlandish realization that I was about to get married. I lay there for a few minutes thinking: Oh. My. God. And alternately grinning and panicking. But when I rolled over and tried to get out of bed, I found that my left foot *just said no,* in the venerable words of a former First Lady of the land. Everything on the left side from the hip down had checked out for the duration. Already on the honeymoon. Flown to the West Coast, metaphorically speaking. I yelled for Ma, and together, we managed to get me up.

I phoned Joe to tell him I just might be seated during the performance. "I'll sit on your lap," was his comment.

"Your mother had polio when she was a child," I said, providing what I thought was the bulletin of the century.

"Yeah. That's how she got into horseback riding."

"You knew?!"

"Sure."

"But Joe, don't you think her having polio was just a tad relevant to her response to me? How come you never told me?"

"I don't know. I never thought about it."

"Oh my." I was thinking, Maybe this clueless man could actually use me in his life.

"I need you for this kind of stuff. Wanna get married?" he asked through a yawn.

It was a day filled with things to do which would take longer now that I was about thirty percent out to lunch. I was damned if I was going to give up my pedicure, however, since it was my first ever. Dee came along and we had a crisis over color choice. She wound up with hot pink polish and I did one foot in melon and one in flaming scarlet. It just seemed that the character of my feet differed to such a degree, particularly today, that they cried out for differenti-

413

ation. My theory was that a lively melon shade might stir some sensation into the numb foot. In any event, this was the sort of thing I permitted myself to think about — now that I was casting my lot in with this man who was practically a complete stranger, and leaving behind a person who had been my sole support and comfort for my entire life.

Somehow the day dissolved and maybe the nail polish worked because I was standing on both feet. My hair was combed, my bag was packed: one bathing suit, one toothbrush, and 420 pills. Ma had been subdued all day. No clatter in the kitchen, very little conversation and then only a single "Damn" when her dress snagged. Every time I looked at her, my eyes filled up.

Some of my father's contribution went into the hiring of a commodious limousine. I backed in easily. "Where's the lap pool?" I called to Ma. She was still outside holding the door open. Big Bob leaned all the way in and handed me a little box. His face was as red as the polish on five of my toes.

"I want to wish you and your husband all the happiness in the world," he recited. I realized that he was waiting for me to kiss his cheek, which I did.

"You've been a godsend, Bob," I said.

"I'm going to miss you."

He grabbed my hand, crushed my knuckles affectionately, and backed out. Ma got in and off we went. I fumbled to open Big Bob's present. It was a bracelet charm, a little silver airplane that looked just like Gus's. A test. If I could get through that, I'd probably be all right.

When we got to the church, the sun was making a slow slide down over the West Side. Ma started to get out of the limo but I reached for her arm. In just a few minutes, our lives were going to change irrevocably. We couldn't hurtle into it without some small recognition.

"Stay a minute," I said.

She turned to scan me with that computer-virus software she had in her head. I knew that no one, not even Joe, would ever read me so quickly, so thoroughly.

"Lock the door," I said.

She did it. I could hear someone on the sidewalk saying, "Are they coming out?"

"Ma —" I began.

She held up her hands. "Oh, no. Don't start."

"It has to be said."

"Nothing fucking well has to be said. You want me to get through this goddamn ordeal in one piece or what?"

"I have to. Otherwise I can't get married."

She sighed, then sat back and waited as if for imminent execution. I hadn't rehearsed this, so it took me a few seconds to gather my thoughts.

"I want you to understand that I'm aware of what it's cost you to take care of me," I started out. "It hasn't been easy and you have never complained. Not once." I felt my voice begin to shake. She put her hands over mine, those soft, caring hands.

"It was a privilege, Anna," she said.

I had to wait a minute before I could go on. "You've made it possible for me to have a life," I said, "and now it's your turn. Even though I know you'll be lonely for a while. Ma, no matter where I am, however far away, I want you to call me whenever you need me. You have to promise, Ma."

She looked at me with wet eyes. "Okay. I promise."

I lifted her hands and put them to my cheek. Somebody rapped on the window. "What's going on in there?" It was Steve. "Are we having a wedding?"

Ma rolled down the window. "What's the goddamn hurry?" She hated being rushed.

"It's all right, Steve," I called past her. "We're coming out."

I caught a glimpse of Joe slipping into the

416

church and remembered the first time I saw him at the photography exhibit. I thought I'd come to terms with my illness then. But the truth was, I was only just now beginning to accept it, acknowledging with certainty the reality and the permanence of it. I guessed that time had had a hand in the process, and Ma, too, but mainly it was Joe. There seemed no doubt at all about that.

Ma caught my eye. "You look ready," she said.

I nodded.

"Okay, babe. Let's do it." She got out of the limo and there was Duncan Reese's hand extended to me once again, this time to lead me up the steps and into the sanctuary. Inside, the little church was lit up with candles. The wedding guests sat on both sides of the aisle in the first few pews. When they turned to us, warm candlelight flickered on their faces. Steve began a simple melody on the recorder. Joe had assured me that he played well, and indeed the sound soared pure and true against the stone of the old church. I walked to the altar, with Ma on one side, Duncan on the other. I could see Joe waiting there, the lines fanning from his eyes as he smiled at me. Not a stranger at all, but my Joe.

"Dearly beloved . . ." said Father

Dewbright. And so it went, in a blink of time, the culmination of so much suffering and laughter and foolishness and agonizing, and ultimately, affirmation.

Joe kissed me shamelessly. It must have lasted a full minute, which is a very long time when you're aware of so many eyes on you, maybe in particular those of your mother-in-law. When we turned to walk back down the aisle, I was simply unable to lift my left foot. Steve was piping away with something that sounded like an Irish folk tune while I stood rooted to the stone floor. Joe looked at me with concern.

"First gear seems to be broken," I explained.

"Oh, that's easy," he said, and swept me up in his arms. Grant whooped in delight as everyone applauded. Joe carried me out of the church and set me down beside the car where we said our good-byes. I couldn't look at my mother.

Then I tossed the flowers high in the air — I still have a pretty good arm — as everybody backed away from Ma. She had no choice but to catch them. There was cheering, and suddenly Joe and I were being pelted with rice. We took refuge in the limo. The door clicked shut, and we pulled away.

Wait, I thought. *Wait*. There's so much

more I need to say to her. But it was too late.

I turned to glance out the back window. There was Ma standing apart from the others on the sidewalk, looking after us in the twilight, her shining face growing smaller and smaller and eclipsing the flowers she held clutched in her hands.

The employees of Thorndike Press hope you have enjoyed this Large Print book. All our Large Print titles are designed for easy reading, and all our books are made to last. Other Thorndike Press Large Print books are available at your library, through selected bookstores, or directly from us.

For information about titles, please call:

(800) 257-5157

To share your comments, please write:

Publisher
Thorndike Press
P.O. Box 159
Thorndike, Maine 04986